Loosening the noose, Bolan leaned closer to the old man

"Why did you send for me, Hakim?"

MacMurphy blinked, as if trying to focus on the dark figure above him. He licked his lips and, his voice a rough croak, said, "Telemetry...act... activation...bloody Russians thought they were so damn clever."

A shudder racked him, and it seemed as if he was summoning all of his remaining strength to husk out one brief sentence. "The Hellfire Trigger."

The old man tried to say more, but his words blurred into a moan of despair. His eyes glazed, he shuddered again and his body went slack on the hard floor.

MACK BOLAN ®
The Executioner

DON PENDLETON'S
EXECUTIONER®
THE
HELLFIRE TRIGGER

A GOLD EAGLE BOOK FROM
WORLDWIDE®

TORONTO • NEW YORK • LONDON
AMSTERDAM • PARIS • SYDNEY • HAMBURG
STOCKHOLM • ATHENS • TOKYO • MILAN
MADRID • WARSAW • BUDAPEST • AUCKLAND

First edition September 1998
ISBN 0-373-64237-7

Special thanks and acknowledgment to
Mark Ellis for his contribution to this work.

HELLFIRE TRIGGER

True hope is swift, and flies with swallow's wings;
Kings it makes gods, and meaner creatures kings.
—William Shakespeare

To hope to be a king or a god is insanity, and far too many people in today's world share that particular madness. Unfortunately there's only one sure cure for it.
—Mack Bolan

THE
MACK BOLAN®
LEGEND

Nothing less than a war could have fashioned the destiny of the man called Mack Bolan. Bolan earned the Executioner title in the jungle hell of Vietnam.

But this soldier also wore another name—Sergeant Mercy. He was so tagged because of the compassion he showed to wounded comrades-in-arms and Vietnamese civilians.

Mack Bolan's second tour of duty ended prematurely when he was given emergency leave to return home and bury his family, victims of the Mob. Then he declared a one-man war against the Mafia.

He confronted the Families head-on from coast to coast, and soon a hope of victory began to appear. But Bolan had broken society's every rule. That same society started gunning for this elusive warrior—to no avail.

So Bolan was offered amnesty to work within the system against terrorism. This time, as an employee of Uncle Sam, Bolan became Colonel John Phoenix. With a command center at Stony Man Farm in Virginia, he and his new allies—Able Team and Phoenix Force—waged relentless war on a new adversary: the KGB.

But when his one true love, April Rose, died at the hands of the Soviet terror machine, Bolan severed all ties with Establishment authority.

Now, after a lengthy lone-wolf struggle and much soul-searching, the Executioner has agreed to enter an "arm's-length" alliance with his government once more, reserving the right to pursue personal missions in his Everlasting War.

1

The alley was full of shadows, and Mack Bolan felt right at home.

The waterfront area of Algiers wasn't the sort of place recommended to tourists, certainly not at midnight. Despite the obvious physical dangers the maze of back alleys presented, the area reeked with the odors of raw sewage, rotting fruit and diesel fuel from freighters. Though some member of the Algerian tourist board could conceivably describe the area as "exotic," to Bolan, the place simply stank.

The Executioner slipped from shadow to shadow, a hand resting lightly on the butt of the Beretta 93-R holstered beneath his black sport coat. He had been drawn to Algiers more than once over the past few years; the first time resulted in the death of Don Cafu, a Mafia empire builder who had stretched his Family's tentacles into the Third World. During another visit, Bolan had orchestrated the utter destruction of a terrorist alliance that could have been formed only in the unstable political climate of North Africa.

His soldier's mind could immediately recall the city's labyrinthine layout, even though many of the old landmarks had given way to modern apartment complexes and office buildings. Urban renewal hadn't reached the narrow, twisting streets of Quali D'Agadir. Bolan figured its residents were happy to be left alone in their ancient houses and back alleys.

A half block away, a whitewashed, two-story Moorish-style cottage gleamed in the moonlight. The light from a yellow lamp peeped through the shutters of the single ground floor window. That was Hakim MacMurphy's arranged all-clear signal.

Hakim MacMurphy had been born of a Muslim mother and an Irish father. The father had fled Ulster during the "troubles" of the 20s, and MacMurphy came of age during World War II when Algiers served as the headquarters of DeGaulle's Free French Army in North Africa.

He provided intelligence to the Allied command and, after the war, he expanded his information-brokering service. For a time, his network was unequaled in Africa. Interpol, embassies, military attachés, spies and even Stony Man Farm had done business with him.

Though MacMurphy's service had been impersonal and politically neutral, he enjoyed a reputation of never selling out or compromising his clients, no matter who they were or what they served. His intelligence-gathering methods were crude by current standards: eavesdropping, bugging, newspaper "milking," and wielding a vast network of hotel porters, longshoremen, taxi drivers and mercenaries.

With the advent of computer databases, modems and satellite uplinks, MacMurphy's little brokerage became quaint and outdated. The last Bolan had heard, MacMurphy intended to retire and sell his files to the highest bidder.

It came as a surprise when a message arrived at Stony Man Farm through a back channel. The message and the back channel itself were characteristic of MacMurphy—a single sheet of handwritten paper slipped into the Sunday edition of *The Washington Post*. The message read simply: Hardman. Blue Noon.

The wording was MacMurphy's personal code for meeting Bolan at midnight on the third day after receipt. So, at midnight on the third day, Bolan paused in the shadows and made a slow visual scout of MacMurphy's house. He checked his watch. Twelve o'clock high.

Then he saw another light, a match that flared in the darkness at the left-hand corner of the house. Bolan pressed flat against the rough surface of the alley wall.

A man stepped around the edge of the house, the match illuminating his face as it touched the end of his cigarette. He was of average build, pale of complexion, with dark blond hair scraped back and tied in an inch-long ponytail. An Ingram MAC-10 submachine gun, outfitted with a Sionics sound suppressor, hung from his left shoulder by a long leather lanyard. Wearing an oversize T-shirt and jeans, the man fit the standard definition of "Eurotrash."

The door to MacMurphy's house opened and a similarly dressed black man stepped out. The square butt of an automatic pistol was visible above the waistband of his trousers. In a loud whisper, he called to Ponytail and the man joined him at the door. They spoke in French, but it was such an obscure dialect Bolan understood only some of what they were saying.

"He's started the questioning. Not much longer now, I hope," the black man stated.

Exhaling a stream of smoke, Ponytail replied, "That bastard Nubbar and the jobs he hires us to do. Who's the guy writing the check on this, Dawi?"

"An American, I think."

"CIA?"

Dawi shrugged as if the matter were of little importance. "Don't think so. At least he's paying Nubbar well. Maybe enough so we can get out of this stinking hole."

Ponytail muttered something in response, and though Bolan didn't understand everything he said, he received the impression that Algiers suited him just fine and he wasn't about to leave.

The two men continued to speak, but Bolan tuned them

out. Most of his attention was occupied with keeping himself invisible, since he was standing less than one hundred feet from them.

Ponytail flicked his cigarette butt into the darkness, and it burst into a shower of tiny sparks. Dawi hiked up his trousers, adjusted the pistol and went back into the house.

Ponytail loitered in front of the door for a moment, then sauntered down the street.

When he'd presented his back to Bolan, the Executioner left the shadows in long strides on the balls of his feet. As he reached his target, Bolan snatched the leather strap of the machine gun and yanked.

Ponytail, grabbing at empty air, fell backward, right onto Bolan's out-thrust knee. He clawed first for the Ingram, but it was beyond his reach, then he clawed at the strap cinched tight around his throat. The only sound he uttered was a gasping grunt.

Bolan kept the pressure on Ponytail's carotid artery until the man's struggling weakened and ceased. He eased him down to the street and dragged him by the strap to the rear of the house. He quickly detached the strap from the Ingram and, by looping and knotting it expertly, he had Ponytail hog-tied in a matter of seconds.

Patting him down quickly, he found no other weapons. Ponytail moaned faintly. Cutting off a man's oxygen and the flow of blood to the brain was usually good for five minutes of unconsciousness, but Bolan took no chances. With a gag made from Ponytail's socks and his belt secured in place, he made sure the man could make no outcry upon awakening.

Tucking the Ingram under his arm, Bolan tried the back door. It was locked. He drew a slender hooked rod from a compact kit of chrome tools in his coat pocket. A moment of manipulating it in the lock caused the door to open silently beneath his hand.

Bolan drew his Beretta, making sure the sound suppressor was threaded tightly onto the barrel. His thumb eased off the safety, and he glided into the house. From a prior visit, he knew a stairwell at the front of the house led up to a large common room that served as MacMurphy's office, den and lounge.

He heard the scuff of footfalls from above, and someone gasping for breath. Reaching the stairwell, Bolan paused to listen. A low, musical voice reached his ears.

In English, with a faint Jamaican lilt, he heard a man say, "You're so stubborn, Hakim. But stubborn or not, you will talk or you will die. I can arrange both."

In a crouch, Bolan crept up the stairs, his body pressing against the wall. He held the Beretta in his right hand, the Ingram in his left. At the top of the stairs, he raised his head above the edge of the floor and took in the scene with one quick glance.

The windowless room was dark except for a goose-necked lamp glowing on the desktop. Ten gray steel filing cabinets lined one wall, bounded at one side by the dials and indicator lights of a powerful radio transmitter, and on the other by a complex tape unit with vertically mounted spools and an eighteen-channel console.

Hakim MacMurphy stood in front of the filing cabinets. He was a short, squat man, barely six inches over five feet tall. His hands were tied behind him with nylon binders. His neck was crooked to one side and looked abnormally long, strained by the noose of silver baling wire that stretched down from the ceiling. The wire was attached to a block-and-tackle contrivance hooked to a rafter. The wire then ran down at a forty-five-degree angle to a small winch held by a pair of huge, hairy hands.

A man with the shoulders of a fullback and a face resembling a catcher's mitt—in texture and color—gripped the handle of the winch. He was well over six feet tall, weighing perhaps 250 pounds. By the Slavic cast to his features, Bolan guessed him to be a Bulgar.

Dawi stood beside him, helping to hold the wire steady as MacMurphy struggled.

The wire around MacMurphy's neck had just enough slack to allow him to touch the floor with the tips of his shoes. He was desperately balancing himself on his toes. His weathered face was dark and congested, his eyes bulged and his sparse gray hair was soaked through with sweat. The wire noose had bitten cruelly into the flesh beneath his jawline; blood flowed in threadlike rivulets down his neck and stained his shirt collar.

From the far end of the room, an area blocked from Bolan's vision by a partition, he heard the lilting voice again.

"You betrayed us, Hakim. You betrayed the confidence of a client. You sent a message. Who is 'Hardman'?"

MacMurphy made a gagging sound. As if that were a cue, the Bulgar gave the winch handle a half turn. MacMurphy fixed his eyes on someone. Hatred and rage shone out of them. He managed to gasp out one sentence. "Kill me and be damned, you shit-faced fairy."

Dawi stepped forward, grabbed MacMurphy's shoulders and pushed downward at the same time the Bulgar cranked the winch.

A scream of pain started from MacMurphy's lips.

Bolan didn't waste time with niceties, but he wasn't about to let loose with the Ingram in such an enclosed space. The silenced Beretta spit once and a 9 mm parabellum round slammed into the center of the Bulgar's chest. He barked out a cry of combined shock, pain and rage. As he fell back against the wall, he released the winch and it was jerked up to the ceiling by the weight of MacMurphy's collapsing body.

As MacMurphy fell at his feet, Dawi made a desperate lunge for cover behind the desk. He clawed at the butt of the pistol in his waistband, but the barrel got fouled in either his shirttail or underwear. He was yelling something in French.

The Beretta snapped twice and clipped the rest of the man's words. One of the slugs drilled through the side of his head, and the other cut a red-edged furrow across the back of his neck.

Bolan turned his attention back to the Bulgar, who was still on his feet. A flat black automatic was nestled in his right hand and he was firing off wild shots. Ducking, Bolan heard the bullets thudding into the wall over his head.

The Executioner realized the Bulgar was wearing a Kevlar bulletproof vest beneath his coat, and when he raised his head and gun again, he adjusted his aim and squeezed off a single shot.

A spot of crimson blossomed on the Bulgar's broad forehead, and part of his skull and scalp floated away behind him. Throwing his arms out wide, the gunner toppled forward on his face.

Bolan heard the sounds of rapidly moving feet behind him. He turned as Ponytail, the leather strap dangling from one wrist, rushed up the stairs toward him. His face still bore the imprint of the makeshift gag.

Bolan had to give him credit; not only had he come to sooner than expected, he'd managed to wriggle free of his bonds in record time. He obviously had more professional experience behind him than the soldier had figured.

The expression on Ponytail's face didn't hint at professionalism; it was a bare-toothed grimace of unthinking, murderous fury.

Bolan pointed the Ingram down the stairway and let loose with a short burst. The muffled hammering of the machine pistol filled the stairway as five holes were stitched across Ponytail's shirtfront.

The Executioner turned his attention to the musically voiced man hidden behind the partition. He assumed he was armed, but since MacMurphy required medical attention, he resolved to wait only a short time for the man to make a move. He wasn't too concerned about neighbors calling the police; the sound of late-night gunfire in this part of Algiers was as common as the squawk of seagulls along the wharves.

Bolan laid the Ingram aside. He guessed that as soon as the man realized his back was to the wall, he would try to shoot his way out. The machine gun wasn't a precision weapon, and he didn't want to risk MacMurphy being caught in a full-automatic cross fire.

An intake of breath came from the far end of the room, then the rustle of cloth. The man was moving. Bolan's finger tensed on the trigger. Then he received a surprise.

A lilting laugh, full of genuine amusement, floated through the semidarkness. "'Hardman,' I presume?"

Bolan didn't reply, but he drew a mental image of the speaker; he pictured a Rastafarian with dreadlocks gripping an Uzi.

"Listen now, Hardman. The old fool betrayed us. You can understand why we did what we did. I'm sure you're a professional. This was business. A matter of policy. Nothing personal in it at all."

Bolan waited.

When the man spoke again, there was a note of impatience in his voice. "There are millions in this. *Billions.* Perpetual wealth. I want to spend some of it, not end up on a slab. Let's talk. I assure you I am unarmed. I despise firearms."

A moan came from MacMurphy, punctuated by a labored wheeze. He was hitched over on his right side, eyes closed, mouth open.

"Your friend Hakim needs attention. The longer we play this game, the longer he goes without it."

Bolan's lips compressed. "Show yourself."

"Ah, Hardman *can* talk. And he's sensible, as well."

"Put your hands behind your head," Bolan ordered.

"Link the fingers. Face the wall. Get down on your knees. One step at a time, crab-walk toward me. If you don't stop when I tell you to stop, I'll put six bullets along your spine."

The man laughed again, but this time there was a nervous edge to it. "Fair enough."

A man shuffled sideways into Bolan's field of vision. Even on his knees, he had to be one of the tallest and skinniest men he had ever seen.

"Stop," Bolan commanded. "Turn around. Face me."

The man did so. Aside from his dark brown skin, he bore no resemblance to the image Bolan's mind had conjured. His bony frame was stretched at least seven feet from the soles of his running shoes to the board-flat top of his peculiar hairstyle. His temples were shaven, and his hair was shaped like a coffee can.

His expensive, canary-yellow workout suit fit poorly; it drooped from his skinny shoulders like clothes from a wire hanger. He couldn't have topped the scales at more than 150 pounds.

His face was alert and intelligent, with a prominent, almost lanternlike jaw. At the moment, the bottom half of his face was split by a wide grin.

"You look just like I pictured," the man said.

"I can't say the same," Bolan replied, rising to his feet. "Who are you?"

The grin widened a bit. "Those who speak of me at all call me Dr. Jest."

"Doctor of what?"

"This and that. It's more of an honorific, even though I studied chiropractic."

Bolan walked toward Jest, the muzzle of the Beretta on a direct line with his head. "Should I kill you, Doctor? Or should I give you the same choice you gave Hakim—talk or die or both?"

Jest sighed. "I knew it would come down to this."

He began to bow his head, as though in resignation.

Bolan's combat senses suddenly came on full alert. He started a backward step.

Simultaneously Jest's head bow turned into a forward somersault. With blinding speed, his head reversed position with his feet, and the soles of his running shoes slammed into Bolan's chest with breath-robbing force.

Bolan's backward step kept the pair of feet from hitting his face. But he was driven off-balance and only the backs of his thighs striking the edge of the desk kept him from staggering across the room. The goosenecked lamp fell to the floor and cast a halo of pale light on MacMurphy's body.

Jest sprang erect like a gymnast coming out of a shoulder roll, and he flung himself on Bolan, clawing with his long fingers, bony knees jacking up to seek his groin.

Bolan tried to swing his gun into position for a body shot, but Jest seized the sound suppressor and twisted it aside. Their arms locked, and they fought for possession of the Beretta. Jest's strength was enormous; it was like struggling with living steel cables.

The soldier felt Jest's bony fingers probing along the base of his neck, searching for a vulnerable spot.

The realization registered on Bolan's face, because Jest's grin returned. Giggles bubbled from between his lips, and he bent his head to snap at his adversary's throat.

As he brought up an elbow to keep those perfect teeth at bay, Bolan glimpsed Jest's left hand curled around the sound suppressor. The fleshy heel of his hand blocked the bore and Bolan squeezed the trigger.

The slug went into the ceiling, but it took a small piece of Jest's hand with it.

The sudden searing pain, coupled with the flash-burn, made the man scream. His body convulsed as he pressed his injured hand to his chest.

Bolan swung the pistol down and around, but Jest springboarded off his torso, driving the air from his lungs. The man flung himself away in a backward cartwheel that turned into a somersault. He rolled down the stairwell, curled in a tight yellow ball.

Struggling erect, Bolan squeezed off a pair of shots, but he knew they missed their target. He was standing at the top step in less than a heartbeat, but he reached it just in time to see Jest launch himself from Ponytail's body toward the front of the house.

Bolan started to pursue him, then thought better of it. Mechanically he checked his watch. Barely six minutes had passed since he had picked the lock on MacMurphy's back door.

He kneeled beside MacMurphy. The old man was barely alive. He recognized the symptoms of anoxemia, a lack of oxygen in the blood. He examined the wire lacerations around his neck. A few more turns on the winch would have severed MacMurphy's arteries, and a few more after that would have decapitated him. As it was, he was dying, either from shock or cardiac arrest brought on by strangulation.

Loosening the noose around MacMurphy's neck, he leaned down close to whisper, "Hakim. It's Hardman. Blue Noon."

MacMurphy's lips writhed. He moved his head from side to side and opened his eyes. Bolan bent low. What was left of the old man's sight was fading rapidly.

"Why did you send for me, Hakim?"

MacMurphy blinked, as if trying to focus on the dark, soft-voiced figure above him. He licked his lips. His voice was a croak. "Telemetry..."

MacMurphy's voice, as faint and hoarse as it was, still held a note of urgency and terror.

"Telemetry...act...activation code...bloody Russians... thought they were so damned clever...telemetry..."

A shudder racked him. It was as if he were trying to

summon what was left of his strength to gasp out one half-gagged sentence. "The Hellfire Trigger."

The old man tried to say more, but his words slurred into a moan of despair. His eyes glazed, he shuddered again and his body went slack on the hard floor.

2

Bolan gently closed MacMurphy's eyes. Though the information broker hadn't been a friend, he hadn't been an enemy, either.

He turned his attention to the Bulgar. The man was flat on his face, arms out-flung. Blood had pooled around his head. Without much surprise, Bolan noted that the automatic in the man's hand was a Russian-made Makarov. His wallet provided the information that his name had been Nubbar Kalashin, and he had indeed been a native of Bulgaria, and he resided at 2332 Rue Gaid Malika, bungalow number 9.

Searching the man's pockets, he found a few coins, some wadded bills and a metal ring that carried only three keys. One was for a car, and the other two were house keys. Bolan detached them.

The Executioner figured Kalashin had been a KGB soldier; the Russians had used Bulgars as cannon fodder for decades. With the collapse of the Soviet Union, a lot of them had turned freelance, and Algiers was certainly the place to seek employment. Terrorist groups were always on the lookout for a few good mercenaries.

Except this didn't smell like a terrorist operation. The torture of a helpless man, and the Kevlar-vested, Makarov-toting Bulgar certainly bore all the earmarks of the Red Brigades or the Front Line, but the man calling himself Dr. Jest was a wild card.

As he ejected the clip from the Beretta and popped a fresh one into the magazine, he examined the filing cabinets. All ten were unlocked and empty. Bolan wondered who had purchased that quarter-ton of files and for how much.

Bolan left the house and took the same circuitous route through the shadows until he reached his rented Volvo.

As he drove down the narrow streets, Hakim MacMurphy's final words echoed in his mind. He knew a "hellfire trigger" was a gadget that turned a semi-automatic weapon into full-auto, but that was strictly American street slang. He doubted MacMurphy had ever heard of one. And "telemetry" and "activation codes" had no connection with a piece of hardware prized by L.A. gangbangers. Nor did the reference to bloody Russians.

After half an hour of navigating torturously twisting streets, Bolan reached the Rue Gaid Malika. The avenue was broad, well-lit and smoothly paved. It took him to El-Biar, a fashionable suburb at the foot of the Sahel Hills. Beyond the slopes, the modern high-rise structures of the Algerian capital raked the night sky. After the waterfront area, it was like driving from the twelfth century to the twentieth.

Bolan found 2332 with little trouble. It was a modern three-story apartment building much like others lining the avenue. Parking the Volvo up the block where he had an unobstructed view in all directions, Bolan sat and checked his backtrack.

A few cars passed him, and a moving van rumbled in the direction from which he had come, but the drivers paid no attention to the dark-haired man sitting behind the wheel of the parked vehicle.

Bolan got out and strode quickly to the apartment building, walked through a breezeway and went to the door marked nine. He didn't go through the routine of knocking and pretending to hear a response. He tried both keys; the first one didn't turn, but the other unlocked the door. He pushed it open and stepped in.

Immediately Bolan dropped into a half crouch, sweeping the room with the Beretta. He saw nothing but a sparsely furnished living room lit by a single table lamp. All he heard were traffic noises wafting up from the avenue. He crept through the apartment. Both the kitchen and the bathroom were small and utilitarian.

At the end of a short hallway was a closed door. He tried the knob. It was locked. His fingers explored the area around the knob, and he lifted an eyebrow in surprise.

The door was made of heavy sheet metal, fashioned and painted to look like wood. It had to have cost Kalashin quite a sum to have it made and installed, either by bribing the landlord or sneaking it in under his nose.

Bolan inserted the second key into the lock. Tumblers clicked, and he carefully eased the door open with the pressure of one foot.

The room was dark. With his free hand, Bolan felt for a wall switch. He found it and nudged it up.

Two things happened simultaneously. An overhead light fixture bearing four 120-watt bulbs blazed into life, and a low mechanical hum began somewhere to his right. Bolan quickly identified the source of the hum. A window-unit air conditioner was wired to the light switch. The appliance was installed at least eight feet up the wall. The long window in which it was placed was bricked up and covered with a sloppy coating of plaster and drywall.

Bolan assumed Kalashin had felt safe from prying eyes; it hadn't been a whim to make the bedroom into a vault. The room was stacked with enough weaponry to turn the dictator of a banana republic green with envy.

Many of the crates bore Russian Cyrillic words. In one corner were at least two dozen assault rifles and a box of hundreds of 7.62 mm rounds. Lying on a workbench was a Soviet RPG-7 rocket launcher. They were tools of Kalashin's trade. He had probably looted an abandoned Soviet armory somewhere in the Balkans before relocating to Africa.

Bolan pushed the door open farther and stepped into the center of the room. Behind him, the door was swung shut by a pneumatic hinge connected to the top of the frame.

Only the bed was free of the clutter of death-dealing ordnance. In the closet, Bolan found two crates of grenades. One crate held the fragmentation type, and the other concussion. A dozen Kevlar bulletproof vests hung stiffly from a coatrack.

Though the sheer volume of weaponry was impressive, none of it was current. Most of it was fifteen or more years old. Bolan doubted that few high-end terrorist groups came to Kalashin's bedroom marketplace, so he had been forced to hire out his muscle.

Bolan turned to leave. Trying the doorknob, he found the lock solenoids had clicked back automatically into place. He also found that the key wouldn't turn the tumblers. He studied the door and stifled a cough. There was a faint, burning sensation in his nostrils and throat.

He became aware of a very light, not unpleasant fragrance. For an instant, he dismissed the odor as coming from one of the customary incense burners in another apartment. Then he dismissed his dismissal and spun toward the air conditioner.

The fragrance was being blown into the room from the wall unit and the closer he walked to it, the more pronounced was the odor. His stomach muscles twisted as he identified the aroma.

Burnt almonds. A cyanide gas or derivative was being pumped into the room. Immediately he realized the mechanics of the trap, but he knew it hadn't been laid for him, even though he'd stuck his head between its jaws.

Nubbar Kalashin's employers had wanted him dead. His payoff was to have been a silent death in an airtight room.

a sort of do-it-yourself gas chamber. Someone had known that the light switch was on the same circuit as the air conditioner, had planted a gas cartridge inside it, then rigged the door. They had probably hoped Kalashin would expire in his sleep and days, maybe weeks, would pass before his body was discovered. By then, the trail leading back to them would have been cold.

All this leaped into Bolan's mind in a fraction of a second. Though the entire set-up smacked of some plot out of a sixties spy show, it was effective. He felt a moment's grudging admiration for the imagination that had concocted it.

His first impulse was to kill the power to the air conditioner, but that would only leave him coughing in complete darkness. The room was already full of the invisible gas.

The overhead lights danced before Bolan's straining vision, and a wave of dizziness rolled over him. His eyes and lungs were burning now.

He knew it was useless to shoot at the door with the Beretta, and his eyes flicked around the room. The RPG-7 rocket launcher would batter down the door, but in such a confined space, the cure might be worse than the disease. If the explosive impact of the warhead didn't flash-fry him, flying shrapnel would slash him to ribbons.

Bolan went to the closet and snatched several bulletproof vests from their hangers, grabbed an apple-size concussion grenade and stumbled to the bed. He was desperately fighting off a coughing fit. He upended the mattress with one heave and arranged it in a horseshoe curve against the far wall. He draped the vests over the outside of the mattress, and pulled one over his head and shoulders like monk's cowl.

Crouching inside the U formed by the mattress, he wrapped a pillowcase around the grenade. Gauging the distance as best he could with tear-filled eyes, Bolan's fingers gave the pin a twist, then a pull. He lobbed the grenade underhanded toward the door. Before he ducked down behind the mattress, he saw it land silently at its base. Hunkering down against the wall, he covered his ears and opened his mouth wide to equalize the pressure.

The explosion was so loud the soldier didn't hear it, but he certainly felt it.

A wrecking ball seemed to smash against the outside of the mattress and slam it violently against the wall. Compressed air crowded Bolan against the baseboard, and the mattress molded itself around him.

When he opened his eyes, he thought for a second he might be blind. After pawing the vest from his head and kicking away the suffocating weight of the mattress, he saw the concussion had blown out the lights, but a little illumination peeped in from the living room. The door was open about six inches. The panels of the door were warped outward, sheet metal peeled back from the frame like cheap tin.

Bolan picked his way through the wreckage of the room and put a shoulder to the door. It squealed open another few inches and jammed. By inhaling deeply and holding his breath, he squeezed through the narrow opening and went out the front door into the breezeway.

His stunned eardrums were recovering. He heard cries of fear and panic from Kalashin's neighbors. They would be phoning the local militia, and Bolan didn't feel like answering any questions.

Not caring if he was seen, he kept the Beretta unholstered and held next to his leg as he walked quickly down the block to his car. He climbed into it and drove away.

Less than a mile down the street, a long line of fire trucks, ambulances and police cars passed him. Bolan wasn't surprised by the immediacy of the response. Algerian officials were so accustomed to explosions in the middle of the night, they probably slept behind the wheels of their vehicles, just waiting for the next inevitable call.

He drove toward the Dar el Beida airport, twelve miles east of the city. As he steered, he took in great breaths of the night air, flushing the last of the gas from his lungs. If nothing else, the trap proved that a terrorist group wasn't involved in the murder of MacMurphy.

It was too convoluted and too subtle. Someone who got a kick from devising clever death traps to snare a single man would have no place in a standard-issue Mideastern terrorist organization.

At the airport, he ditched the car in the lot and headed toward an airside terminal. Two of the few perks of being "on call" to the American government were doctored diplomatic papers and a private jet with a trusted pilot provided by Stony Man Farm. Since Bolan rarely made personal requests, not even Hal Brognola had questioned his covert flight to Algeria.

As he strode between parked cars, a woman, her body sheathed in heavy blue robes and her face veiled, hurried toward him from the direction of the terminal. They came within a few feet of each other, and, as Bolan passed her by, she cast her dark eyes to the ground. He hadn't taken more than another five steps when a gun touched the back of his neck. He froze.

A husky female voice whispered, "Keep walking or I shall certainly shoot you."

The gun barrel prodded him, and Bolan began to walk, not looking behind him. He could have taken the woman; she was too close for her own safety. But if she truly intended to blow out his brains, she would have done it, not threatened it. Besides, he detected an accent in her voice, but not French nor Mideastern nor even British.

It was Russian.

Bolan allowed himself to be directed across the parking lot. The woman walked a few paces behind him, as was traditional for orthodox Muslim women. In the dim light,

and to a casual observer, the pair would appear to be a
Muslim man and wife.

Before they reached the edge of the lot, the woman
touched Bolan's back with the gun and whispered, "To
your left. The truck."

They marched toward a moving van, parked diagonally
so the cab was pointed away from the nearest light pole.
The aluminum body was emblazoned with the cartoon image of a green elephant pulling a house with its trunk. The
corners of Bolan's mouth quirked in a faint smile. He recalled seeing the van while he sat outside Kalashin's apartment building.

Bolan climbed into the cab. In the narrow wall space
between the pair of bucket seats was a rectangular door
panel. It swung open, and, ducking his head, he entered the
cargo compartment. A hand grasped his shoulder, spinning
him deftly so he was facing a steel reinforced wall. Another
hand unsheathed his Beretta and relieved him of his wallet
and passport.

"Turn around slowly," the woman said.

Bolan did as ordered. She had removed the veil and head
covering. The woman looked to be in her early thirties, and
was a little over medium height. Her complexion was a
smooth, dark olive. Her slightly slanted eyes were such a
dark brown they appeared black. Sleek black hair was
swept back from a pronounced widow's peak at the center
of her hairline. Even the billowing folds of the robe
couldn't completely conceal the swell of her breasts and
hips.

"*Salaam Aleikum,*" Bolan said.

"Shut up," the man standing beside her growled.

He was a brawny man with tousled brown hair, wearing
a gray coverall bearing the green elephant logo. He had the
Beretta pointed at Bolan's belly.

The cargo compartment was packed with module after
module, console upon console of some of the most ad-

vanced electronic equipment Bolan had ever seen outside of the operations center at Stony Man Farm.

"Don't even think about raising an outcry," the woman said, lifting the barrel of the Glock 19 compact automatic in her hand. "I am an excellent shot. Do you understand?"

Bolan nodded.

The man was perusing the contents of Bolan's wallet and passport. "Michael Belasko," he announced in a voice not quite as deeply accented as his companion's. "Of Washington, D.C. Full diplomatic credentials and a top-level UN security pass. With these, you could have access to any embassy in the world."

The man's eyes narrowed as he scrutinized Bolan's features. "If that's so, why have I never heard of a Michael Belasko?"

Bolan shrugged. "I guess we don't travel in the same social circles."

"Or we don't travel in the same circle of forgers."

"Enough," the woman said sharply. "You have guessed correctly that we are Russian nationals, and I have guessed correctly that you are an American. Let us assume we are all professionals, shall we, and go on from there."

"Okay," Bolan replied.

"Who are you and what are you doing here?"

"Those should be *my* lines."

The knuckle of the woman's trigger finger tightened. "I lose my patience easily, Belasko. A bullet from this gun wouldn't kill you—provided it only entered a kneecap or a wrist or a testicle, for example."

Bolan made no reply.

The woman took a deep breath and asked, "What is your connection with Deveroux?"

"Who?"

"Dev-er-*ou*," she repeated, carefully enunciating each syllable. "Nubbar Kalashin was in his employ. You visited Kalashin's home less than an hour ago, and for some reason, blew it up. What evidence were you trying to destroy?''

"Why would I destroy evidence?"

In a tone ragged with impatience, the woman said, "To keep it from us. Didn't you think we'd still be on Deveroux's trail, even after all this time?"

Bolan was rapidly gaining interest in the topic, but just as rapidly losing all tolerance for the circumstances of the discussion. He had skirted the edges of the international intelligence community before, and in the past had more than once gone head-to-head with KGB operatives. Past experience had taught him that little was to be gained from continuing to play the roles of either ignorant innocent or tight-lipped adversary.

As if he had picked up on Bolan's thoughts, the big man rumbled, "I've had enough of this stalling-around horseshit."

He took a menacing step forward and poked the Beretta's sound suppressor hard into the pit of Bolan's stomach. "Answer her questions, or I'll gut-shoot you and stake you out in the desert so the jackals can unwind your intestines. I'll make sure you're still alive while they do it."

In one swift motion, Bolan back-fisted the sound suppressor away with his right hand and sprang forward to head-butt the man in the face. The woman's voice rose in a frightened shout, and the soldier pivoted on his right foot and kicked up his left leg horizontally. The toe of his shoe caught the butt of the pistol in her hand, sending the weapon spinning upward.

Before she could react, Bolan had stretched out a hand and snatched the gun from the air. He whirled to cover the big man with it.

He was sagging against a communications console, both hands vainly trying to staunch the flow of blood from his nose and mouth. His eyes were squeezed shut, and tears of pain dripped down his face, cutting tracks in the crimson smear. The green elephant on his coverall was slowly turning red. The Beretta lay on the floor plates at his feet.

Bolan kicked the sound suppressor and sent the pistol skittering toward the rear of the truck. As he did so, he noticed that the weight of the Glock in his hand felt an ounce or two short of a full load.

The big man lurched to his feet, eyes, nose and mouth streaming. He bared blood-filmed teeth, swore roundly in Russian and started toward him. Bolan aimed the gun at the man's right thigh and squeezed the trigger. He wasn't overly surprised when the only sound was the dry click of a firing pin striking an empty chamber.

The man reached for the lapels of his sport coat, and Bolan chopped at his left hand with the flat of the pistol. He heard the crunching of knuckles, but the man was already in so much pain from a broken nose and split lips that to him the blow was hardly more than a twinge. He pounded a right into Bolan's body, just below the heart.

The Executioner swallowed a grunt of pain and staggered against a monitor rising from a computer console. The big man rushed for him, and Bolan rolled aside, grabbing a handful of coverall and using his momentum to pitch him forward. The man's hands flew instinctively out to catch himself, but Bolan kicked his feet out from under him.

His head crashed into the monitor with a splintering of glass and a loud cracking of plastic. The man's body turned to rubber, and dropped to the floor.

Bolan retrieved his Beretta and faced the woman, who was glaring at him while nursing her hand.

"There was no reason for that," she spit. "Sergei was just bluffing, and you might have broken my finger."

Bolan waggled the extended barrel of the Beretta at her. "This one is loaded," he said quietly. "Pick up my wallet and passport."

She obeyed, and as she handed them to him, he told her, "I thought you said we were all professionals. Trying to get the bulge on an armed man with an unloaded weapon is not only unforgettably amateurish, it makes you too stupid to live by just about anybody's standards."

Her eyes stared into his defiantly. "Will you kill me, then?"

"Lucky for you I'm not anybody. Do you have a name?"

She ran a nervous hand through her wealth of black hair. "Anastasia Kirchov. *Professor* Kirchov, of the Russian Institute of Applied Astrophysics."

"Pretty high-flown cover identity, and an easy one to blow if you run into an expert in that field."

"I *am* an expert in that field. It is not a cover."

"I know times have changed, but since when does the Russian Foreign Intelligence Service use academics as field agents?"

Kirchov hesitated a moment before saying, "Since their knowledge and expertise make them invaluable when certain circumstances arise."

"And those certain circumstances are what?"

She shook her head. "A matter of internal security. I was dispatched on this mission because the former excesses of Sergei's fraternity are no longer countenanced."

"In other words, Sergei didn't have kill permission for this job, and you came along to make sure he didn't reinterpret his orders. That's why you were waving around an empty gun."

Bolan smiled thinly. "Times *have* changed. Well, I have a flight to catch, and I don't have the time to pump you for information. I'll use my own resources."

A sudden alarm came into her eyes. "You have nothing to go on."

Bolan pushed past her to the entry panel leading to the cab. "Not much. References to telemetry, activation codes, and—I'm sure you'll appreciate this one—bloody Russians who think they're so damned clever."

Kirchov made a contemptuous gesture with one hand. "Nonsense words."

"Oh, I almost forgot." Bolan paused and said blandly, "The Hellfire Trigger."

Fear flooded her face. She reached out for him, thought better of it and dropped her hands to her sides. She plucked agitatedly at her robe. "Forget you heard that. Do you wish to instigate a major diplomatic incident? I am convinced you have nothing to do with our investigation. This…misunderstanding will not even figure in my report to my superiors. Leave it at that."

"Afraid not, Professor," Bolan responded, holstering the Beretta. "You've given me way too many questions to simply walk away into the sunset."

As he left the truck, he could hear her calling after him, first threatening to report him to the State Department, then to the Algerian government. He kept walking.

Bolan didn't know what kind of stew was boiling around him, but his meeting with Professor Anastasia Kirchov had given him a good idea where he could find the answer.

3

Stony Man Farm, Virginia

Aaron Kurtzman wheeled his chair away from the computer terminal and knuckled his eyes. Text scrolled across the monitor screen.

"I wish you had more to go on than just a name," he said. "There are only about five hundred Deverouxs in the database and out of that, about a hundred variant spellings."

Bolan leaned against a desk and crossed his arms over his chest. "Sorry, Aaron, but I doubt Professor Kirchov would have been kind enough to spell out the name for me."

The lighting in the computer room was dim for security reasons. Here and there glowing monitor screens provided squares of eerie light. The room was Kurtzman's private domain, so Bolan didn't comment on the risk of eyestrain.

After arriving at Stony Man Farm three hours before, Bolan had commandeered the computer expert from another project to open up the main database. Bolan could have done it himself, but there was protocol to observe.

Kurtzman tapped a sheet of hard copy inside a laser printer's output tray. "At least Anastasia Kirchov's credentials check out. She's who she said she was."

"But not what she *is,*" Bolan replied. "Even a kinder

and gentler SVR wouldn't send an academic into the field unless a situation was desperate.''

The computer beeped softly and the wild scrolling stopped. On the screen, pixels slowly grouped and built the mug shot of a mustached, middle-aged Hispanic man. Leaning forward, Kurtzman read the curriculum vitae beneath the image.

''Salvador Deveroux. Low-level cocaine trafficker out of Haiti. He's been dead for two years.''

Kurtzman cursed and punched a button, clearing the screen and starting the search process over again. ''That was a cross-referenced DEA file. Why don't they update their damn files?''

''Patience, Bear.''

Kurtzman heaved his broad shoulders in a shrug. ''I've got to admit the name Deveroux rings a faint bell. But I don't associate it with anything criminal.''

The beep came again. The scrolling stopped, and the pixels built another picture. The image that formed wasn't a mug; it was a candid, head-and-shoulders shot of a young, slim man with long, blond hair that tumbled past his shoulders. He was sharp-featured, with a pair of round-lensed sunglasses masking his eyes.

When the vital statistics came up, Kurtzman snorted. ''Here's a real golden oldie, cross-referenced from the Justice Department database, no less.''

Bolan moved closer, eyeing the screen. ''Oh, yeah.''

''Dexter Hewitt Deveroux,'' Kurtzman said, reading off the vitals in an amused tone. ''Chairman and chief stockholder of Deveroux Multi-Industries. He formed the company over twenty-five years ago and spread it out into a dozen different fields—entertainment, construction and alternative energy sources, primarily soltech.''

''Soltech? Solar technology?''

''Yeah. He built an experimental solar power station on a no-name island in the Gulf of Mexico, just off the west coast of Florida. The station was a public-relations effort. He was trying to get government contracts.''

"He was trying more than that, as I recall," Bolan said.

"Yeah. He got involved in radical chic politics. You might remember that tour he took of Cambodia during Pol Pot's regime, claiming it was a business trip since he only dealt with winners. The Khmer Rouge wined and dined him like he was an emperor or something."

More and more memories were coming back to Bolan. "He publicly supported groups like the Weather Underground and the Tigers of Justice, didn't he?"

"As long as they were chic and the darlings of the media, yeah," Kurtzman replied. "Before they were exposed as being engaged in terrorist activities. Then they weren't so chic anymore. And neither was Deveroux."

Kurtzman pressed a key and more text appeared on the screen. "Deveroux tried his hand at fashion design. His clothing line, Dex's Durables, failed miserably. He opened a chain of discos, and those were as short-lived as his other enterprises."

Bolan grunted. "Sounds like a man who tries to keep in step, but always manages to stumble."

Kurtzman nodded. "The horses break loose from his bandwagon and he's stuck in the driver's box all dressed up with no place to go."

"That Intel is pretty old. What's the latest we have on him?"

"Not a thing. Even this picture is over twenty years old."

"Then why is he in the database?"

Kurtzman smiled sourly. "Probably the same reason as Salvador Deveroux is—someone was too lazy to purge the file. I mean, aside from his old radical connections, Dexter Deveroux is a forgotten man. A counterculture Missing In Action. Kirchov was obviously talking about another Deveroux. This guy seems about as dangerous as a tie-dyed T-shirt.''

"Can you get me something more current?''

Kurtzman shifted in his wheelchair. "This particular Deveroux can't be connected to what went down in Algiers.''

"Humor me.''

Sighing, Kurtzman tapped the keys. "Okay, I'll check known associates.''

The screen bisected and in one corner the color image formed of a beautiful young woman with huge, haunting dark eyes. Straight red hair fell past her bare shoulders. It was obviously a posed studio shot.

"Deveroux's first wife...a fashion model named Christa Clay. She was the spokesmodel for Dex's Durables. She died almost fifteen years ago.''

"Of what?''

"The main health threat to models. Anorexia.''

Kurtzman's fingers manipulated the keyboard, and the picture of Christa Clay was replaced by that of another woman. Though she was pretty, her nostrils were pierced by golden studs and her short, white hair was cut in asymmetrical spikes. She was wearing a black leather dominatrix outfit, standing on a stage and holding a microphone. Her lips were curled in a carefully calculated sneer.

"Deveroux's second wife,'' Kurtzman announced. "Barbie Bizarro, a.k.a. Meriem Jackson, a punk rocker with the Microcephalics. The band had a brief vogue in underground clubs several years ago. Deveroux was their manager. She's dead too.''

Bolan eyed the image. "Not anorexia?''

"Nope. She was found dead in a London hotel room, the victim of an apparent heroin overdose.''

Another tap of a key and another picture resolved on the screen. It was of a lovely black woman, smiling sweetly.

"Deveroux's third wife," Kurtzman announced. "Erica Quiller, a clothing designer."

"Let me guess. Deceased?"

"No, disappeared. Eight years ago. Deveroux filed for divorce on the grounds of desertion."

Smiling thinly, Kurtzman hit another key. "Let's try for number four."

The image the pixels built was not that of a woman. It was a publicity photograph of a scholarly black man, one long-fingered hand crooked beneath a pronounced chin. The man wore wire-rimmed glasses and his expression was meditative. Thick hair surrounded his head in a dark halo.

Bolan leaned forward as Kurtzman said, "Jesse El-Hamid. Took his cybernetics degree from M.I.T. at age eighteen. A real whiz kid. He was involved in Deveroux's soltech research."

"Anything in there about a degree in chiropractic?"

"What?" Kurtzman swiveled his head to stare at Bolan. "What would a cyberneticist need with that?"

"To learn about the human nervous system, maybe."

Kurtzman's answering, "Maybe," was doubtful.

"Can you manipulate the image?" Bolan asked. "Take away the glasses and about thirty pounds, give him a new hairstyle and add about ten years to his face?"

With deft motions of the mouse and following Bolan's instructions, Kurtzman carefully altered Jesse El-Hamid's appearance. Within fifteen minutes a different face was staring out of the screen.

"Dr. Jest, I presume," Bolan muttered.

"This is the guy who got away," Kurtzman said. "Your Algerian connection."

Bolan straightened. "Bear, I want you to squeeze the database for everything that might relate to Deveroux or El-Hamid, no matter how minor or silly it seems. Got it?"

"Got it," Kurtzman said. "Just give me a few hours."

Leaving the computer center, Bolan took the elevator to

the second floor and walked down the carpeted corridor to the room he called home when he was at the Farm. He paused for a moment to gaze out a window at the rolling Virginia hills. Midafternoon sunlight gave the grounds of Stony Man Farm a bucolic, peaceful glow that was almost magical.

He couldn't see the elaborate system of heat-sensing warning devices, night-vision scopes and trigger alarms surrounding the acreage. There were armed guards posted around the clock, although the guards seemed like farmhands idling about the grounds looking for something to do.

Bolan turned from the window and continued down the corridor. Both Phoenix Force and Able Team were away on missions, so he had the Farm more or less to himself— except for Barbara Price, the mission controller, Kurtzman and his cybernetics team, and the Farm's support staff, not to mention a small army of guards.

The place had all the comforts of home, if your idea of home was a military base.

In his room, Bolan stripped and showered, washing away the faint odor of burnt almonds that still clung to him. He closed the blinds of the window and hit the rack. Though he was accustomed to going without sleep for long periods, he was also accustomed to catching sleep whenever he could, to build up a backlog.

Bolan was awakened almost immediately by the sound of rotor blades. The Farm, apparently, had a late-night visitor. Several minutes later he received a call from Price, requesting his presence in the War Room.

PRICE AND KURTZMAN were already seated at the table. The atmosphere of the room was electric with tension. An attaché case lay on the table beside Price's elbow. Kurtzman was busy at the computer terminal and glanced up when

Bolan entered. The deep crease across his broad forehead was a dark slash of irritation.

"What's going down?" Bolan asked, taking a chair.

Hal sent someone to see us—a Professor Anastasia Kirchov of Russia. She's brought some Intel that he says has the potential to be pretty damn explosive. Unfortunately he's tied up in D.C. We have to handle it."

"My system is interpolating the encrypted disk she had in her briefcase," Kurtzman broke in. "She said she didn't have the proper code to read it, so it's taking some time."

"I had a close encounter with the professor in Algiers. Interesting that she shows up here. Where is she?"

As if on cue, the door panel of the elevator opened and a security guard escorted the Russian woman into the room. Price dismissed the security guard and waved Kirchov toward a chair in the center of the table. The woman seemed taken aback when she caught sight of Bolan.

Kirchov smiled hesitantly. "I am here in a joint cooperative effort between Russia and America. I remind you that the intelligence services of our respective nations are no longer at each other's throats. There has been a limited trade of certain pieces of information over the last few years, and the situation Russia finds herself in demands access to a great deal of Intel and resources my country does not have. We need help stopping someone called Dexter Deveroux."

"Just what do you know about him?" Bolan asked. "Aside from the fact that he supported leftist radical causes and isn't much of a businessman?"

The smile faded from Anastasia Kirchov's face. "I do not wish to sound melodramatic, but if any man exists who currently has the means and the desire to destroy the world, Deveroux is that man."

"That's a pretty stiff ambition for anyone," Price replied wryly. "Even for a capitalist."

Kirchov knew she was being mocked, but she didn't

seem offended. "Deveroux is not a capitalist in the strictest sense, not even by my culture's admittedly broad definition."

"Why not?"

"Because he is not motivated by a desire for money, love or even territory."

"I'll bite," Bolan said. "What *does* motivate him?"

Kirchov took a long, deep breath. "All his material desires have been transcended by a consuming fire to attain godhood."

4

Tampa, Florida

The Double D building punched its way five hundred feet above the streets of Harbour Island, Florida. It wasn't listed as the Double D in the city directory. Its formal name was the Osiris Tower. The tower was rented and maintained by the Tiamat Management Company, which was retained by Deveroux Multi-Industries. Deveroux Multi-Industries kept the building on a ninety-nine-year lease from Ra Soltech, which was a holding company owned by Lastlight Entertainment.

The building was called the Double D by residents because the exterior of the penthouse sported a huge pair of bright red, overlapping capital *D*s.

Dexter Deveroux flew over one of the *D*s. He was seated in a small, delicately designed helicopter, which was sinking gracefully toward the landing pad on the roof of the building.

His green eyes, masked by the dark lenses of designer sunglasses, scanned the haze-veiled skyline of Tampa. He murmured into the transceiver of his headset, ''Another age will see all this in quite a different perspective.''

''Sir?'' The pilot turned his head toward him.

Deveroux pointed down toward the flat roof.

The chopper landed with a gentle bump, and Deveroux stepped out with loose-limbed ease. He didn't bother to duck beneath the spinning blades, though they beat the air furiously barely two inches above his head. He walked to the entrance cupola, wending his way among a dozen solar energy panels. Eight feet long and tilted upward at forty-five-degree angles, the heat reflected from their glassy surfaces was fierce. Deveroux didn't flinch, though judging by the pallor of his complexion, even limited exposure to direct sunlight would result in a painful burn.

Deveroux was wearing a midnight blue shirt, trimmed with gold thread. Around his waist was a wide patent leather belt with a huge "god's-eye" buckle made of brass. His pale hair was brushed back and knotted at the base of his neck.

At the cupola, he placed the palm and five fingers of his right hand over a lit panel. The door opened, and he walked down a short flight of stairs. The stairs opened into the operations center of Deveroux Multi-Industries.

The two dozen people manning computer consoles and sitting at desks were of different races, genders and nationalities. They shared two common traits; one was their age. They were all young, none over thirty. The other trait was the anxiety that shone in their eyes at their first sight of Deveroux.

It was his preference to employ young, talented people; he believed if they were suitably influenced when young, their gifts and abilities could be turned in any direction he wished. Privately Deveroux referred to them as "knobs," and often thought of the entire room as Knob Row.

Deveroux didn't so much as nod to them. He walked to a huge Mercator projection map of the world that covered an entire wall. Spots of light flickered in almost every country, and a network of glowing lines crisscrossed it like a web spun by a deranged spider.

He studied the spots of light, traced one of the glowing lines with a long finger and said, "Get back to it, children."

The people in the operations center went back to their

individual endeavors, and Deveroux walked to a far door. His fingerprints unlocked it, and he walked into the King's Chamber. His employees didn't call it that; they referred to it as his private office or his inner sanctum. It made them too nervous to apply their boss's designation to that room.

But a King's Chamber it was, and it was the only intentional affectation Deveroux had ever adopted. It was furnished with Egyptian objets d'art, all manner of statues and wall hangings.

A skylight allowed a shaft of sunshine to blaze upon a massive, marble-topped desk. The marble was inlaid with colorful cartouches. Even the intercom keys were hieroglyphs.

Hanging behind the desk, suspended by thin steel wires, was a huge gold disc in the form of the Re-Horakhte falcon. The upcurving wings were inlaid with colored glass. The sun disc atop the beaked head was a cabochon-cut carnelian.

One wall was covered by a huge illustrated section from the Eighteenth Dynasty *Book of the Dead,* depicting animal-headed gods and goddesses from the Egyptian pantheon.

Arrayed on a long shelf on the opposite wall were a dozen *ushabtis* figures, small statuettes representing laborers in the Land of the Dead.

Against the right wall was a granite six-foot replica of the seated figure of Ramses the Third, artfully copied from Egypt's Abu Simbel valley.

In another place, another time, Deveroux might have been a Ramses, an Akhenaton or, at the very least, an Alexander. But in this place and time, Deveroux was an entrepreneur, an aesthete, an artist and a man who despised the limitations of mortal flesh and bone.

He had followed many paths trying to find the key that would unlock his warrior-king spirit from the frailties of the flesh. Meditation, macrobiotic dieting and a wasteful—

and expensive—experiment with hypnotic regression hadn't even shown him the door, much less a glimpse of the key.

He had found the key on his own, after reaching the conclusion that all the spiritual advisers he had sought out in the past were deliberately directing him down the wrong path.

The key lay in amassing personal power, taking control over his environment, over each and every component that influenced his life. Deveroux knew he wasn't unique in his drive for power. He dealt on a daily basis with people who shared the same obsession; they were chairmen of international corporations, government executives, princes, kings and self-proclaimed presidents-for-life.

Unlike these people, Deveroux didn't subscribe to the belief that power was an end, not a means. He believed in the exact opposite.

At his desk, he sat and lifted the stack of hard copy from his "in" basket and began to read. From long practice and concentration, Deveroux could read two thousand words per minute and, as he possessed almost total recall, he retained everything his eyes scanned.

The sheets of hard copy were the daily reports filed, gleaned, stolen and sometimes traded from data sources as diverse as the Navy's SR-1 channel to wastepaper baskets in the Rwandan embassy.

A select group of operatives—Deveroux called them conduits—monitored all the information and passed it on through several layers of personnel, dead-drops and back-channels to the Double D, where it was entered into computers, collated, cross-indexed and then spit out as hard copy. The hard copy was printed on a special flash paper of Deveroux's own manufacture, and after he was finished with it, the copy was routinely incinerated. He oversaw the incineration himself.

No bit, byte, gram or germ of intelligence that came into

Deveroux's hands was ever discarded. Something that to-day seemed innocuous, even foolish, could be of enormous consequence a year down the road. He had learned that through hard and costly experience when he first established himself as an information broker.

Deveroux read the hard copy quickly, turning each absorbed page facedown on the desk. There were reports about new alloys, the hybridization of grains, pages upon pages picked up from the AP news wire, gossip and innuendo about various public figures, nearly half a ream supplied by his conduits inside the FBI, the CIA, the NSA, the ONI, the IRS, Interpol and a score of other institutions across the world that had a monomania about secrecy. The data was eclectic, spanning topics from new antibiotics to gasoline additives.

Much of it appeared nonsensical, but for every scrap of data there was a buyer, or a group of buyers.

A soft chime sounded somewhere in the room. Without raising his eyes from the sheet of paper, Deveroux pressed a colored inlay on the desktop. With a hydraulic hissing, a panel in the wall slid aside and Jest stepped out of a narrow elevator. It was one of four lifts situated around the penthouse. Only Deveroux knew the locations of all of them.

Jest folded his long body into a chair facing the desk. He cradled his bandaged right hand in his left. He was smiling.

"Hakim?" Deveroux asked.

"Dead."

"And Hardman?"

"Never learned who he was, but I learned *what* he was."

Deveroux looked up from the printout, face expressionless, eyes masked by dark lenses.

Jest shifted in his chair. "A hardman, all right. A real pro. He took out Nubbar and his team and damn near took me out."

"I see." Deveroux steepled his fingers. "Nationality?"

"American. He could be connected."

"Connected or not, he saved you the problem of dealing with Nubbar."

Jest's smile turned into a scowl. "I went to a lot of trouble rigging Nubbar's apartment. Finding him with a bullet in his head instead of dead in bed is bound to get some notice, even in Algiers. And if our Russian friends get wind of it—"

Deveroux's snort cut off the rest of Jest's words. "The thieving bastards are only concerned with keeping a twenty-eight-year-old skeleton in its closet. They couldn't care less about the telemetry."

"Except for me and you," Jest ventured, "nobody even knows about it."

"Unless," Deveroux replied, a steel edge entering his voice, "Hakim had time to make a statement to Hardman. He obviously trusted him enough to send him a message, even suspecting we were keeping an eye on him."

"Nubbar was our only intermediary when we bought Hakim's files," Jest said. "As far as Hakim knew, he sold his files to the Bulgarian version of *The Enquirer.*"

Tapping his fingers on the stacked hard copy, Deveroux asked, "What about the courier Hakim used to get word to Hardman?"

Jest gingerly rubbed his bandaged hand. "According to Phildercost, the courier was traced to a dead-drop in a Richmond shopping mall. He lost him after that."

Deveroux's lips compressed in a tight line. "Hardman could belong to anybody...the Agency, the Bureau, the Mob—"

"Not the Mob." Jest displayed his bandaged hand. "He had the perfect opportunity to blow my ass away, but he didn't."

"Maybe he should have," Deveroux snapped. "One less loose end to distract me."

"Come on, Dex." Jest forced a smile. "We're brothers.

I've been at your side from the beginning, up or down, thin or thick, busted or flush. I've gotten you out of three bad marriages, six patrimony suits—''

"Enough." Deveroux raised a hand. "I don't need a reminder of how much I owe you."

Jest sighed. "Sometimes I think you do, Dex. Remember, wife number three, the lovely Erica, was my first cousin."

Deveroux pushed his sunglasses down his nose and stared at Jest over the rims. "First rule of security. A balance of check and countercheck. She failed the countercheck. Because you lied to me about her ability to keep secrets. Her loose lips put you at as much risk as they did me."

Pressing an intercom key, he called his secretary in the outer office. "Has Phildercost checked in this morning?"

"Yes, sir. He said he'd been in around ten or ten-thirty."

"Let me know the moment he arrives."

Deveroux stood, stacked the hard copy carefully, tucked it under his right arm and said, "Let's go. Feeding time for the baby."

He crossed the room to the seated statue of Ramses. As he fingered a cartouche at the base of the sculpture, the entire stone figure slid to the left, pushed by small hidden pistons. Behind the statue was a narrow doorway and Deveroux and Jest stepped through it. The dimly lit passage beyond was a tight squeeze, even for men of their thin physiques.

The end of the passageway was blocked by hanging Plexiglas strips. Both men took a pair of white, hooded sterilized coveralls from a hook on the wall. They slipped them on, adjusted the surgical masks over their noses and mouths, pushed the static guards aside and entered the room.

None of the various pieces of data that floated through the Double D in hard copy could be touched by hands other than Dexter Deveroux's. It was all downloaded and stored in a machine five feet high, three feet deep and sixteen feet long.

The Cheops Alpha was a one-of-a-kind computer, utilizing the prototypical processing system known as teraflops. The Cheops required such a vast memory that chips with the capacity of one billion bits—the equivalent of four hundred pages of newspaper—were required to operate it. The chips were pieces of silicon not much larger than a thumbnail.

Deveroux and Jest had developed the technology to etch circuit lines in the chips through X-rays rather than the standard optical lithography. As a result, the Cheops processed information and performed various tasks at one trillion operations per second. Thousands of these chips were inside the guts of the computer.

The Cheops was hidden inside a special strong room. The entire penthouse had been designed around it, built solely to protect the machine. The strong room didn't show up on floor plans or even on the architect's blueprints. The room itself wasn't spacious, and the computer and its support systems covered almost every inch of space.

Deveroux fed the stack of hard copy into a scanner as Jest took a seat at one of the Cheops's three keyboard stations.

"On-line, Dex," Jest said after a moment.

Deveroux turned on the scanner, and the hard copy was converted into raw electronic bits and fed into the database. The Cheops cross-referenced and indexed every piece of information, deleting duplicate items. The process required less than ten seconds.

Deveroux left the stack of hard copy in the scanner's tray. Later, he would take it to a specially designed incinerator in the King's Chamber and dispose of it.

Turning to Jest, he said, "Access design program Remora Three."

Jest moved over to the master keyboard, his long fingers flying over it. The four-foot Super VGA monitor screen blazed with color. "Program on-line."

Deveroux watched as a jumble of geometric shapes, straight lines and cones swirled across the screen, then attached themselves to one another. The schematic of a single-stage rocket appeared, and specifications scrolled down beside the image.

"It's an improvement over Remora One and Two," Jest said, gesturing to the screen. "Still have propellant problems, though."

Deveroux grunted. "We're only dealing with Newton's Third Law. We're not trying to invent warp drive."

"Yeah, but this single-stage design has too many unstable variables. It's easier to use a multistage set-up."

"We can't risk the stages being detected by radar as they're dropped," Deveroux replied. "A single stage is smaller, faster."

"A rocket only ten yards long won't have much of a problem achieving escape velocity if our launch window is at optimum, but we still have the payload problem to deal with."

Jest pointed to the nose cone. "See, we've got the flight direction system and antennae directly above the diffusion chamber. The turbo-compressor feeds right into the solid-chemical propellant chamber. With only one stage and ten yards to work with, that's like a car consisting of ninety-nine percent gas tank and one percent left for the driver."

Leaning forward, Deveroux traced the image on the screen with one gloved finger. "The payload is only a magnetic grappler and a microwave tight-beam transceiver. The whole apparatus weighs less than five hundred pounds. However, we may be able to reconfigure the air intake of the combustion chamber. Get to work on that redesign and modem it over to Eberhardt and let him tinker with it. We've got less than a week before we lose our window."

The intercom on the wall crackled and a woman's voice said, "Mr. Deveroux? Mr. Phildercost is here. Mr. Nyung is with him."

"Five minutes. Then I'll buzz them in."

Leaving Jest at the keyboard, Deveroux walked out of the strong room, stripping off the coverall. Returning to the King's Chamber, he touched the cartouche at the base of Ramses and the statue slid back into place.

He sat at his keyboard, pressed a hieroglyph on its surface, lock solenoids clicked open and his office door swung wide. Bertram Phildercost and Billy Nyung entered.

Phildercost was a slob. He was of medium height, narrow in the shoulders, wide in the hips, with a big belly that sagged over his loose gray slacks. His sparse gray hair was combed over a bald spot on his head. The white shirt beneath his cheap sport coat was soaked through with sweat.

Billy Nyung was short, barely five feet five. He was at least twenty-five years younger than Phildercost, and wore a white linen suit. As he always did when he entered Deveroux's office, he peered around the room through wire-rimmed spectacles and grinned.

"He lives in a museum," he intoned in singsong cadence, "when people come to see him, he really is a scream, Dex-ter Dev-ah-RO!"

Nyung punctuated his song with a sharp double-hand clap.

"Shut up, Billy," Phildercost growled. He plopped in the one chair in front of the desk. "We need to talk, hoss."

"We do indeed," Deveroux said. "I understand you lost Hakim's courier—in a shopping mall of all places."

Phildercost shook his head. "I subcontracted that gig to Billy-boy here. He just don't have the shadowing experience. 'Sides, what difference does it make? Heard that old Hakim got himself whacked, right?"

"He had some help," Deveroux replied. "And a witness."

"That's just the topic we got to discuss, hoss. I picked up some word from the station in Algiers. Word is your witness has heavy connections. It's just a buzz, but where there's smoke, there's fire. From what I been told, your witness may've been a guy named Belasko. Seems he might have worked covert ops for the Justice Department. Anyway, he's a heavy hitter used to playing in the big leagues. Or so I hear.

"If this guy gets on to you, hoss, you're in big trouble. From all my sources, all I hear is that he's bad news."

"I begin to understand," Deveroux said. "You'll be in the line of fire and will compromise your oh-so-eminent position in the Agency if Belasko connects you to me."

Phildercost scowled at the sarcasm. "Something like that. I put in a lot of years with the Company, starting with the ZRIFLE operation in Miami, working against Castro. I got my equity to consider."

"Not to mention your access to laundered, and therefore untraceable, cash. Tell me, Bertram, why aren't you worried about compromising your position as one of my conduits?"

Phildercost barked a harsh laugh. He took a Havana cigar from an inside jacket pocket and jammed it between his teeth.

"Don't smoke."

The CIA man ignored him. He set fire to the cigar with a burnished steel butane lighter and blew a wreath of smoke toward Deveroux. "I'm not worried about my position, hoss, because I got you by the balls."

"I hope we're not talking blackmail, Bertram, because I assure you that whatever happens to me will certainly happen to you."

"I got no reason to blackmail you, hoss. I just want to be released from my contract. With a severance package included, of course. Sort of an out-of-court settlement. A hundred grand ought to do it."

Deveroux sat silently for a moment, then said, "I have a counteroffer. I'll simply kill you and forget about you."

Phildercost grinned behind the cigar. He snapped the fingers of his right hand. "Billy-boy."

Nyung gave the left sleeve of his coat a little shake. His hand whipped up, the five-inch blade of a butterfly knife dancing over his fingertips.

"Thought you might need more persuading than just a talking-to, hoss," Phildercost said. "You know Billy-boy, right? How he has only one marketable job skill, and that's cutting throats slicker than warm snot on a cold doorknob?"

"Or I could slide it in his ear," Nyung said with an enthusiastic smile, swishing the knife through the air.

"That's right, you could," Phildercost agreed. "Make it look like a cerebral hemorrhage. Man carrying the load you're carrying, nobody'd question it, hoss."

Deveroux continued to sit quietly.

"Well?" Phildercost asked. "Are we going to be reasonable?"

"Yes, we are."

He stood and carefully walked around the corner of the desk, stopping about six feet from Billy Nyung.

"Do it, Billy-boy," he said in a husky whisper. "Give me a cerebral hemorrhage."

Nyung blinked in surprise. The smile faded from his face, he bared his teeth in a silent snarl and he moved. The knife blade darted forward like the head of a striking viper.

Deveroux's entire torso bent backward at the waist, his head nearly brushing the floor. The butterfly knife whiffed the air his throat had occupied a fraction of a second before.

Deveroux's long right leg came up, the foot smashing brutally into Nyung's face. The young man screeched a protest as he went staggering backward into the wall.

Recovering his balance gracefully, Deveroux stood and smiled. Nyung's face changed. His cheerful, naive expression became one of undiluted hatred and fury. His black eyes glittered from behind the cracked lenses of his spectacles. Saliva and blood drooled from his mouth.

Raking his ruined glasses from his face, Nyung lunged forward, sunlight glinting from the steel blade in his fist. The knife cut a figure-eight pattern in the air.

Deveroux leaned away from the steel edge, reached out, plucked the cigar from Phildercost's surprise-slacked lips and skated away from Nyung's rage-crazed charge.

As the young man passed, Deveroux mashed the red, glowing end of the cigar into Nyung's right eye.

He howled, clawing at his face. The knife fell to the floor and he went to his knees, pawing madly at his eye.

Deveroux snatched up the knife with his right hand, grabbed a handful of black hair in his left and wrenched Nyung's head to one side. The narrow knife blade dipped into and out of his ear in two smooth motions.

Nyung's howls of agony were cut short. He stopped clawing and writhing, and when Deveroux released his grip, he toppled face-first to the floor with a sound like a wet towel slapping against concrete.

Turning to face Phildercost, Deveroux tossed the red-stained knife atop the marble desk, where it chimed with a clear musical note.

Phildercost was breathing heavily, sweat pouring down his face, dripping from his double chins and running down his thick neck. His eyes were wide and wild.

"Bertram, do you know why I despise violence so much?"

Phildercost didn't respond for a moment. He licked his lips, then he exhaled a querulous, "No."

"Because I'm so fucking good at it, that's why. I resent being forced to display an art I've already mastered. It's undignified, like demanding Houdini perform cheap sleight-of-hand magic tricks at a cocktail party."

Stepping over Billy Nyung's body, Deveroux returned to

the chair behind his desk. He smiled, but it didn't reach his eyes. Like an animal smelling blood, he sensed Phildercost's terror and responded to it with pleasure. "You're a sweaty, fat fool, Bertram, who scares much too easily. And you want me to share your weakness. However, you *are* useful to me. Do you still wish to sever our relationship—one which even I have to admit has been rewarding?"

"No." The single word passed Phildercost's lips like a bubble of gas.

"Good. I want more information about this man Belasko. A picture if possible, or a sketch. I want it by this afternoon. Is that doable, Bertram?"

"Yes."

Deveroux flipped his hand dismissively. "I will attend to Billy-boy. You may go now."

"Thank you." Phildercost heaved himself out of the chair and shuffled to the door. He waited for Deveroux to free the lock solenoids.

"Bertram?"

"Yes." He didn't dare turn.

"In the future, do not address me as 'hoss.' And do not smoke. Is that doable as well?"

"Yes. Yes, sir."

The locks clicked open. The door swung wide on its hinges.

"Good seeing you again, Bertram."

5

Stony Man Farm, Virginia

The thing on the wall was dark, squat and ugly. It looked to be about ten feet long by ten wide, consisting of a flat platform and a long cylinder encased in some dark, heavy metal. CCCP was painted in white letters on the rivet-studded skin. Men in white coats and coveralls bustled around the platform.

"I converted this internal security film to videotape," Anastasia Kirchov stated. "The quality is not of the best, but you can recognize its historical significance."

"Maybe you can," Price replied. "What's so significant about an old home movie?"

One wall of the War Room was covered by the flickering black-and-white image. It was grainy and spotty and occasionally out of focus.

"An orbiting nuclear platform, like the old BAMBI systems," Aaron Kurtzman announced. He cast a glance at Kirchov. "Am I right?"

"You are. This film was made over two decades ago, right before the platform was launched."

"In direct violation of the Outer Space Treaty of 1967," Price said.

"And so are many aspects of your government's Strategic Defense Initiative," Kirchov replied calmly. "I am not here to engage in a finger-pointing contest."

"Go on," Kurtzman urged.

"One of the Israeli technicians coined the term *Gehenem fayer Peron,* which, in Yiddish, translates loosely as the Hellfire Trigger. The platform carries a thermonuclear payload."

"An H-bomb? A fission-fusion-fission bomb?" Kurtzman asked incredulously. "Good God."

"Yes, you might say that," Kirchov said dryly. "Since it was launched, the platform has been nestled securely at the apex of a Lagrangian point—a suborbital point in space at which a small body, such as a satellite or platform, under the gravitational influences of two large ones, like the Earth and the moon, remains approximately at rest. Relative to them, anyway."

"What kind of yield are we talking about here?" Price asked.

"Nothing too spectacular," Kirchov responded. "The warhead is of average size, with the usual mixture of beryllium and plutonium 239. A fission trigger is connected to a fusion device made of uranium 238 and lithium deuteride. The explosive power is approximately that of 300,000 tons of TNT."

"So a 300-kiloton fusion bomb has been hanging above our heads for over twenty years," Bolan said. "I can't say I'm shocked, but I am a little surprised your government is admitting to putting one in orbit."

"We have no choice but to admit to it, since the platform is no longer under our control."

"And you suspect it's under the control of Dexter Deveroux?" Bolan inquired.

"Yes."

"Why?"

"Several years ago, Deveroux approached my government with a proposal to launch satellites inexpensively and economically. To this end, he wanted us to finance the construction of a special single-stage rocket prototype."

"What was so special about the prototype?" Kurtzman asked.

Kirchov used the flat of her hand to push against the surface of the desk. "Present-day rockets push themselves by ejecting mass at high speed, using a liquid propellant as fuel. As the propellant is pushed out, the rocket is accelerated forward."

"Yeah, right," Kurtzman said impatiently. "We're all familiar with Newton's Third Law of motion."

Kirchov smiled wryly. "Since American education standards are far below those of my homeland's, I wasn't sure if you were. At any rate, the heavier the rocket, the heavier the payload, the more propellant is needed to push it. Liquid chemical fuel is itself heavy. Most of the propellant in conventional rockets is wasted by being used to achieve escape velocity."

"Deveroux's prototype solved that problem?" Bolan asked.

"At least in his proposal papers. Mr. Kurtzman, have you accessed that file yet?"

"Yes," he responded gruffly. "If you intended us to view it, why didn't you provide me with the encryption key?"

"Precautions. I could have been intercepted before I reached you, and my superiors didn't care to make matters easy for the opposition." A grin of genuine amusement crossed Kirchov's face as she added, "Besides, I was told by Mr. Brognola that you were one of the premier computer experts in the world."

Scowling, Kurtzman started to retort, then laughed. "Always nice to have one's talents recognized."

On the wall screen a schematic appeared, a scale drawing of a double-walled circle with a piece branching off at the top, giving it the semblance of an upside-down *Q*. The text stated that the diameter of the circle was a quarter of a kilometer.

"Looks like a particle accelerator," Price observed.

"In a way, you're correct," Kirchov acknowledged, "but more accurately, it is a gigantic centrifuge. According to Deveroux's proposal, the particle to be accelerated would be his lightweight, single-stage rocket. Theoretically the projectile would be propelled around the vacuum tube, gaining speed with every revolution."

"What propels it around the vacuum tube?" Kurtzman asked.

"Solar-powered turbines and jets of pressurized water. When the rocket had built up sufficient centrifugal force and achieved its maximum speed, it would be ejected from the launch tube. The proposal stated that the velocity would be about eleven kilometers per second, sufficient to break free of the Earth's gravity well. The limited amount of fuel aboard would be burned to maneuver it into position, and not wasted on the launch itself."

"Pretty efficient," Bolan observed. "A disposable pocket rocket. Why did your government pass on it?"

"Despite the man's reputation as a supporter of leftist causes, our background investigation found him to be unprincipled, thoroughly self-serving and self-deluded. He was deemed too untrustworthy to deal with, too impulsive to control. In fact, we learned his sole passion was amassing a collection of ancient Egyptian artifacts."

"Knowing the KGB's methods," Bolan commented, "they realized that passion was difficult to satisfy. Bribing or blackmailing Deveroux with genuine artifacts was beyond their means."

Kirchov shot Bolan a slit-eyed glare, but she didn't respond to the remark. "A few years later," she continued, "we heard of Deveroux again. He had devoted his resources to building an intelligence and data-gathering network. A few KGB officers were discovered to be on his payroll, working as conduits for his information brokerage."

Bolan grunted. "I'm starting to get it now. During the transition phase of the Soviet Union, a lot of classified Intel was sold off by suddenly unemployed Russian spooks. A piece of that Intel had to do with the Hellfire Trigger."

Kirchov nodded unhappily. "Exactly, but we had only one piece."

"Explain."

"The operating codes and triggering telemetry were binary—two pieces for security purposes. One code was be fed into a ground-based communications array and then transmitted to a satellite. Once the uplink was established, the satellite would broadcast the second part of the program telemetry to the platform's onboard operating computer. The first part of the code, the ground-based one, was destroyed when cooler Kremlin heads prevailed."

"And the second part?" Price wanted to know.

"That is evidently in Deveroux's possession. We surmise that he somehow became aware of the platform during his negotiations with the government. He tried to buy the telemetry when the data market opened a few years ago."

"Only to find that Hakim MacMurphy had already purchased it," Bolan said grimly. "Deveroux bought Hakim's files to get his hands on the code, and he kept Hakim under surveillance just to make sure he didn't pass along what he knew of that tidbit."

"MacMurphy wanted to pass it along to you," the woman said. "And that is how and why our paths crossed. I had no idea you were connected to the American authorities until I saw you in this room."

"So, the Russian government suspects Deveroux will put this code to what use?" Price demanded.

"I believe what they suspect is obvious," Kirchov stated blandly. "Deveroux has the means to activate the platform's operating systems. With a single-stage rocket, he could link up with the platform, more or less manually put it on-line, and drop it on whomever's head he chose."

"Why would he do that?" Kurtzman asked. "What's his motive? Blackmail?"

"I don't think it's that simple. As I said before, our investigations proved Deveroux to be dangerously unbalanced. He is not technically insane, but his self-delusions of attaining godhood are such that he will follow his own agenda, no matter what destruction he might wreak."

Kirchov paused, licked her lip nervously and added, "The platform's payload is programmed to trigger at 900 meters above sea level. At that height, the yield effect of a 300-kiloton thermonuclear detonation is roughly eight kilometers. Within 1,500 meters of the hypocenter of the explosion, a metropolitan center the size of downtown Washington would be destroyed instantly. Within four kilometers, ninety percent of the population would be killed, and all multistory buildings would collapse. Within 7.5 kilometers, virtually everyone exposed to the blast and its thermal effects would die."

"Any ideas on his proposed target?" Bolan asked.

Kirchov shook her head. "None. Does it matter?"

Clearing his throat, Kurtzman said, "If Deveroux's vacuum launch tube is solar-powered, there's only one possibility for his rocket site."

Bolan nodded. "If he actually built the thing."

Barbara Price sighed, glanced from Bolan to Kirchov and declared, "I suppose there's only one way to find out."

6

Florida

It was late afternoon, and Bolan was on the final approach to Tampa International Airport. He had occupied himself during the two-hour flight reviewing the contents of an Intel jacket hastily compiled by the Sensitive Operations Group of the Justice Department.

There was very little in it beyond what Aaron Kurtzman's computers had dredged up. There were copies of Deveroux's many patent applications for solar energy receptors and generators, a report about his public business interests, but no mention and no photographs of the island he had allegedly converted to a solar power station.

His various companies were listed in the weekly NASDAQ stocks, and none of them, from Ra Soltech to Lastlight Entertainment, seemed to be on the move. The net changes column had more minuses than pluses.

Jesse El-Hamid had no criminal record, and beyond six patrimony suits that were settled out of court, Deveroux was clean as well. Not even his fingerprints were on file. He had maintained a remarkably low profile, at least in the eyes of the law-enforcement and intelligence communities. There was very little information on the man either as a personality or a potential adversary. He was like a wraith, a ghost drifting through the shadows of international wheeling and dealing.

There was no mention whatsoever of his career as a data broker. Bolan reflected that the omission was probably by design. Some of the people who put the jacket together might well be on Deveroux's payroll. It always amazed and irritated Bolan that files an inch thick could be kept on private citizens who sympathized with nonpartisan causes like rain forest preservation, but almost nothing could be known about terrorists who dealt daily in death.

Money might not buy happiness, but it could, if properly spread, buy a sizable portion of anonymity. Deveroux had evidently invested heavily in it.

Looking out the port-side window, Bolan saw the Tampa Bay area sprawled out below. The sandy coastline meeting the Gulf of Mexico was white, and the vast spread of blue water shimmered in the late-afternoon sunshine. He saw a few irregularly shaped islands rearing from the mirrored surface of the Gulf, and he wondered which one might house Deveroux's solar power station.

The day before, after Anastasia Kirchov had returned to the Russian embassy in Washington, Hal Brognola had promised to devote his Sensitive Operations Group to finding the island's location. Brognola, who served as the official liaison between the federal government and the Farm's covert operations, had also found the lack of Intel about Deveroux deeply suspicious.

The jet made a smooth landing on the small airstrip and taxied to an airside reserved for private aircraft. Commercial jets boomed and thundered overhead.

Bolan's ordnance case was on the seat beside him. The leather and brass-reinforced box contained his big .44-caliber Desert Eagle, a half-a-dozen clips of ammunition, his multipocketed blacksuit, a tin of combat cosmetics and a broken-down USAS-12 Remington autoloader shotgun. It was one of his favorite close assault weapons, chosen because of the gun's manageable weight and gas-system operation, which suppressed the recoil and allowed it to be manipulated with one hand. A pair of rotary drum magazines containing twenty rounds of 12-gauge ammunition were nestled in foam-cushioned hollows at the bottom of the case. There were also a half dozen magazines for his Beretta. Each magazine contained fifteen 9 mm parabellum rounds.

Having visited Florida in the summertime before, Bolan knew better than to carry the 93-R in its shoulder rig. He had it tucked into a simple leather-belted slide holster at the small of his back, covered by the tail of his short-sleeved navy blue shirt.

After the jet rolled slowly to a stop, and while attendants were chocking the wheels, the pilot emerged from the cockpit. The tall man's name was Travis, and because of his weather-beaten, rawboned looks and the drooping leonine mustache he wore, he looked more like one of the Earp brothers than a pilot. Over the years, when Jack Grimaldi or Charlie Mott weren't available, he had flown Bolan in and out of hellzones across the world.

"Received a message from the Farm," he said laconically. "The location of your island has been pinpointed. Your contact team has all the Intel."

"Who's my team?"

Travis shrugged. "That's all I was told, Striker. You're supposed to meet them in the rental car area on the ground level of the airport."

After digging into his pocket, Travis handed Bolan a picture ID card identifying him as Mike Belasko of the Justice Department. "Flash that at the security checkpoints. It'll get you through the metal detectors and X-ray stations. The airport police are expecting you, so you shouldn't have any trouble."

Travis opened the hatch and a wall of hot, humid Florida air crowded in, overwhelming the cool interior of the cabin. Heat waves shimmered from the runway surface. The pilot whistled and said with a wry grin, "Welcome to the Sunshine State, by God."

By the time Bolan had completed the short walk across the tarmac, he was perspiring. It had been cooler in Algiers. The sunlight was so dazzling, even at close to six o'clock in the evening, he was forced to put on a pair of sunglasses.

At least the interior of the airside was comfortable. Bolan carried his equipment case in his left hand, and attached the ID card to the breast pocket of his shirt. He kept his right hand, his gun hand, free. Behind the dark lenses of his sunglasses, he scanned the faces of tourists and travelers. No one gave him more than a passing, disinterested glance, but his soldier's instinct was on the alert. He knew, on a gut, subliminal level, that he was entering enemy territory.

True to Travis's words, his ID badge got him through every security checkpoint. At the final one before the main terminal, one of the uniformed officers stared a bit too long, a little too intently at the photo on the badge and at Bolan's face.

The officer was middle-aged and middle-size, thick of gut and heavy of shoulders. Bolan guessed him to be an ex-deputy sheriff or a former city policeman. His eyes held the cold, cynical gleam of a man who suspected everyone of everything.

Though he waved him through, Bolan cast a glance backward; the officer was speaking into a cellular telephone he had taken from his belt. He was staring at Bolan, and for a moment, their gazes locked. Though the man quickly turned away, Bolan knew he had been made.

He had been expected.

Wending his way past the duty-free shops and restaurants, Bolan reached the escalator, which took him to the bottom level. He walked through the baggage claim toward the row of automobile rental booths. Standing near the Dollar-Rent-A-Car cubicle was a big, brown-haired man with unshaven jowls. His eyes were rimmed by black crescent moons, his nose was red and swollen, as were his lips. He was wearing a short-sleeved Hawaiian print shirt and he scowled at Bolan's approach.

"Sergei," Bolan said. "You're my contact team?"

"Half," the burly Russian replied. His speech was somewhat slurred due to the stitches in his lower lip. "Let's go."

Sergei Nimchov led the way through a double set of sliding glass doors to the arriving passengers pickup area. Though the long strip of roadway was protected from the direct blast of sunlight by an overhang and palm trees, the humidity, mixed with the fumes of idling car engines, made breathing difficult.

A late-model dark green Chevy Lumina was parked at the curb. Nimchov put Bolan's case in the trunk and climbed in behind the wheel. Bolan slid in beside him. Anastasia Kirchov sat in the back seat. Because of the light dusky hue of her complexion and her high-cut white shorts, sleeveless blouse and sandal ensemble, she appeared better suited to the subtropical climate than either Nimchov or Bolan.

As Nimchov steered away from the curb, down the curving one-lane road leading to the exit, Kirchov said, "You don't seem surprised to see us."

Bolan half turned toward her. "I am, a little. How did you get authorization to operate on foreign soil?"

Kirchov lifted her bare shoulders in a shrug. "A carryover from glasnost. I am the only field expert on the platform, and your government recognized the threat posed by your fellow countryman."

"So, you'll deal with the platform and I'll deal with my countryman?"

"That is an equitable division of labor, is it not?"

Bolan answered the woman's question with one of his own. "You have the coordinates of Deveroux's island?"

Kirchov patted her handbag. "Yes, on a nautical chart. However, we have no pictures. Your Mr. Brognola indicated he would have that matter rectified by tomorrow."

The Lumina moved toward the tollbooth, and Nimchov fumbled in his pockets. Bolan withdrew a dollar bill from his wallet and handed it to him. "It's on me."

The driver paid the attendant and guided the car toward the exit. "You should've gotten a receipt," Bolan told him. "It's deductible."

Nimchov didn't respond. He steered the Lumina to the entrance ramp of Interstate 275 and headed north. The drive along the six-lane highway seemed like a direct route to the sun, even though it was sinking in a welter of crimson and orange on their left. For some reason, Nimchov didn't turn on the air conditioner, but the wind blowing through the open windows at least flicked the sweat off Bolan's face before it could drip onto his shirt.

"Where are we going?" he asked, speaking loudly to be heard over the rush of the wind.

Kirchov leaned forward in her seat. "To a commerce center called Harbour Island."

"Why?"

"That is where your fellow countryman maintains his corporate headquarters. It is a good idea to take a—what is your word?—look-see at our adversary's base of operations."

Nimchov's driving, though not particularly reckless, made Bolan a little nervous. He changed lanes every few seconds, accelerated around any vehicle that was traveling under seventy and passed on the shoulder of the road.

As they swooped down the Ashley Street exit ramp, they passed a sign reading: To Harbour Island.

"How long have you been in town?" Bolan asked.

"Only a few hours," Nimchov answered.

"You seem to know your way around."

"I've visited here before, on a diplomatic mission. I accompanied an agricultural delegation to a convention. Afterward, we went to Disney World.''

Nimchov sent the Lumina through an amber light and into the traffic stream swirling around the museum. There was an outraged symphony of car horns behind them.

They reached Bayshore Boulevard, and the Lumina dipped sharply to the left as the Russian cut the wheel toward the turn lane. He raced the engine while he waited for the green turn arrow. On the left side of the boulevard was another sign pointing toward Harbour Island.

''Do we even know if Deveroux is in town?'' Bolan asked.

Before either Nimchov or Kirchov could answer, the green arrow appeared and the Lumina rocketed across the opposite traffic lanes and down Bayshore. They crossed a drawbridge spanning a channel of the Hillsborough River and reached the entrance of Harbour Island. The wide bridge was mobbed with a gleaming snarl of bumper-to-bumper madness.

Even as the Lumina crept along, Bolan could see the red, overlapping double *D*s affixed to the top story of the Osiris Tower.

''Dexter Deveroux isn't too concerned about keeping his profile low,'' Bolan commented.

''Why should he?'' Kirchov asked. ''To the business community, he is just another entrepreneur.''

Harbour Island was roughly tear-shaped, and there appeared to be very little uncovered land anywhere on it. The surfaces were paved, manicured and asphalt-covered. Scattered around the island were buildings, businesses, shops and a huge luxury hotel.

Nimchov circled the block occupied by the building; the parking garage was manned by a quartet of uniformed security guards wearing Sam Browne belts and the red DD logo emblazoned on a sleeve patch. Their side arms were semiautomatics. Though they were snugged into vacuum-formed plastic holsters, Bolan identified them as 10 mm Colt Delta Elites.

There were still quite a few cars parked in the garage, even though it was long after business hours. Bolan recalled the Intel jacket listing Deveroux's various enterprises: recording, opinion polling, entertainment, publishing, merchandising, and so forth. There were probably a number of secretaries, night agents, receptionists and executives working late.

As they made another slow pass, this time past the glassed-in lobby, they saw another pair of guards sitting at a video monitor station. A camera was clamped above the sliding glass doors, and Bolan noticed the lens swiveling as the Lumina swung by, following its path.

"Let's move on," he suggested. "No point in advertising our presence."

"We're not drawing any attention to ourselves," Nimchov retorted.

"Yet. Do as I say."

For a moment, the man looked as though he were going to argue, but with a mumbled curse, he turned the wheel and redirected the car away from the building.

As they headed back toward Bayshore Boulevard, Bolan asked, "Do we have any hard Intel on that building—like how many offices and floors are occupied, how many people work there, where Deveroux's office is?"

"That is something else Mr. Brognola will obtain," Kirchov answered. "However, by the location of his initials, one may adduce that Dexter Deveroux's office is on the top floor, the penthouse."

"The god seat," Bolan said.

"Exactly. To affirm the Olympian nature of his personality." The woman didn't smile as she spoke.

As Nimchov drove back toward the interstate, it occurred to Bolan that the Russians may have been jumping to conclusions. There was no doubt Deveroux was a shadow-walker; MacMurphy's murder attested to that, but whether the man was actually attempting to gain control of the so-called Hellfire Trigger was another matter entirely. It seemed too complicated an undertaking for one man, no matter how resourceful or self-deluded. Still, Bolan knew from bitter and bloody experience that men with grand dreams often used venal schemes to achieve them.

By the time the Lumina was rolling up the on-ramp of I-275, it was 7:45 p.m., and a warm dusk was settling over Tampa. Nimchov switched on the headlights as they merged with the southbound traffic. A smack against the rear window of the car and tinkling of glass caused the Russian to jump, swear and swerve. "What the hell was that?"

Both Kirchov and Bolan turned. A bullet hole starred the glass, a spiderweb pattern of cracks surrounding it. Behind them was a weaving tangle of headlights; there was no way to tell from which car the shot had come.

"We've picked up a tail," Kirchov said calmly.

"We've picked up worse than that," Bolan replied, unholstering his Beretta from the belt rig.

"Who?" Nimchov demanded, a mixture of fear and anger in his voice. "Who's after us?"

"I think we'll find out shortly," Bolan stated, still peering behind them. "Get us off the interstate, to a place where we can maneuver."

Nimchov jammed down the gas pedal, and the Lumina leaped ahead.

"Are either of you armed?" Bolan asked.

"No," Nimchov grunted, hands tight on the steering wheel. "Your government wouldn't allow it."

The Russian took the next exit, cutting off a pickup loaded with machine parts. The angry bleating of a horn came from behind them, as well as a few shouted curses. Nimchov sent the Lumina roaring through a red light, then slewed it around a corner onto a residential side street. The speed limit was posted at thirty-five miles per hour. He threaded the automobile between double rows of parallel-parked cars at close to fifty.

A charcoal gray Ford Bronco lunged around the corner. The windows were tinted a smoky hue. Tires squealing, it barely avoided sideswiping a parked Hyundai Excel. It roared down the narrow side street in pursuit. Bolan heard a faint, rapid hammering noise, and the Lumina shuddered from three heavy impacts against the rear bumper. Though he couldn't see the weapon or its muzzle-flashes, the Executioner figured it was a submachine gun equipped with both a sound suppressor and a flash-hider.

Nimchov took the next corner in a two-wheel skid that brought them onto Dale Mabry Boulevard. Traffic was a slow-moving cluster, held up by stoplights every hundred yards or so. A solid bank of cars blocked their way and reduced their speed.

The Russian wrenched the wheel to the right and aimed the Lumina for the nearest sidewalk. People scattered, yelling and swearing as the car hurtled the curb and did a crazed back-and-forth slide. Nimchov maneuvered the vehicle down the sidewalk for a few hundred feet, then shot off a parking apron to an adjoining side street. The car careered wildly, fishtailing with a screech of tortured rubber. The driver fought the wheel and tapped the brakes as the car bounced and rocked violently.

The Bronco raced after them, its unseen driver mimicking the Lumina's maneuvers expertly. Another storm of shots struck the car, and the rear window collapsed in a rain of glass fragments. Kirchov ducked low, but she didn't cry out. Nimchov did, however. His body jerked at the impact of a bullet plowing through the back of his seat and ripping a long, bloody furrow along his rib cage.

Bolan took his eyes off the Bronco long enough to give Nimchov's wound a quick examination. Though the blood loss was heavy, it wasn't critical. The bullet had slid along his ribs, probably cracking, maybe even breaking, a couple of them.

Gritting his teeth, the Russian still had his hands wrapped around the wheel, ignoring the pain and flow of blood.

"We need to make a stand," Bolan said. "Whoever they are, they outgun us and can probably outrun us."

Nodding tersely, Nimchov turned the steering wheel sharply to the right, and the car sped down a wide avenue between looming warehouse walls. They passed beneath a sign that told Bolan they were entering the Bayside Park Industrial Complex.

The Bronco easily maintained the pace, and was creeping up alongside them. Nimchov swerved back and forth, blocking each attempt to pass. A yellow, diamond-shaped sign flashed by, which read: No Outlet.

"We'll be running out of road soon," Bolan said. "Park us somewhere. Fast."

Nimchov turned the wheel, hit the brakes and swerved all at the same time. The car jumped a curb, its rear-end slithering in a 180-degree turn, the right back fender smashing against the brick facade of a printing supply business.

Bolan had braced himself, so the sudden jolting stop didn't fling him into the dashboard or through the windshield. He unlatched the seat belt and saw that the passenger-side door was jammed shut by the wall. He didn't hesitate. Reaching across the bleeding driver, he opened the door and pushed him out. Kirchov remained hunkered in the back seat.

Nimchov clung to the door for support. His face was filmy with sweat, and his breath came in harsh gasps. Bolan maneuvered him down beneath the Lumina's chassis. Grimacing in pain and swearing, the Russian squeezed himself between the asphalt and the car's undercarriage.

The Bronco had overshot their position, but now it was lurching in four-wheel-drive reverse, engine roaring, tires screaming and spurting smoke. Bolan vaulted into the narrow space between the Lumina's engine block and the building's wall. The bodywork of the car offered scant protection against armor-piercing rounds, but there was no better cover available.

A series of staccato pops filled the air, and bullets blasted chips from the warehouse wall. Fragments of brick and splinters of mortar showered Bolan as he lined up the Bronco in the sights of the Beretta. He adjusted the fire selector switch to burst mode.

The gunner was in the back seat, and judging by the barrel jutting from the window, it appeared as if a modified Heckler & Koch 94 autocarbine was his weapon of choice. A 40 mm modular muffle-type sound suppressor was attached to the muzzle. Equipped with a 15-round magazine, the HK-94 was a compact, but exceptionally lethal killing machine.

Steel-jacketed, 9 mm bullets hosed the building behind Bolan, ricochets screaming in all directions. There was a pause as the gunner adjusted his aim, trying to catch the Executioner in the steady stream of subsonic autofire. Four or five more rounds caromed off the wall.

The Beretta in Bolan's fist spit out three wads of lead at 375 meters per second, and the left front and rear tires of the Bronco exploded. The vehicle slewed sideways at forty miles per hour, all direction and control gone. Sparks showered and metal screamed as the wheel rims slashed deep gouges into the asphalt.

With a crash of breaking glass and the squeal of crumpling bodywork, the rear end of the Bronco rammed an aluminum light post. The post bent and broke at the point of impact, the halogen light fixture erupting in a flash of blue flame.

Leaping over the Lumina's hood, Bolan sprinted broken-field style toward the vehicle. The engine noise died, and the driver's-side door swung open. A blond-haired man wearing a black T-shirt and baggy white cotton pants struggled out.

He stood behind the shield of the door, a long-barreled Smith & Wesson Model 629 revolver held in both hands. In a smooth, practiced motion he drew a bead on Bolan.

The Beretta chugged out three bullets that drilled through the exterior of the door and center-punched the man standing on the other side of it. He staggered the length of the Bronco, arms windmilling. As he fell, the left rear door was flung open.

A short, Hispanic man tried to retreat from the vehicle in a fast backpedal, putting the Bronco between him and the Executioner. He swung the Heckler & Koch toward him, a fusillade of muffled shots skimming over the charcoal gray hood, chewing up the paint job.

As the burst of bullets ripped the air above his head, Bolan hit the ground, sliding on the seat and right leg of his jeans. He rolled under the Bronco's front bumper, squeezing the Beretta's trigger. Three hollowpoint rounds broke the top of the man's head into three pieces. The triple impact lifted him off his feet and flipped him backward, as though he were performing an acrobatic trick. A bloody mist surrounded his head like a halo. He slammed down against the asphalt, the autocarbine clattering end over end across the road. He made no movement afterward, not even a foot twitch.

Getting to his feet, Bolan made a quick, 360-degree circuit of the killzone, saw it was secure and sprinted toward the Bronco's driver.

"Belasko!" Kirchov shouted from behind him.

"Stay there," he commanded.

The driver was still alive, breathing heavily and irregularly. Three wet stains were spreading across his shirtfront. The Smith & Wesson revolver lay near his outflung right hand. Bolan toed it away.

The man's eyes were glassy with pain, but he managed

to twist his lips into a smirk when Bolan bent over him. "Fuck you," he grated.

Bolan went to one knee beside him and planted the bore of the sound suppressor in the fleshy underside of the man's chin. The man flinched at the heat.

"You know who I am?" Bolan's voice was a low, deadly monotone, his face a shadowed mask.

"Fuck you," the man rasped out. "You'll get nothin' out of me, Belasko."

"How do you know who I am?" He dug the hot bore of the Beretta into the man's flesh, twisting it a little. The man was going rapidly into shock, and Bolan needed to keep what little cogent thoughts he had left focused on him. The discomfort would help to do that.

"I don't rat on a contract," the man muttered.

"Who do you work for?" Bolan pressed.

The man didn't answer. His eyelids were fluttering. Patting the man down, Bolan found a pack of Marlboros in his pants pocket, a handful of loose change, but no wallet and no identification. Bolan started to toss away the cigarettes, but saw a card with perforated edges slipped in between the plastic wrap and the package. He removed the card, glanced at it, slid it back in place and put the pack in his shirt pocket.

The man mumbled something inaudible, then his chest rose and fell several times. His eyes snapped wide. The pupils enlarged and engulfed the brown irises. He expired very quietly and quickly.

Bolan returned to the Lumina. Nimchov had crawled out from beneath it and was leaning against the hood, supported by Kirchov. In the distance was the sound of sirens, growing louder by the second.

"Who were they?" Nimchov asked from between clenched teeth. He was pressing a hand against his side,

74 *Hellfire Trigger*

blood glistening between his fingers. His eyes were glazed and wet with pain.

"I don't know," Bolan answered grimly. "But it's safe to say we've been formally announced."

7

Deveroux stood before the big blue chroma-key screen, struggling to make himself look relaxed and forceful at the same time. He wore a beige, artfully tailored business suit, pale yellow shirt and a red "power tie."

He would have preferred to have worn his cream-colored herringbone blazer and a black turtleneck, but Jest told him the coat's pattern would cause a strobe effect and the turtleneck would make him look thin and sinister.

As it was, Deveroux's lean face was caked with makeup to conceal his pallor, and his hair was blow-dried and styled to make it look fuller and shorter. After catching a glimpse of himself on the playback monitor, Deveroux thought he looked more like a shoe salesman moonlighting as a pederast than a savior.

Jest dollied the video camera closer, checking the angles of the overhead studio lighting. He peered through the viewfinder. "You're off your mark, Dex."

Deveroux moved obligingly to the left, aligning his toes with the X taped to the floor.

"Okay," Jest announced. "Scene two, take two. We're rolling in three, two, one. Cue backdrop."

The red light shone on the camera and on the playback monitor, it appeared as if Dexter Deveroux were standing before a hazy, smog-choked city skyline. In a clear, conversational tone, he said, "Yes, my friends, now more than ever before, the secret is energy. Locating it is easy, exploiting it is the hard part. Inasmuch as the world's energy consumption keeps doubling every decade, easily attainable reserves of petroleum and natural gas will be consumed by 2005. Even without the recent tragedy in the Mideast to contend with, alternative energy sources would still need be found. Ra Soltech has already found them.''

On the playback monitor, the haze faded from the skyline, revealing a clean expanse of blue. Sunshine glinted brightly from the tops of building.

''Fossil fuel supplies have been diminishing at an alarming rate over the past century. It took millions of years to form them and only a few hundred to use them up.'' Deveroux paused, smiled and continued. ''Now, I'm not a mathematical genius, but it doesn't take one to see that solar power is the cleanest and most generous available source to provide our country, even the world, with all its energy requirements.''

The skyline dissolved, to be replaced by a filtered, cheery view of the sun hovering over an ocean horizon. Deveroux gestured to the empty blue backdrop behind him.

''Oh, I know your first reaction is to say solar power is too expensive, too difficult to tap. Hasn't the government spent millions of dollars researching it?'' The smile faded from his face, and he shook his head sadly. ''In fact, all the money diverted to solar-energy research represents less than three percent of the overall energy budget. In truth, the government, in tandem with big oil interests, can't monopolize the sun, therefore they don't want you, the average citizen, the suffering taxpayer, to take advantage of a renewable and economical power source. They prefer us to continue to rely on imported foreign fuels, despite the recent accident in Saudi Arabia that has, for all intents and purposes, cut off that trade.''

Deveroux frowned, folding his arms over his chest. ''Very soon, energy will be a luxury rather than a birthright. Electricity, gasoline and even heat will be available only to the elite, the ultrarich, the insiders. Is this the twenty-first century you want your children to grow up in?''

The image of the sun disappeared and several different scenes built on the playback monitor, arranging themselves in a checkerboard pattern. Each square showed something different: an array of parabolic mirrors stacked like a pyramid, satellites with huge, winglike panels stretching out into space, speeding automobiles equipped with glassy solar cells instead of combustion engines.

Deveroux gestured behind him at the blue screen. ''Ra Soltech holds patents on solar-power collector satellites, solar-power collection antennae, solar-power conversion stations, automobiles and even appliances. Rather than continue to pollute our rivers and cities with soon-to-be superexpensive fossil fuels, it makes perfect business sense to redirect the budget to making America sun-powered and independent. Think of the new industries to be developed, all the new job opportunities that will be available. For instance, cloudy countries such as the United Kingdom would import our solar-generated electricity, and that would substantially decrease America's international trade deficit and even the national debt.''

On the monitor, Deveroux watched several center squares slide around until they built into an image of the American flag, the stars and stripes fluttering in the breeze. Clasping his hands together, almost as if in prayer, Deveroux chose his closing words carefully, emphasizing the trigger words, the ones carrying the most visceral impact.

''I *implore* our government, our industries, our business community, our citizens to replace fossil fuels with solar power. We'll no longer need to wage war over *oil,* sacrificing the *lives* of our young men in foreign lands. The world economy will *stabilize,* and we will truly live in a land of plenty. The possibilities are endless, and *Ra Soltech* will make them *realities.*''

Deveroux paused, smiled and stared directly into the camera lenses, saying quietly, "Thank you for listening."

The red light blinked off. Jest straightened, his angular face split by a grin. "That ought to hold the little bastards."

Deveroux pulled a handkerchief from a breast pocket and wiped at the rouge on his cheeks. "How long will it take you in the editing room?"

"About a week. I've got music to add, opticals, titles—got to make sure all our dissolves don't pixel out on us."

"Good," Deveroux said. "I'll reserve the airtime for the weekend after next."

Jest's grin widened, as if he'd never felt better in his life. "You'll pull in some of the highest ratings of the year, Dex."

"Of the year? Of all time." A smile touched the corners of Deveroux's lips. "I will have arranged it that way, won't I?"

THE DAMAGE to the Lumina was superficial, primarily cosmetic. With Bolan at the wheel, it circled the warehouses in search of a rear exit from the industrial park. Patrol cars with sirens and lights blazing blue were roaring into the main entrance.

On the far side of the complex, Bolan spotted a gate in the chain-link fence, secured by a padlock. He nosed the car up to it, shot away the lock with the silenced Beretta and drove the Lumina through.

He followed a maze of side streets until he reached Westshore Boulevard and drove to the motel where Kirchov and Nimchov were registered.

The Russians had taken a ground-floor room, and Bolan found a parking space directly across from it. He was careful to back the Lumina into it, butting the bullet-riddled rear-end against a hedge.

Kirchov carried Bolan's case while he helped Nimchov into the room. Once inside, Kirchov examined her partner's injury and pronounced it minor, though she diagnosed one cracked rib.

While she cleaned and bandaged the wound with material from a first-aid kit she had stowed in the closet, Bolan put in a call to Stony Man Farm. He waited impatiently while the scrambler circuits were engaged. When Barbara Price got on the line, he dispensed with the amenities and asked to be connected to Hal Brognola. He had assumed that he would have to wait until Price cross-linked the circuit and patched it through to Brognola's secured line in his Justice Department office. Fortunately Brognola was at the Farm and picked up the call immediately.

Tersely Bolan told him everything that had transpired since arriving in Tampa. The big Fed was unhappy with the report and said so.

"That makes two of us, Hal," Bolan said into the receiver. "I was made before I got out of the airport. I was expected."

"Impossible, Striker. We followed all of the standard security measures. Your little sight-seeing cruise past Deveroux's office probably put the hair up the asses of the hounds."

"I doubt Deveroux just happened to have a hit team on standby."

"All right, what do *you* think happened?"

"Deveroux has tentacles in a lot of intelligence pies. Someone working for Deveroux could have put feelers out and passed along that info to him."

"Any ideas on who that someone might be?"

"Is there an Agency station in Tampa?"

"Not that I'm aware of."

"What about a contract agent?" Bolan asked. "With all the anti-Castro factions in town, there's got to be a spook keeping tabs on them."

"Anti-Castro? The ZRIFLE station was dismantled years and years ago."

"Just find out if there's a Company spook in the local woodpile," Bolan replied. He gave Brognola the motel's telephone number and room number and hung up.

Kirchov had followed Bolan's side of the conversation as she worked on Nimchov's wound. She had disinfected the gash and was applying a pressure bandage.

"You suspect a leak in your organization?" she inquired.

Bolan shook his head. "No, but there may be a leaky Intel pipeline feeding into it."

Checking his equipment case, Bolan noticed a couple of scars and rips in the leather sheathing. A couple of bullets had struck it, but the metal beneath the leather had deflected them. The contents were intact.

"What did you take from the assassin?" Kirchov asked. She handed Nimchov a glass of water so he could wash down a pain reliever.

"This." Bolan showed her the pack of cigarettes.

"I didn't know you smoked."

Removing the card from beneath the plastic wrapping, Bolan passed it to her. Kirchov's face drew into a frown of disgust. The card bore crude pen-and-ink cartoon renderings of a pair of nude women with huge, gravity-defying breasts. The logo of the Bottoms Up Club ran along its length. Beneath the illustrations, the card asked the burning question: What's So Lewd About Dancing Nude?

Turning the card over, Kirchov read aloud, "'VIP parking pass.' I don't understand."

"Very Important Person," Bolan explained. "The hit man must have been a regular at the club."

The telephone rang. Bolan picked it up and waited through the electronic beeps and squawks of the scrambler circuit.

"Striker?" Brognola's voice was harsh and testy.

"What've you got, Hal?"

"The only spook operating out of your zone is a war

horse named Bertram Phildercost. He's one of the old guard from the Alpha 66 operation.''

Alpha 66 was the code name of a group of Agency-sponsored militant Cuban exiles who had been trained to invade Castro's island domain, before and after the Bay of Pigs fiasco.

"He's more or less semiretired,'' Brognola continued, "though he still holds a contract agent's status. He's helped out the DEA a few times, arranging drug stings and the like. He's also been suspected of helping himself to confiscated cash.''

"Why?''

"Because he holds interests in a few businesses in the Tampa Bay area. A couple of Cuban-cuisine hash houses, a car wash and a men's club.''

"You mean a strip joint,'' Bolan said. "By the name of the Bottoms Up.''

"If you knew that already, why'd you have me check it out?'' Brognola asked with some irritation.

Bolan chuckled. "I didn't know who owned it. Are these places fronts for Agency activities?''

"Sometimes, maybe. Who knows? What kind of activities?''

"Like recruiting hit men. One of our wanna-be assassins was a Latino. He could've been Cuban.''

Brognola sighed. "What are you going to do about it— or do I need to ask?''

Ignoring the question, Bolan asked one of his own. "What about the aerial recon of Deveroux's island?''

"It's scheduled for midmorning tomorrow.''

"Good. I think I should take a look-see myself, by water if possible.''

"Go to the Sunset Marina,'' Brognola replied. "It's at the far west end of Tampa, on Rocky Point. I'll arrange for a boat.''

"Can you arrange for another car? The one you provided for Professor Kirchov is a little conspicuous."

"That means it's shot full of holes, right?" Brognola asked wearily, but not without humor. "Okay, I'll have a new set of wheels delivered."

"Tonight. Right away."

"Try to keep the new one intact."

"I'll try. Thanks, Hal."

Bolan hung up and consulted his watch. It was half-past nine. He reckoned that it would take Brognola at least a half hour to persuade the local FBI office to deliver a new car, and another forty-five minutes to an hour before it would arrive. For what he had in mind for the rest of the evening, the later the better.

The motel had a restaurant, and Bolan phoned in a take-out order for the three of them. Before he went to pick it up, he removed the Desert Eagle from his equipment case, jacked a round into the chamber and handed it to Kirchov.

"I know you don't like guns," he said, "but I'm positive you like being dead even less."

Though her eyes were expressionless, her voice contained a note of anxiety when she asked, "Do you think we may have been followed here?"

"First rule of walking the hellfire trail, Professor. Always assume the worst."

Bolan left the room and walked to the restaurant, the Beretta in his belt rig, covered by his shirttail. He saw nothing and no one suspicious. He carried the three foam containers balanced in the palm of his left hand, and he kept his right resting casually on the butt of the 93-R.

Neither Kirchov nor Nimchov complained about the cheeseburgers and fries that served as their dinner. Nimchov's only comment was that it was better than airline food, but not by much.

Bolan was eating the last of the fries when he heard a car horn outside. It beeped a "shave and a haircut" rhythm.

Going to the window and peering through the blinds, he saw a casually dressed black man getting out of a parked turquoise blue Mercury Sable. The man strode across the parking lot and climbed into the passenger side of a pale gray Chevy conversion van. The interior light didn't come on when he opened the door, but Bolan glimpsed a man wearing a suit and tie behind the wheel.

The van sat for a moment, then the horn beeped out the "two bits" finish of the signal, then rolled away, out of sight. Bolan glanced at his watch. It was nearly eleven o'clock.

From his equipment case Bolan took out a lightweight, white linen sport coat. Removing the Beretta from his belt, he held it out to Kirchov. "Trade you."

For a moment she stared at him uncomprehendingly, then handed over the .44-caliber Desert Eagle, taking the 93-R from him. "Are you going someplace?"

"I am. I don't know how long I'll be gone. If I'm not back by dawn, call that number I gave you."

"Where will you be?"

"If I don't come back, then you'll find out. Right now, the less Intel you have, the less you can spill."

Anger flared in Kirchov's dark eyes. "I will not compromise you. We are working together!"

"But separately. My job is to handle my fellow countryman, remember? Put out a Do Not Disturb sign and don't open the door for anyone. I don't care who it is or where they say they're from. Understand?"

Nimchov, though a bit groggy from the pain reliever, snarled, "We are not children or amateurs!"

"Neither are the people we're up against."

Bolan tucked Desert Eagle into the belt slide rig and shrugged into the sport coat. His shirttail wasn't long enough to hide the long-barreled .44. Without a word, Bolan left the motel room and crossed the parking lot to the

Sable. The temperature was hovering around eighty degrees, and the humidity was close to the same.

He bulled the vehicle out into the traffic river, heading again for Dale Mabry Boulevard. The traffic increased when he reached it. Neon signs that glared words like The Pearly Torso, Diamond Lil's, 69 Club and the Mons Venus lit up both sides of the six-lane thoroughfare. There were more sex joints along the boulevard than Bolan had ever seen, outside of Berlin or Hamburg.

The parking permit card he'd taken from the hit man carried the address of the Bottoms Up Club. It was farther out on the boulevard, away from the competition. Since the club was private, it wasn't as lit-up or as gaudily decorated as the others. It was a narrow, two-story building with the words Bottoms Up outlined in a queasy neon-pink against the night sky.

The parking lot was surrounded by a high chain-link fence. Down a short, sandy driveway was a gate and a gatekeeper. He was a big man, several inches over Bolan's six foot three. His face was deeply tanned, square and blocky of chin. A thick, reddish-blond mustache drooped past his chin, the weight of two gold beads tied to the ends dragging it down. A pinch of white powder was caught in the hairs beneath his right nostril. His wavy hair was parted in the middle and braided at his nape. He wore very tight jeans, and a vest with nothing on beneath it. His chest was covered by a thick, reddish-gold mat, and gliding through it was the tattoo of a cobra, tinted in brilliant hues of vermilion and yellow. A Browning B-80 autoshotgun was cradled in the crook of his right arm.

"Private club," the gatekeeper said when Bolan braked to a stop. He had a small walkie-talkie clipped to the waistband of his jeans.

Bolan handed him the parking permit. The man glanced at it, then at Bolan's face. "Don't remember seeing you around here before, pal."

"With the amount of pixie dust you shove up your nose, how reliable is your memory?"

The gatekeeper thought that over for a moment. Then the mustached man spit in the direction of the Sable's rear tire, handed the permit back and waved Bolan through.

He circled the lot twice, checking out the zone for egress and escape, and parked in the shadow provided by an wide-boughed oak tree. Bolan climbed out of the car, not locking it. He made sure the Desert Eagle was hidden by his coat and moved toward the door.

Disco music that sounded as though it were being played at the bottom of a swimming pool pounded at him. A red spotlight shone in the darkness, pinpointing a G-stringed girl who flounced across a poker chip of a stage at the far end of the main floor.

Smoke, like streamers of dirty chiffon, hung above the crowd of men. They were drinking, and puffing on cigars and roaring with laughter. Bolan stood in the archway and watched the dancer. Perspiration sparkled on the girl's skinny limbs. She had breasts like a pair of porcelain door-knobs. Despite her overdone makeup, Bolan estimated her age at barely eighteen.

The Executioner moved away from the door and toward the side of the stage. Several members of the audience glanced at him incuriously as he made his way past. Bolan spotted several who should have had the word Mob stenciled on their foreheads. He didn't see anyone who would fit the general outline of a bouncer. As a members-only club, the Bottoms Up management probably saw no need for one.

He pushed aside a hanging curtain and stepped into an alcove. At the rear of the stage, sitting in a chair on a small runway, was another dancer, wearing a towel draped around her body. She was an unbelievably obese woman, with her red hair styled in a high bouffant. Behind the runway was a narrow corridor.

Stepping across the runway, Bolan entered the corridor, which terminated in a closed door. A hand-lettered sign tacked to it read Private No Admittance. A big man whose face consisted primarily of an out-thrust jaw sat in a chair in front of the door. A bright red polyester shirt was stretched tight over huge biceps and swelling pectorals. When he saw Bolan, he arose and moved toward him at an ominous gait. By the way his eyes sparkled, Bolan could tell he boasted an IQ well into the double digits.

Putting a goofy, inoffensive smile on his face, Bolan slurred his words as he asked, "Hey, pal, where's Bert?"

The big man kept strolling toward him. His massive right hand pulled a leather-encased blackjack out of a hip pocket. The blackjack was also massive. He slapped it lightly against his thigh as he walked. "Bert's busy, sport. Get out of here."

"No, I gotta see Bert. Got a perpasition for him. A business perpasition, you know?"

Lifting the blackjack and waggling it Bolan's direction, he asked, "You want this upside your head, sport? You want a hangover that'll take you a fucking year to get over?"

"No, not especially," Bolan replied in his normal voice.

The man's eyes narrowed in suspicion. "Then get the fuck out of here."

"Say please."

As the bouncer growled and lifted the blackjack, Bolan kicked him as hard he could in the groin. The man clutched at his crotch and folded in the middle. His face screwed up in astonished pain, and a gassy wail keened from between his lips. Bolan swept his legs out from under him with one of his own, and the bouncer sat hard on the corridor floor.

He had dropped the blackjack, so Bolan scooped it up and struck him expertly across the back of the neck with it. The bouncer's torso listed forward, head sinking between his legs.

The soldier quickly patted him down and found no other weapon. He dropped the blackjack and drew the Desert Eagle. Grabbing a fistful of polyester, he dragged the unconscious man down the corridor and heaved him back into his chair. Though his head lolled and his hands dangled between his knees, the bouncer would pass a quick inspection.

He stood at the door, listening. The murmur of male voices reached him. Trying the knob, he found it was unlocked and he eased the door open a crack and peered around the frame.

It was a fairly large room, one wall taken up by a long bar. A middle-aged, casually dressed man was seated at a round, varnished table. He was smoking a cigar and drinking from a highball glass. A chandelier-like light fixture hung over the table, the yellow illumination casting wavering reflections from the polished tabletop on the man's face. Bolan recognized him.

Standing behind the bar, pouring liquor into a silver jigger, was a sweating, heavyset, balding man. He was chewing the wet stub of a cigar and speaking in a rough, boasting voice. Bolan didn't recognize him.

"I told that scrawny bastard to shove his job up his ass. He begged me to stay on with him, so I cut him a break."

"What kind of break, Bert?" the man at the table asked.

"The usual, you know. I set up a hit for him. All I did was let Ramon and Tony bid on it, and I skimmed an easy two grand off the top. A finder's fee. I don't know how it worked out, though. Ramon and Tony haven't reported in yet."

Bolan stepped swiftly through the door and closed it behind him. "That's why *I'm* here," he said coldly. "It didn't work out."

8

Bolan knew the man sitting at the table. He was Leo Paleotti, a born survivor. He'd lived through gang wars, attempted assassinations, Congressional investigations and indictments for tax fraud. He had also survived Bolan's assault on his Mob family's Massachusetts stronghold.

Paleotti's hand dipped inside his cardigan. His mouth was open in a silent scream of terror. Bolan squeezed the trigger of the Desert Eagle. The sound of the shot was very loud, but muffled by the racket out in the club.

The .44-caliber wrecking ball punched a crater in the ceiling, knocking loose the hook that supported the chandelier with a spurt of plaster. The heavy light fixture crashed down noisily atop Paleotti's head and shoulders, the weight of it slamming his face against the tabletop. Sparks jumped and glass flew in fragments.

Paleotti lunged from his chair, wrestling with the metal-and-glass construction. Face scarlet-streaked and pinched with fear, he flung the fixture away from him. Falling to the floor, he clawed a .32-caliber revolver from beneath his sweater and hurled it into a corner, shrieking, "I'm unarmed, I'm unarmed!"

The man mixing the drinks spit the cigar stub from his mouth and reached under the bar. Bolan fired the big gun in his direction, and the bullet smashed into the rack of liquor bottles behind him. Bottles danced, glass dissolved and liquor sprayed. Flying splinters of glass stung the man's face and he screamed, clapping a hand over his cheek. His eyes showed terror of the big, ice-eyed man with the dark hair and the big gun. Bolan moved to the left of the door, putting his back against the wall. The sounds from the club were muted and muffled. The private room was equipped with soundproofed paneling.

"You're Bertram Phildercost." Bolan wasn't asking a question.

The man tried to speak, only squeaked, then nodded several times.

"Hands on the bar, palms down. Leo?"

"Yeah?"

"You'll want to stay where you are, on the floor. Sit on your hands, palms up."

Phildercost wiped liquor and blood from his face and tried to glare. He had to show how tough he was, how much in control he was, even if he didn't feel tough or in control at the moment.

"You bastard," he grated. "Do you know who you're screwing with? You are so dead. What do you think you're going to do?"

From his position on the floor, Paleotti fought against a spasm of trembling, lost and shuddered in fear for his life. "Jesus, Bert," he croaked. "Don't play around with this guy. Don't fuck with him!"

Clearing his throat, Phildercost said, "Hey, look, hoss. You want a deal, I can deal."

Bolan chuckled, a sound like the distant rustling of leathery wings. "Why should I make a deal with you, Bert? You're a small-time penny-ante. You take orders, you cheat, you lie, you betray and you think you're a big man. I ought to blow you away right now, just on general principle."

Bolan was playing a psychological game he had played many times before—Hoodlum Psychology 101. The tougher a man thought he was, the more of a bad-ass image he'd built around himself, the more devastating the realization when he encountered someone who was tougher and more of a bad-ass. Though Bolan thought of it as a game, it wasn't a bluff.

"Tell me what you want," Phildercost said, a pleading note entering his voice. Blood from the laceration on his right cheek oozed down his fleshy jowl.

"You're a Company man, Bert. With your contacts, I'm sure you've made yourself very useful to certain people over the years, like old Leo here. One of those certain people put out a contract on me. I want a name."

"I don't know what you're talking about." Phildercost's response was quick and by rote.

"The names of the hit team were Tony and Ramon. I hit them instead. I was expected in town, and I imagine you used Agency contacts to let your employer know about me. I already have a pretty good idea of your employer's name, but I want to hear it from your lips."

Phildercost tried a comradely smile on him. "Come on, hoss. Me and you, we're professionals. You know I can't spill anything. It's not how business is done. I got to get paid."

Bolan put the sights of the Desert Eagle on a direct line with Phildercost's sweat-sheened forehead. "This isn't a question of money. It's a question of life or death."

Phildercost attempted a derisive grin. "The way I hear it, Belasko, you do work for the Feds. You got rules to play by."

"The same rules you play by, Bert?"

The grin faltered, and the man's eyes flickered in sudden fear.

"If you know as much about me as you say you do," Bolan continued, "then you know *I* make the rules."

From his place on the floor, his hands sandwiched between his plump buttocks and the carpet, Paleotti screeched, "I'm too old for this shit! Tell him, Bert, or he'll kill us both! Goddamn it, tell him it was that hippie freak job!''

The door behind Bolan burst open violently, the hinges jumping in their brackets. The big man in red polyester lunged into the room, roaring in baffled rage. Bolan stepped forward, swinging the Desert Eagle from high behind his ear, bringing it down hard on the man's skull, knocking him forward into the table.

Back-kicking the door shut, Bolan moved close to the man as he pushed himself up and away from the table. As he whirled, the Executioner backhanded the .44 across his face. There was a dull meaty sound of metal striking flesh. The big man's eyes rolled up, and he staggered to the side as though he were rolling out of bed. He hit the floor unconscious, right beside Paleotti.

Amid the crash of 250 pounds of deadweight hitting the floor, Phildercost had snatched a pair of objects from behind the bar. In his left hand he held a small walkie-talkie, a mate to the one connected to the gatekeeper's waist. He was shouting into it. Bolan couldn't make out the words, but the tone was sheer, undiluted panic and terror.

In his right hand he gripped an Astra Model .45-caliber revolver. It was a big gun, with a heavy, six-inch barrel, far too big and heavy a pistol to fire accurately with only one hand. The gun kicked, pulling up toward the ceiling as the first shot boomed and echoed in the enclosed room. The bullet dug into the wall a foot above Bolan's head.

Bolan tightened his two-handed grip on the Desert Eagle. "Drop it!"

He didn't want to shoot Phildercost. The big .44 was a powerful gun, and it was almost impossible to shoot to wound with it. Shoot a man in the leg with it, there was no way he'd ever walk right again. Aim for an arm or a shoulder, and the .44-caliber round was as likely to tear the arm completely off.

Phildercost dropped the walkie-talkie and adjusted his

aim with the Astra, wrapping both hands around it. Paleotti was screaming wordlessly, scooting backward on his hands and the seat of his pants. Bolan had no choice but to squeeze the trigger of the big pistol. The recoil of the Desert Eagle was light, allowing for a quick recovery and fast second shot if necessary.

It wasn't. The single shot was loud, sending out a wave of ear-shattering sound. The wad of lead caught Phildercost dead center. He didn't cry out. He just left his feet, flying backward into the bottle rack behind him, bouncing off it, then slumping forward over the bar. Bottles fell and broke on the floor behind him. The bullet crushed Phildercost's chest, smashing ribs and clavicle, ripping both lungs apart and probably pulverizing his heart.

Spinning on Paleotti, Bolan stood over him, the Desert Eagle pressed hard against his skull. "The name, Leo. The name of the hippie freak job." Paleotti squeezed his eyes shut. Tears worked their way down his face. "A guy named Deveroux. He's a fruit. Jesus, you killed Bert."

"Yeah. How connected is Deveroux?"

"Connected to what?"

"The Mob, the Agency, the Bureau."

Paleotti shook his head. "I don't know. He's protected, though. Bert said he pays well for it."

Stepping away from Paleotti, Bolan went to the door. "Sit there for a while, Leo. Think about how lucky you are."

Back out in the corridor, Bolan put his gun hand inside his coat. Everything seemed the same; the loud distorted music and roar of laughing voices. As he crossed the runway, he saw that the skinny girl had completed her dance, and now the fat woman was boogying across the stage. Her rolls of fat undulated like jelly in an earthquake, and the customers laughed and threw catcalls at her.

Bolan managed to make it to the door without anyone noticing him. He opened it and stepped out, coming face-to-face with the tattooed gatekeeper. He was holding his shotgun in front of his body. The volume control on the walkie-talkie was turned to maximum, and it hissed with static. The expression on his face was grim and worried. Beyond him, Bolan saw that the gate to the parking lot had been closed.

"Excuse me," Bolan murmured, trying to step around him.

The gatekeeper put a hand on his chest and pushed him back toward the door. "Got a call about some trouble inside. Nobody leaves until I find out what it is. Club policy."

"Nothing going on in there," Bolan said, carefully pushing the man's hand away. "I've got to get home or the old lady'll have my ass."

"Son of a bitch," the gatekeeper snarled, "you heard me!"

He grabbed a handful of lapel and tried to body-block Bolan back into the club. Casually, as though he were pulling out a handkerchief, the soldier took out the Desert Eagle and pressed the bore against the man's lower belly.

"I heard you," he said in a quiet, calm voice. "Now hear me. Turn around and walk back toward the gate."

Rage and fear fought a quick, hot battle in the gatekeeper's eyes. Bolan saw his face turn hard as rage won out over fear. The man moved, his arms whipping upward in a practiced explosion of nerve endings, reflexes and muscles. The stock of the shotgun arced toward Bolan's face.

The Executioner leaned back from the waist, and the butt of the weapon stroked empty air. As he leaned away from it, he slashed the long barrel of the Desert Eagle across the tattooed gatekeeper's forehead, a practice known in the Old West as "buffaloing."

The front blade sight split the man's skin, and he was immediately blinded by a flood of blood. He staggered, screaming, "I'll kill you!"

Bolan didn't want to kill him; he had been in town barely six hours, and he had already turned three men into corpses. Statistically that was a high body count, even for him. He was disinclined to add a fourth body to the list if it could be avoided.

The gatekeeper stumbled backward on rubber legs, swiping at the flow of wet warmth pouring into his eyes. He surprised and impressed Bolan. He didn't fall, and he didn't drop the shotgun. Instead, he fumbled with his weapon, brought it to hip level and triggered a blast in the Executioner's direction.

Bolan had already shifted position, and the 12-gauge buckshot pounded a ragged, plate-size hole through the door. From somewhere in the club, a man screamed in agony.

The gatekeeper echoed that scream with one of his own, a shriek of rage. He jerked the shotgun's trigger twice, swinging the barrel in a short semicircle.

As the two rounds blasted into the night, Bolan dropped flat in a hurry, rolling across the sandy ground, stopping when he hit a tire, then crawling beneath the elevated rear-end of a customized Camaro. He heard screams and shouts from within the club, but no one dared to come outside and investigate the reasons for the gunshots.

The gatekeeper cleared the bloody haze from his vision with a swipe of a forearm. Blinking and squinting, he roared, "I'll blow your fuckin' balls off!"

Crawling clear of the Camaro, Bolan crept at a diagonal angle to where he had parked his Sable. It was at least twenty yards away, and though it would be possible to reach it by crawling and scrambling among the parked cars, he didn't want to invest that much time or effort in an escape.

By habit, Bolan had counted the number of rounds the gatekeeper had fired. The Browning B-80 held only five shots, so there were two more to be triggered.

In a half crouch, Bolan rose from behind a Corsica and called, "Hey, dip shit!"

The gatekeeper pivoted on one heel and pumped the trigger of the shotgun. The side windows of the car turned into fragmented spiderwebs as buckshot shattered them.

As the weapon boomed, Bolan left his feet in a dive, aiming his body toward a sedan. The tattooed man glimpsed the blur of motion and squeezed off another round.

Bolan landed in a crouch, catching himself on his left hand and right knee, hearing the buckshot rip deep into the bodywork of the Corsica. Immediately following the deep-throated boom came an impotent click-click.

Lifting his head above the hood of the sedan, Bolan watched the gatekeeper shake the shotgun and heard him curse. He looked from it to the sedan.

Rising to his full height, Bolan walked around the car toward the area he had parked the Sable. The gatekeeper was directly in his path.

The tattooed man roared in a mindless, berserk rage. Reversing his grip on the shotgun, he grasped it by the barrel and raced toward Bolan, clubbing the weapon like Davy Crockett at the Alamo. Though more than half blind, he rushed Bolan with the wrath of a demented tiger.

Sidestepping the first blow of the shotgun's stock, Bolan ducked the backswing, and drove his left elbow, with all his weight behind it, into the gatekeeper's right kidney.

The man uttered a gargling cry. Already off-balance from the momentum of his shotgun swing, he swatted empty air. Bolan hooked his fingers in his belt and put his heel into the back of his adversary's left knee. The guy stumbled and fell forward to his hands and knees. Bolan jumped and came down hard on the back of the man with both feet. The air rushed out of the tattooed chest with an agonized *whoof!*

Bolan left the gatekeeper lying facedown in the sand,

gasping, gagging and writhing. By the time he reached the Sable and started the engine the man was still down, wheezing and bleeding. No one had stirred from the interior of the club, and the Executioner didn't blame them.

He wheeled the Sable around the lot, pressed down hard on the gas pedal and crashed through the gate. It was a flimsy thing, made of aluminum tubing and galvanized metal wire. The vehicle smashed it loose from its hinges and sent it clattering across two lanes of Dale Mabry Boulevard traffic.

He had left a hell of a mess at the Bottoms Up Club, but it was part of the job. At the very least, he had sent a direct message to Dexter Deveroux, one that didn't need to be deciphered.

9

Deveroux sat immobile in the King's Chamber, a silent figure behind the massive desk. The room was dark, the panes of the skylight above him polarized to deflect the early-morning sunlight.

His eyes were closed in meditation, in accordance with the teachings he had learned in India. After hearing what had happened the night before, he desperately needed an uninterrupted period of quiet contemplation.

As per his order, Bertram Phildercost had provided him with a composite sketch of Belasko. Deveroux had sent the sketch to his agent in the airport police department. Sooner than expected, the agent had called in with a report that the man had arrived in Tampa.

Deveroux had contacted Phildercost, who in turn, contacted a team of hitters, stationing them at Harbour Island. It was supposed to have a been a simple, no muss–no fuss elimination, of the type he had orchestrated many times before.

Then the news came in, first from his conduits on the police force and then from his agent at the Bottoms Up Club. Deveroux hadn't needed the secondhand report from the terror-stricken Leo Paleotti to realize who had brought forth so much hell in so little time.

A soft chime drew Deveroux from his altered state. Without opening his eyes, he touched the inlay key on the desktop and heard the pneumatic hiss of the lift doors opening. Deveroux kept his eyes closed even when he heard Jest say in a quiet, flat voice, "Phildercost is dead."

Deveroux nodded once. "I know. And Belasko isn't. A difficult situation."

"I just reviewed the security video tapes our airport contact supplied," Jest continued. "A man and a woman were with him."

He opened the folder and fanned out several eight-by-ten photographs on the desktop. "I had these enlarged and enhanced from the video record."

Deveroux leaned over them, head thrust forward, like a bird of prey searching out its next meal. Tapping a key on the desk, the skylight reversed its polarization effect and allowed sunshine to shaft down.

"It's Kirchov," he announced after a moment. "Anastasia Kirchov. She sat on the review board of my proposal to the Russians."

Jest's eyebrows rose. "A Russian scientist working with Belasko?"

"Why not? A unification of resources. She has more information about my plans than the American government. She's the top scientific thief of all scientific thieves. The other man is probably SVR. *Fuck!*"

Deveroux swept the photographs from the desk with a furious swipe of one hand. "Do you know what this means?"

Jest said nothing.

"If Belasko tracked down Phildercost so fast, he'll show up on the island with his Russian scientist sidekick." Deveroux's voice trembled with anger and frustration.

Swallowing hard, Jest said, "Then we should shut down the operation. We're in a corner."

Deveroux shook his head and took several deep breaths to center himself. "Too late for that now. We'll lose the launch window for at least a month. We'll simply have to kick up the schedule."

"Dex, they're on to us. If Phildercost talked—"

"They're on to shit," Deveroux declared. "Bertram didn't know shit, so he couldn't talk about shit. If we stick to the original schedule, we'll be giving the Feds all the time they need to put together warrants and assault teams. Right now, Belasko has no proof of anything. All he has are suspicions."

"He doesn't *need* proof!" Jest exclaimed. "From what we've learned he hits first and asks questions later!"

"Exactly my point. He's only one man, operating on his own. We can handle one man, regardless of his reputation."

Jest exhaled noisily, a sigh of resignation. "What's the plan?"

Deveroux leaned back in his chair and steepled his forefingers beneath his chin. "We made our move, he made his. His move has told us he wants blood. Very well. He'll get blood. We'll let him drown in it."

Jest wiped the back of his hand across his wide mouth, dropping his gaze to the floor. He was a study in nervous gestures. "We don't have the time for vendettas, Dex. We have a day, maybe a day and a half of an optimum launch window before a storm front moves in. Eberhardt has completed the modifications on the Remora and our systems are green. We get our act together in the next twenty-four to thirty hours, or we don't act at all."

Deveroux pressed an inlay on the surface of the desk. "Kindzierski?"

A male voice responded crisply from the intercom. "Yes, sir?"

"Warm up the chopper. You're flying me to the island in thirty minutes."

Standing up, Deveroux walked around the desk, his footsteps echoing on the marble floor. He stopped before the statue of Ramses, his back to Jest. Quietly, calmly, he said, "Your life depends on what I do, Doctor. So does my empire. Everything I own, everything I am or ever dream of attaining, is at stake. I can't think of a more appropriate time for a vendetta."

THE PREDAWN DARKNESS was breaking up with scraps of pale orange when Bolan, Kirchov and Nimchov arrived at the Sunset Marina near Rocky Point. When he had returned to the motel the night before, he had apprised the Russians of the situation.

The woman seemed shaken by the story of violence, but Nimchov was unimpressed. The Russian had insisted on accompanying he and Kirchov that morning, even though his injury was still causing him pain. Bolan suspected that Nimchov distrusted him; perhaps the SVR agent was under orders to act as Kirchov's bodyguard.

Leaving the Sable parked near the office, they walked along the concrete pier, past sloops, speedboats, cigarette boats and cabin cruisers. In one of the last slips, rocking slightly on the swells, was a twenty-foot luxury runabout. On the planing forward hull the name *E.G. Robinson* was painted in bright, cobalt blue.

A black man wearing a khaki work shirt, jeans and a Greek fisherman's cap was on deck. He greeted them with a casual, "You're the Belasko party?"

Bolan recognized him as the man who had delivered the Sable the night before. "That's right. Permission to come aboard?"

The man gestured. "Granted. Feel free to take a pew, spit on the floor and call the cat a bastard. This is Liberty Hall."

"What?" Kirchov asked faintly, confusion furrowing her brow.

Smiling, Bolan told her, "Forget it."

Stepping into the boat, he clasped the man's outstretched hand.

"I'm Heath. I've been told to extend you every courtesy on today's outing."

Bolan made quick introductions and Heath ran a fast check on the craft's systems and supplies: compasses, autopilot, life jackets, flare gun. The CIA contact took the wheel, and, following his instructions, Bolan cast off the mooring lines. The runabout backed out of the slip, the engine making bubbly, burping noises.

"Nice recreational craft," Bolan commented.

"Part of a property confiscation," Heath replied. His tone was less formal. "A local coke dealer had a whole fleet of them. The DEA divided them up between some of the agencies."

Heath turned the bow toward the sunlight-flecked waters of McKay Bay. "Do we have a destination, or is this just a pleasure jaunt?"

Kirchov handed him a folded square of paper. "An island."

"What's its name, ma'am?"

"It does not have one," she replied.

Heath nodded and opened the chart. "Figures. Most of the islands out in the Gulf are so small they don't have names, and they're only about a hundred of them."

Raising her voice to be heard over the throbbing engine, Kirchov said, "The one we're looking for is indicated on the chart."

Looking it over, Heath found a small speck circled in red with a felt-tip pen. He studied it a moment, then reached beneath the control console and brought out the microphone of a shortwave transceiver.

Thumbing it to life, he announced, "Sonny, this is Bubba Boy. Come in, Sonny."

A male voice crackled over the speaker. "This is Sonny. Go ahead, Bubba Boy."

"Got the coordinates of our recon target," Heath replied.

He rattled off a series of numbers and degrees. "Copy that, Sonny? Acknowledge."

"Acknowledged, Bubba Boy. Transmitting coordinates to Falcon Station."

As Heath rehooked the microphone, Bolan asked, "Falcon Station?"

"Yeah. Mr. Brognola said you needed aerial recon. We've got a first-class method of getting low-profile, high-flight Intel without drawing attention."

Gunning the boat toward open water, the runabout bounced roughly in the chop until Heath eased off on the rpm. Glancing behind him, Bolan saw that Nimchov was wearing a life jacket over his shirt. He seemed to be in pain. The salt spray was probably penetrating the bandage over his ribs and irritating the bullet wound. One hand gripped a cleat so tightly his knuckles showed white. Though it was hard to tell in the shifting, postdawn light, it looked as if his swarthy face was several shades paler than normal.

Full daylight arrived, bringing with it some of the most cloying, oppressive heat Bolan had ever felt outside of the jungles of Southeast Asia. Kirchov shrugged off her blouse and wormed out of her shorts. She wore a black scrap of a bikini beneath her clothes. Though it wasn't particularly daring by Florida standards, the bikini was more revealing than Bolan figured an astrophysicist might care for. Her body, though not slender, was beautifully proportioned. The wind ruffled her long, raven's wing hair, and she somehow managed to look both wild and reserved at the same time.

Nimchov growled something at her in Russian, and she shot back with a sharp, short retort that made him look away.

It was after nine by the time Heath had navigated the vessel through Intercoastal Waterway and reached the Gulf proper. The sun reflected blindingly off the water as if the

Gulf were a huge mirror, forcing everyone to put on sunglasses.

They spent the long, hot morning powering from one clump of dirt and vegetation to another. Fortunately there was an ice-filled cooler down below, stocked with soft drinks.

A large number of pleasure crafts headed out of the channel into the Gulf. The traffic was heavy and diverse: outriggers, Hobie-cats, sailboats, chartered fishing boats. Heath pointed to a cabin cruiser about the size of the *E.G. Robinson* that was full of thong-bikinied women and laughing, beer-guzzling men. "That's where I should be," he said with a grin.

Tuning into the weather channel on the radio, they listened to a forecast about a major storm front moving into the area by late evening. A small-craft advisory was expected.

Bolan was scanning the massive blue expanse of sky and sea with binoculars. Turning the lenses toward the southwest, he saw an irregular hump rising above the horizon. Unlike most of the islands he'd seen that morning, this one was fairly symmetrical in shape, resembling a black saucer floating upside down. Though it was at least three miles away, Bolan estimated it was much larger than the other no-name islands they'd passed. Something flickered and flashed on the surface of the black saucer. It wasn't an optical illusion. Squinting through the eye-piece, he tightened the focus. Light flickered again, white and bright, far too bright to be outdoor lighting. It was like sunlight reflecting from a highly polished surface. At that distance, the polished surface had to be gigantic, and the reflected light had to have been blinding on the island.

"I believe we've reached our destination," he told Heath.

The agent nodded and fed more power to the engine. The boat pushed through the waters, skipping on the chop like a flat stone on a pond. Nimchov cursed and gripped the edges of his seat. Kirchov stood and lifted her arms, laughing as the spray from the bow showered her.

Bolan tried to keep the binoculars trained on the island. What with the spine-compressing jolts of the boat bouncing up and down, it wasn't easy. The bridge of his nose was sore by the time he was able to pick out more details. At a half mile from the island, he told Heath to slow the craft to a crawl.

The engine roar became a low growl, and the runabout rode the swells as it circled the island. Bolan studied it through the binoculars. It was about two, maybe three miles wide. Unlike the majority of the other islands, this one had a crescent moon of white beach, bracketed by stunted palms and mangrove trees. The needle tips of Spanish bayonet plants poked out of the undergrowth at irregular intervals. There was no hint of light flashes, not even a flicker.

Planted in the sand of the beach was a big wooden sign. Painted on it, in three-foot-high red letters were the words: Private Property. Owner Authorized To Use Deadly Force Against Trespassers.

Below the warning, in smaller letters, Bolan read *A Ra Soltech Property*.

"This is definitely the place," he said to Kirchov. "What exactly are we looking for?"

She came up behind and to the side of him, and he felt the warmth of her near-naked body at his back. "We'll know it when we see it."

The runabout continued its circuit around the island. Every so often another sign warning away trespassers reared out of the undergrowth. Suddenly Bolan saw a thinning in the jungle, and a low building across an open space, beyond the edge of tangled vegetation. It was a long, single-story building without windows, and the far end of it seemed to merge into the undergrowth. It was made of whitewashed concrete, and the flat roof was painted in a camouflage pattern and colors. There were two other smaller outbuildings like utility sheds near it.

It was a compound, surrounded by a high cyclone fence topped by curls of razor wire. There were big security lights on poles inside the fence, and Bolan saw a flat concrete circle off to one side, obviously a helicopter landing pad.

The boat swung casually in a parallel course with the compound. Through the binoculars, Bolan saw a long pier jutting out over the water. It bore warning signs, too, and beyond it, where the pier joined the island, was a chain-link fence, separating the dock from the land. So far, there were no signs of people.

"There's our falcon," Heath announced.

Tilting his head back, Bolan peered through the lenses at the clear blue sky. For a moment, he saw nothing, then a white, winged shape skimmed into view. Bolan lowered the binoculars, stared, then put them to his eyes again. "What the hell is that?"

"It's a SWIFT—Swept Wing with Inboard Flap for Trim."

Gazing at the craft high in the sky, Bolan estimated the sleek, streamlined fuselage to be about twenty feet long. The "wings" were one piece, swept back at a twenty-degree angle, resembling a nineteen-foot-long boomerang joined in the center by the body of the craft. As he watched, the SWIFT banked gracefully and circled, tilting to star-board. There was no sign of an engine or a prop or a turbine or even external wires. The SWIFT was a cross between a hang glider and a sailplane.

Though its altitude was a little over a thousand feet, Bolan was able to discern small flanges on the wings that rose and fell rhythmically. They were secondary winglets, supplying more lift and stability.

"We lease it from its inventor," Heath said, "whenever we need unobtrusive aerial surveillance. Not as noisy or as conspicuous as a plane or a chopper."

"It can carry a camera?"

"In the belly, right below the cockpit. Its average cruising speed is around fifty miles an hour, the stall speed is twenty. Eighty is redline. It puts too much stress on the superstructure and the composite wing."

"How many people does it carry?" Bolan asked.

"Only one. A pilot and maybe an extra hundred pounds of equipment, depending on the weight of the pilot."

"How'd it get here?"

"Tow plane from a private airfield, about twenty miles away," Heath replied. "At the proper height and speed, the SWIFT is released. It can fly all day, make a perfect soft landing back at the airfield. Its range is damn near unlimited."

"But it's fragile," Bolan ventured. "Rough weather would chew it up."

"It wasn't designed to be a war plane," Heath responded. "Strictly recon."

Suddenly Bolan felt Kirchov's fingers bite into his arm. Her voice full of alarm, she said, "Something's happening."

10

A twenty-foot-long cabin cruiser swung around the headland. The steady thud of its diesel engine had been swallowed by the purr of the *E.G. Robinson*'s motor.

The boat was about a quarter of a mile away, and Bolan hazarded a quick glance at it through the binoculars. Two men stood behind the steel-framed windshield. One was dark-complexioned, and his companion was a crew-cut, goateed man with the build of a weight lifter. He was handling the wheel. Both men wore mirrored sunglasses and long-visored caps bearing the Double D logo.

On the deck behind them, Bolan spotted a shortwave radio mast and a canvas-shrouded object with metal tripod legs. Judging by its shape, he guessed it to be a U.S. M-60 mounted machine gun. Though he couldn't see the men's bodies, he was certain they were armed with the Delta Elite pistols.

"Shit," Heath growled, giving the wheel a spin. "Let's get out of here before we're made."

"We're made already," Bolan said, handing the binoculars to Kirchov. "They haven't spotted me, so I'll lie low below. Professor, try to be as sexy and as brainless as you know how to be."

Kirchov scowled at him. "I do not understand. I probably do not want to understand."

As Bolan ducked into the little cabin, he said, "Don't talk. Your accent is a dead giveaway."

Taking up position beside a rectangular Plexiglas port just above the waterline, Bolan drew his Beretta from the belt rig. He listened to the approaching pulse of the patrol boat's engine. He was irritated with himself. When he saw the pier, he should have realized there was no need for a dock without a boat. After last night's bloodletting, the security patrols around the island probably had been tightened and their frequency increased.

He could only hope Kirchov wouldn't be recognized. She was wearing big sunglasses, and if she behaved in the manner Bolan had suggested, the guards wouldn't be looking at her face.

Peering out of the port, he saw the bow of the cruiser knife through the water as it pulled alongside and slowed its engines.

"Good morning, folks," he heard a friendly voice say. "I'm very sorry, but this is a controlled and restricted area. May we ask your business here?"

In a cheerful, insouciant tone, Heath replied, "Just soakin' up the rays, my man. Cruisin' the day away on a charter. Hey, since when is this area controlled?"

Bolan shifted position and saw the goateed man smiling a fake smile. "It's regulated by the state," he replied politely, "to protect environmentally sensitive areas, like the island. Besides, drug dealers have been known to hide their stashes on the islands out here in the Gulf."

"Yeah?"

"Yeah. Do you have identification, like a boating license?"

Though he couldn't see it on his face, Bolan heard the frown in Heath's voice. "Hell, you aren't Coast Guard. You're rent-a-cops."

"My company is licensed by the Southwest Florida Water Management District to question boaters in restricted areas. You can check with the state attorney's office." A flinty hardness entered the man's tone. "Let's see some ID."

Through the port, Bolan watched Heath reach over and hand a laminated card to the man on the patrol craft. He carefully examined it, then handed it back. "You'll wait for just a moment, please."

The guard pulled a microphone from the control console, turned his back and talked into it for a time. The answering voice crackled, shot through with so much static, Bolan couldn't understand a word.

The man lowered the microphone, turned and asked, "Who are your passengers?"

"A couple of tourists," Heath responded.

A drunken, female giggle floated down into the cabin. Craning his neck upward, Bolan glimpsed Kirchov stumbling unsteadily across the deck. She bent over to paw through the cooler, the fabric of her bikini bottom stretching taut over her backside, outlining every curve.

"Tourists from where?" the guard asked.

"Montreal or some damn place." Heath's voice was impatient, annoyed. "They hired me to take them out on a day cruise. They been drinkin' since dawn, and both of them are so drunk they wouldn't know if we got deep-sixed."

Bolan saw Nimchov sitting in his chair, head nodding, eyes closed, a stupefyingly stupid smile on his lips. He admired the Russians' skill at improvisation.

"Is there anyone else aboard?"

Silently Bolan moved back to the port.

"Uh-uh. Just us three."

"Would you object if we looked for ourselves?"

Heath sighed gustily, in exasperation, in resignation. "If it'll get this bullshit over with, come ahead on."

Bolan's finger tensed on the Beretta's trigger. No one spoke for a long moment, then, "My apologies, sir. Go ahead. I suggest you put in before dark. A storm front is on its way.''

The cruiser's engine-rumble quickened and the boat accelerated, moving toward the pier on the island. The runabout rocked in the backwash.

Bolan stayed below until Heath reversed course and put a half mile between the *E.G. Robinson* and the island. He sent the boat leaping ahead.

Coming cautiously topside, Bolan smiled at Kirchov and Nimchov. "Good work."

Kirchov returned the smile; Nimchov didn't. He glared at Bolan for a moment, then looked away, gazing at the boat's foaming wake as if it were a unique phenomenon. Kirchov put on her blouse and shorts.

"If they work for the SWFWMD," Heath said, "then I'm J. Edgar Hoover under deep cover."

"They work for Deveroux and Deveroux alone," Bolan replied. "They were checking on us, probably to see if I was aboard."

Heath shrugged. "I think we satisfied them."

Bolan wasn't so sure. He scanned the skies and saw no sign of the SWIFT. "Where's our aerial surveillance?"

"Probably heading back to Falcon Station. By the time we get back to shore, they'll have some hard Intel for you to look over."

Before Bolan looked away from the sky, he saw a small, dark shape zipping from the mainland. He identified it as a helicopter, a small two-seater, its course angling away from their own. It was too far away and too high up for even the binoculars to focus on it.

They arrived back at the marina at a little after one o'clock. After berthing and locking down the *E.G. Robinson*, Heath offered to go with them to Falcon Station.

Bolan followed the agent's directions as he drove across the Gandy Bridge and into the sparser areas of Pinellas Park. Turning off the main highway, he drove down a narrow road, cutting through acres of palmetto scrub and pine trees. The road led to an airfield, one the many private little fields that dotted the area for the use of the wealthy, the weekend flier and for crop-dusting aircraft. It had a single hangar, and a small, aluminum-walled shack served as an office. At the end of the runway was a trailer doing double-duty as a control tower and caretaker's quarters. There were several Piper Cubs tied down near the hangar, and an ancient biplane in the process of being restored. As Bolan swung the Sable around to park near the office, he saw the long, white shape of the SWIFT inside the hangar.

Two men were inside the tiny office, and Heath made introductions all around. The medium-size, middle-aged blond bearded man was Ian Akins, Heath's partner. The youngish, slightly built Asian man was George Tam, the SWIFT's designer and pilot. He was also a videographer.

Indicating a modular television-VCR unit on the desk, Tam said, "I taped about thirty minutes of footage, with a camera bolted beneath the cockpit. I hope there's ten worth-while minutes in there somewhere."

"Let's see it," Bolan said.

Inserting a cassette, Tam pushed the Play button and the screen flashed with color. The first few minutes were of a view looking down upon shining blue water, studded with whitecaps. With no point of reference, it was impossible to tell from what height the footage had been shot.

The edge of the island crept down from the top of the screen. It was an excellent view, encompassing the island's entire circumference. The upthrust of vegetation and sand was roughly oval-shaped. The patrol boat could be seen churning up a white wake near the far end of the island.

Tam thumbed the Fast Forward button. "I was sailing at four thousand feet at this point. I decreased my altitude to fifteen hundred feet and increased the camera's magnification."

He pressed the Play button again. The perspective was

much tighter, the details sharper and cleaner. Since he knew what to look for, Bolan easily picked out the green-and-brown-streaked flat roof of the long building. Within the compound was a pair of ungainly looking vehicles. It took a moment to identify them as swamp buggies.

"That's a damn big place," Tam commented. "I'd judge the building alone is three hundred yards long, maybe fifty wide."

"What the hell is it doing there?" Akins demanded.

"It looks like a manufacturing facility," Kirchov said. "An assembly plant of some kind."

"Manufacturing what?" Heath asked. "There's no record of any type of industrial complex on the island. I'd imagine a private enterprise would be illegal as hell out there in the Gulf. According to our records, all he's supposed to have is an experimental solar power station. And I don't see anything like that."

Tam smiled, pushed the Fast Forward button again and said, "Watch."

At a certain point, he slowed the tape's speed to normal. The scene was the same as before, but suddenly the roof of the building split in the center along a precise line. The two parts of the roof rose, revealing an array of hexagonal concave mirrors. There appeared to be over a hundred of them, fifty on each side.

"Solar cells," Kirchov said, "converting sunlight to electric power by semiconductor chips."

"That explains the flashes of light I saw when we approached the place," Bolan said.

As they watched, the solar cells pivoted upward and reflected sunlight blazed from them in such brilliance that the screen was filled with a white incandescence.

Tam fast-forwarded through the sequence, pushing the Play button only when the solar cells pivoted downward and the two halves of the roof rejoined.

"What was the point of that?" Akins asked.

"It is probably a timed hourly program," Kirchov replied, "to charge the cells and store the energy."

The next scene was a slow pan up the building. When the far end of it was reached, where the building appeared to join with the undergrowth, Bolan suddenly saw it. "Freeze it there."

Tam quickly complied. Stretching out a finger, Bolan traced a circle on the screen, at the end of the building. "Professor, what do you think?"

She moved closer, squinting at the image, then her eyes widened. *"Bozhe moi,"* she breathed.

"I don't get it," Heath said.

"Look close," Bolan suggested.

At first glance, the scene appeared to show nothing more suspicious than some shabby groundskeeping, with no one bothering to trim back the undergrowth from building. By eyeing the image closely, the jungle seemed to be growing and spreading in a peculiar, but strangely symmetrical, fashion. It looked like much of the vegetation had been planted in a very wide, very circular pattern. It fact, there was a hint of a depression in the center of the giant, overgrown circle, as if intertwining leaves, vines and shrubbery were sagging down slightly.

"Camouflage netting," Bolan announced. "Damned big netting, but it's there."

"Camouflaging what?" Tam wanted to know.

"A vacuum tube accelerator," Kirchov answered crisply.

Tam glanced at her quizzically and opened his mouth to ask another question, but Akins held up a hand. "I'm sorry, George. You're not cleared for this. Would you mind waiting outside for a few minutes?"

Tam smiled good-naturedly and moved to the door. "The SWIFT needs servicing, anyhow."

After he had shut the door behind him, Akins turned to Bolan. "Washington fed us some Intel on this situation,

Belasko, but not enough to give us a solid notion of the main buzz. Care to enlighten us?''

Before Bolan could make up his mind about how much to reveal to the Feds, Sergei Nimchov started to talk. ''It meets the same design specifications Deveroux submitted to my government.''

With some irritation, Kirchov interrupted him and picked up the story. When she was done, both Akins and Heath wore expressions somewhere between apprehension and disbelief.

Akins sighed, dry-washing his face with his hands. ''So you suspect Deveroux, with the telemetry he got from your people, intends to launch a rocket from his island, hook up with the Hellfire Trigger platform and drop—or at least threaten to drop—an H-bomb on somebody's head.''

''That's the abbreviated version,'' Bolan said. ''He has the means, and though it's a little murky, he has the motive.''

''This is all supposition,'' Heath said. ''You don't have a shred of supportive evidence. There's not enough here to invite Deveroux in for a chat, much less swear out a warrant.''

Bolan thought it best not to mention the three men who had died under his gun in the past twenty-four hours. ''I can get the evidence, but by then, a warrant may be a moot point.''

''Why?''

''Deveroux has already made me. If he's working on a timetable, he'll push it up.''

Shaking his head, Akins said, ''I can't take this to my section chief, Belasko. Since the last Congressional hearings, we've got stiffer guidelines to follow, more marks to toe. We can maybe provide you with some covert support in a soft probe, but storming Deveroux's office or landing troops on his island is out of the question.''

Bolan nodded, expecting no less. He doubted even Brognola could pull the necessary strings, not without more to go on. "I understand. I'll need the use of your runabout. Can you supply me with a rubber landing raft and a night-vision system, preferably a Startron headset?"

"Sure," answered Heath. "Anything else?"

"A firearm," Nimchov put in. "I have no weapon."

Akins angled an eyebrow at him. "From what I've been told, you're not supposed to have one. You're an agent of a foreign intelligence service operating on our soil, by our rules."

"In cooperation with your government," Nimchov reminded him. "My country has extended similar courtesies to members of your agencies in times past. Can you do less?"

Akins glanced at Bolan. "Your call, Belasko."

Bolan nodded. "I'll accept the responsibility."

"Thank you," Nimchov said, not trying to conceal the sarcasm.

Akins opened a desk drawer, rummaged inside and produced a holstered Colt .45 Government Model automatic. "It's got a full 10-round magazine," he said, handing the blunt, bulky pistol to the Russian. "I don't have any spare rounds at hand."

Nimchov clipped the holster to his waistband and pulled out his shirttail to cover it. The bulge was very noticeable.

"I'll have the raft delivered to the marina," Heath said. From a pants pocket he withdrew a set of keys and tossed them to Bolan. "I'll make sure the runabout is fueled and ready for you."

They shook hands all around, and Bolan and the two Russians left the office. Before he climbed into the car, the Executioner walked to the hangar to get a closer look at the SWIFT. It was propped up on stanchions. George Tam sat in the bubble-enclosed cockpit and when he saw him, he crawled out through a hatch in the belly. After thanking

Tam for his surveillance services, Bolan commented, "This is quite a craft. Very unusual."

Tam shrugged, but pride shone in his eyes. "Combining a glider and a sailplane isn't a new concept, but I'll go out on a limb and say the SWIFT pushes the envelope. It took me five years and damn near a million bucks to develop her, and I'm still working on improvements. Are you a pilot?"

"I've flown some," Bolan replied, thinking about all the seat-of-the-pants flying he'd performed over the years.

"Maybe you'd like to take her up."

"Maybe, when I have some free time."

Nimchov and Kirchov were waiting for him in the car. Nimchov was in the back seat, and he and the woman were arguing, exchanging rapid-fire streams of Russian. Though they both subsided into silence when Bolan slid behind the wheel, the angry tension between them filled the car like an electrical current.

No one spoke until they were back out on the main highway, heading toward Tampa.

"What is the plan?" Kirchov asked tersely.

"I'll make a soft probe of the hardsite tonight."

"Hardsite?"

"The island."

"I'm going with you, of course."

"As am I," Nimchov rumbled.

"Not necessary. I don't intend to make a strike."

"You may have no choice," Kirchov replied.

Braking at a red light, Bolan glanced over at the woman sitting beside him. "Why not?"

"If Dexter Deveroux intends to launch a rocket to link up with the platform, tonight will have the optimum conditions." She paused and added, "Green light."

11

Bolan pressed down on the accelerator. "Explain."

"A storm front is moving into the area tonight," she said.

"And?"

"And, the best time to stage a covert launch is immediately after the front has passed. The atmosphere will be temporarily ionized, and combined with heavy cloud formations and condensation, radar tracking will be unreliable."

Bolan thought that over. "Radar operators may think the trace they receive of the rocket is an anomalous signature, a ghost-reading due to weather conditions."

"Precisely," Kirchov declared.

"Even if that's true, your presence isn't required."

Kirchov's lips compressed. "Don't be a fool. What do you know about rocketry?"

"Very little," Bolan admitted, swerving the Sable around a slow-moving panel truck. "Since this is a new system, prototypical in design, I doubt your expertise is any greater than mine."

Kirchov didn't reply for a long moment. When she did, her was voice was grating. "Take my word for it, Belasko. It is."

Suddenly Bolan wrenched the wheel to the left, cut across two lanes of oncoming traffic and squealed to a stop in the parking lot of a shopping center. He put the car in

Park and turned to face Kirchov and Nimchov, who sat directly behind her.

"There's something you're not telling me, Professor," he said coldly.

He and Kirchov locked gazes. Though her eyes were masked by sunglasses, the woman was the first to look away.

"Very well," she said. "If you must have it, have it then."

"Nyet," Nimchov snapped.

His right hand made a clawing grab for the big pistol holstered at his hip. By the time he had dragged up his shirttail and unsnapped the holster flap, Bolan's Beretta was trained on his chest. Nimchov's clumsy attempts to draw the automatic ceased.

"Cross your legs, left over the right," Bolan commanded. "Hands around the knee. Link the fingers and don't move."

His face a mask of dark, frustrated rage, Nimchov complied.

Not shifting the barrel of the Beretta, Bolan said, "I'm waiting, Professor."

Taking a deep breath, Kirchov began to talk. "The reason I know so much about Deveroux's system is that we—my government—appropriated its design for our own uses. A prototype launch tube accelerator was built at the Plesetsk Cosmodrome installation for the sole purpose of placing suborbital satellites. I worked on the project for several years."

Bolan had heard of the supersecret Plesetsk complex; it was the Russian equivalent of the Area 51 proving grounds in Nevada. For years, Soviet officials denied the existence of the Cosmodrome. "What was your success ratio?"

Kirchov shrugged. "Quite high, around sixty percent. Unfortunately, when my country underwent its governmental upheaval, funding for the project was curtailed."

"What kind of satellites did you launch?"

Kirchov hesitated, her tongue dabbing at her lower lip. "I believe you would call them 'killer' satellites. I'm sure you're aware of the number of spy satellites put into space by your own and other governments that were blinded when they passed over Russia."

"I've heard stories," Bolan said.

"Our satellites contained very weak nuclear warheads. They were programmed to detonate when an enemy surveillance satellite passed within the effect radius of the explosion."

"When did this program end?"

Kirchov smiled bitterly. "I said it had been curtailed, not ended. It continues."

Bolan fixed his eyes on Nimchov. "And you're the man who was sent to protect the secret."

"It is my duty," he growled. "Many things have changed in my homeland, but internal security is still paramount."

"Why didn't you use Deveroux's system to deactivate the Hellfire Trigger?" Bolan demanded.

Kirchov shook her head. "Many reasons," she replied wearily. "Many of them contradictory. Officially the platform does not exist, therefore it cannot be deactivated. Unofficially it was simply too much trouble, too expensive, too risky. Besides, we did not have the entire telemetric code in our possession."

Bolan smiled without humor. "Besides, since an American has the entire code in his possession, it makes more sense to allow the American government to clean up a mess left over from the cold war."

Addressing Nimchov, Bolan asked, "Were you going to shoot Professor Kirchov for spilling the secret, or me for hearing it?"

"I don't know. I was moving on reflex, simply reacting. I was not thinking ahead."

"Think ahead now. Do you want me to put you in an FBI holding tank until the next flight to Moscow, or do you want a shoot-out here in the car?"

Nimchov forced a smile. "Is there a third alternative?"

"In fact, there is. You can still do your duty and help me stop Deveroux."

The Russian agent inclined his head in a half bow. "I prefer to perform my duty."

"Glad to hear it. Just the same, I'd rather you give me your gun until it's time to do your duty."

Nimchov's forced smile faltered. Carefully he removed the holstered pistol from his waistband and handed both over to Bolan. Though Bolan took his gun off Nimchov and steered the Sable back out onto the street, he kept glancing back at the man in the rearview mirror. The Russian continued to sit perfectly still, his legs primly crossed, hands around his knee.

"Since you have hands-on experience with this system, Professor," Bolan said, "what will be Deveroux's procedure to launch his rocket?"

Tapping her chin contemplatively, Kirchov replied, "Solar power is not my field, but I know a little about it. Extrapolating from our operations at Plesetsk, Deveroux has to have a method of pumping vast amounts of pressurized water into his vacuum launch tube. As I told you in Virginia, I imagine he has a series of turbines moored off the shore of the island. With the stored solar energy converted to electricity to turn the blades, he has an untraceable source of massive power. The possible output is around forty-three megawatts."

"So he doesn't have to worry about his bill with Florida Power and Light," Bolan said impatiently. "What's that got to do with anything?"

"I'm trying to explain. The turbines drive the seawater into the vacuum tube accelerator, creating a vortex flow. The flow follows the curve of the tube, surrounds the projectile and comes together at the rear, pushing the thing forward. As the projectile moves, the vortex flow bends backward, and the water rushing past is pulled into the vortex, adding to the volume. By then, the missile is inside a shell of moving water, spinning in a great circle. As the water moves faster, additional propulsive energy is produced by centrifugal force. Then the rocket is launched from an ejector chute.''

"And achieves escape velocity," Bolan said. "But Deveroux has to guide the missile to the platform, and he can't do that without very sophisticated and big directional antennae."

"True."

"Though one wasn't visible on the surveillance tape, he has to have one someplace, either at his building or on the island. Maybe we should make the antennae our target."

"Maybe," Kirchov replied hesitantly. "But if he manages to make a successful launch, uplinks with the platform through a computer and alters its programming, we'll need the antennae functional."

"Exactly what does Deveroux need to lock on to the platform?" Bolan asked.

Kirchov sighed, shaking her head. "The simplest and most cost-efficient way is to equip the missile with some kind of a magnetic docking manipulator. Once the rocket makes hard contact, a junction link can be tied into the platform's targeting and detonation circuit terminal. Deveroux transmits the telemetric code to the missile and the missile's computer piggybacks the transmission to the platform."

"And the Hellfire Trigger is primed and armed," Bolan said grimly. His hands tightened on the steering wheel. "What kind of guidance system did your single-stage rockets use at the Cosmodrome?"

"Upper vectored thrust nozzles, which direct the exhaust products at the proper angle for the desired maneuvering."

"You make it sound very simple."

"It is," Kirchov said. "In a way."

"Yeah," Bolan replied quietly. "As simple and as uncomplicated as a 300-kiloton thermonuclear explosion can be."

DEVEROUX STEPPED from the helicopter, followed by Kindzierski, the pilot. He strode quickly across the compound, toward the corner of the concrete block building. The door was steel, recessed a half foot into the wall. It had no knob, no keyhole and no visible lock.

Reaching into a pocket, Deveroux produced a tiny oval-shaped instrument made of black plastic. He held the instrument against the door and pressed a button. There was a loud click of solenoids and the door swung inward.

Deveroux and Kindzierski walked into a reception room. The floor was carpeted in burgundy, and colorful Degas lithographs hung on the walls. The track lighting was subdued, the air fresh and cool, unlike the humid oppressiveness outside.

A red-haired man wearing horn-rimmed glasses and the uniform of the Double D security force sat at a large mahogany desk. A compact walkie-talkie rested at his elbow. When he saw Deveroux, he hastily got to his feet, trying to hide the copy of *Florida Swingers* magazine.

"Anything to report?" Deveroux asked.

"No, sir. That is, not really."

Deveroux stared at the man over the rim of his sunglasses. "Not really, Burtis?"

Burtis made a feeble, dismissive gesture. "Three people on a boat about a half hour ago. The patrol questioned them and confirmed their nonbelligerence. Since the man who you told us to watch out for wasn't aboard, and they really weren't all that close to the compound—"

"Who were the three people?" Deveroux broke in.

"A black man—a local, and two Canadian tourists, a man and a woman."

"What did the woman look like?"

Burtis shrugged. "The patrol said she was dark-haired and really drunk. So was her husband. The black man, the charter captain, had no objections to his boat being searched, so—"

"Was the boat searched?" Deveroux's voice was like steel.

Beads of perspiration formed on Burtis's forehead. "No, sir. Because he gave his permission, you see, and because his answers to the patrol's questions were satisfactory, they were allowed to go on their way." Burtis licked his lips and added, "You did instruct us to be discreet, sir."

"So I did." Deveroux turned abruptly on his heel and strode for a door in the far wall, leaving behind the pilot in the reception room. Pushing open the door, he walked down a lofty, bare-walled corridor, lit at frequent intervals by soft-white, low-wattage bulbs in wall brackets.

As much as he wanted to, he couldn't blame the patrol for not recognizing Anastasia Kirchov. Since he had only become aware of her presence in the mix a short time before, he couldn't expect his employees to be any more precognitive than himself. They were on the alert for a man fitting Mike Belasko's description, but that was it. They didn't have the photographs.

At any rate, he rarely involved his security people in his low-profile affairs. As far as most of them knew, he was a legitimate businessman, a rather eccentric entrepreneur, but he wasn't dangerous. He certainly wasn't a criminal. He was simply a stickler for procedure. However, he retained a handpicked crew of a dozen to act as his personal extermination squad. They were privy to his most important dealings, and he had made sure they were too deeply involved to feel they could back out and live.

He walked a hundred yards down the corridor, past doors

labeled Design Engineering, Vehicle Systems and Electronics Testing. He turned right through an archway and entered a vast, barn-size room. Its overhead light was indirect, and of a bright blue intensity. The room was filled with all the complicated and delicate high-tech instrumentation of an assembly area: strain gauges, vacuum chambers, heat-molding presses. Along the far wall were glass panels, covering a separate, slightly elevated observation deck. The left end of the room was punctured by a giant, perfectly cut circle, five feet in diameter. A metal-collared hatch gaped open to one side, hanging by thick, stainless-steel hinges.

Deveroux wended his way through rows of drafting tables, frowning at the wads of paper bearing scribbled calculations spilling out of wastebaskets. There were only two people in the room. The young Chinese woman, barely out of her teens, was stunning. She sat at one of the drafting boards, efficiently working on a blueprint. Liu Weng was one of Deveroux's most treasured "knobs," turning her brilliant mathematical skills in the direction he chose.

Fredric Eberhardt wasn't a knob; he was a sixtyish, balding man who suffered from eczema. He was an brilliant rocket scientist, but NASA hadn't appreciated his intelligence. Actually it was his predilection for underage females that NASA hadn't appreciated, and the agency had regretfully terminated his contract.

Dexter Deveroux distrusted physical scientists as a general rule. Outside of journalists, he had never met a more hidebound, dense, play-by-the-numbers bunch. Most of them had the imaginations of tree stumps. Eberhardt was incapable of visualizing anything unless it was within the pages of a scientific journal. He had come to work for Deveroux a few years before, and though he wasn't above trying to seduce the female population of "knob row," he did his job exceptionally well. But he was such a neurotic little man, Deveroux found that just being near him for a short length of time lowered his energy levels. Eberhardt smelled of bad karma, and after everything was in place, he intended to put the man out of sight and out of mind.

At the moment, Eberhardt was standing beside a thirty-foot-long, blunt-nosed metal cylinder painted a nonreflective black. Its diameter was in proportion to its length. The cylinder was resting in heavy iron mounts equipped with hard rubber wheels. He glanced up from tightening a bolt when Deveroux approached.

"Dexter," he said, trying to disguise the apprehension in his voice. "I didn't expect to see you today."

Deveroux didn't respond to the greeting. "Have you incorporated the modifications into the air intake of the combustion chamber?"

"Almost. Another couple of days."

"Make it a couple of hours. We launch tonight."

Eberhardt's shoulders jerked as if he had received a blow between them. "You can't be serious."

"Why not?" Deveroux snapped. "The modifications are simple, a matter of retooling. The payload has been ready for weeks."

He gestured to a metal-sheathed cube resting on a nearby table. It was about the size of a Volkswagen engine. A side panel was propped open, revealing a shining network of circuitry and looping coaxial cables within.

"The antennae leads can be connected," Deveroux continued, "and we have plenty of time for a final simulation. The solar cells are charged and the launch tube can be prepped."

"The weather report forecast a bad storm moving in tonight," Eberhardt protested.

"As one does nearly every single day during the summer," Deveroux declared. "The issue isn't debatable, Eberhardt. The Remora goes up tonight, or you go down tonight. As in six feet down. Clear?"

Eberhardt swallowed, fidgeting with the precision torque wrench in his hand. "Clear."

"Repeat it back to me so I will know you are not without basic comprehension."

"The Remora goes up tonight, or I'll go down."

"How far down, Eberhardt?"

"As in six feet."

"Good. Over the next few hours, if you feel your concentration faltering, just keep repeating that over and over, like a mantra."

Spinning on his heel, Deveroux stalked away. Eberhardt gazed after him, blinking back hot tears of rage and humiliation. He saw Liu Weng smiling at him over her shoulder. It wasn't a smile of sympathy.

12

Bit by bit the starlit sky was slowly swallowed by huge dark thunderheads. Sergei Nimchov looked at the gathering clouds and muttered something in his own tongue.

Bolan was at the wheel of the *E.G. Robinson,* guiding it at a moderate speed through a moderate chop. Far in the distance and dimness, the floodlights surrounding Deveroux's island compound glowed. Anastasia Kirchov stood next to him at the controls, staring straight ahead.

Cloud mountains massed in the east. A crooked finger of lightning arced across them. Bolan consulted his watch, counting the ticks of the second hand. It was few minutes shy of nine o'clock. When the air shivered to a clap of thunder, he said, "The front is about fifteen miles away. We've got maybe forty minutes before it reaches us."

Within a mile of the island, Bolan throttled down the rpm, and the boat coasted quietly through the water. The sweep of white beach was about a thousand feet off their bow, when he turned the craft at an oblique angle to the island, cutting the power. The runabout bobbed on the swells as Nimchov eased the heavy galvanized steel anchor over the side.

Bolan pulled the case containing the night-vision headset from the cabin and ran a quick inventory of his personal ordnance. He was wearing his multipocketed, form-fitting blacksuit, a Fairbairn-Sykes combat stiletto hung from his web belt and the Desert Eagle was holstered at his hip. Four magazines of 9 mm rounds hung from the leather combat harness over his high-necked tunic. Attached to a metal ring on the harness between his shoulder blades was the Remington shotgun. Though it had a shoulder strap, he had hooked it behind him so it wouldn't snarl the strap of his war bag. It was a zippered, watertight pouch looped over his left shoulder, containing two drum magazines of 12-gauge buckshot, a flashlight and a pair of wire-cutters. From the bag, he took the holstered Colt and gave it to Nimchov, who clipped it to his belt.

Bolan blacked his face from the tin of combat cosmetics and handed it to Kirchov. After she smeared dark designs over her face, she passed it on to Nimchov who applied it liberally. Both Russians wore dark clothing and high, laced boots.

The Executioner dropped the package containing the rubber landing raft overboard and yanked the lanyard connected to the oxygen bottle. The hiss and pop of its inflation sounded very loud, even though he knew no one could hear it. His warrior's mind was on full alert, sharpening unconsciously, instinctively on the edge of danger.

The three people carefully climbed into the floating raft, and Bolan and Nimchov took up the paddles. Small waves slapped softly against the rubber sides as they stroked in unison.

In a matter of minutes they felt the tug and push of the surf, and they made speedy and steady progress toward the pale strip of sand. When their paddles dragged on the bottom, they slid overboard into knee-deep water and hauled the raft ashore, stumbling across the beach toward the undergrowth and dropping it in the shadows. They concealed the raft under a foot of soft sand.

Bolan peered into the labyrinth of foliage. Bright lights stained distant treetops with unwavering bands of blue-white. He listened and heard nothing but the chittering of insects and the clacking screech of a seabird.

"Let's get it over with," Nimchov said in a whisper, hand on the butt of the pistol at his hip.

Bolan glanced at Kirchov. Her eyes shone out of the dark smudge of her face. She nodded once.

Unhooking the Remington from the harness, Bolan removed an ammo drum from his war bag and clicked it into place. With the close assault weapon hanging from his right shoulder, he donned the night-vision headset and turned it on. Two infrared beams shone from the twin projectors on the helmet. Viewed through its lenses, the jungle seemed to be lit by a lambent, ghostly glow. Where only black had been before, there were various shifting shades of gray.

"I'll take the point," he whispered. "Stay close."

Bolan went in the direction of the compound, a quarter of a mile distant. The three people walked carefully, doing their utmost to be stealthy, despite the vines snaring their ankles and the thorns snagging their clothing. Insects whirred around their faces. The footing was soft and marshy, and reeked of the rotten-egg odor of sulfuretted swamp gas.

The soldier's eyes watched everything, studied the slightest motion in the dim jungle. He was especially on the lookout for trip wires or snares or motion detectors. He saw nothing, yet he had the feeling they were being watched, or at the very least, they were expected.

He stepped into a depression and very nearly stumbled. Two deep parallel grooves had squashed and flattened the vegetation beneath his feet. The outside edges of the grooves showed a tread pattern, the tracks obviously made by one of the swamp buggies. He warned Nimchov and Kirchov to watch their steps.

Through the brush, the white lights of the security floodlamps cast lakes of illumination across the darkness. Seen through the night-vision lenses, they looked like seething pools of molten lava.

Lowering himself to his belly, Bolan whispered to the

Russians to wait for him. He crept forward, pushing aside leaves and dangling liana. He scanned the perimeter of the cyclone fence for any point not splashed by the floodlights. So far he saw no signs of flaws in the defenses.

Propelling himself by elbows and feet, Bolan followed a slow course parallel to the fence. Eventually it was a sound, the low, steady rumble of an engine, that alerted him to the penetration point he was after.

A swamp buggy rolled from around a corner of one of the outbuildings, its headlights fanning white cones ahead of it. The buggy was a tractorlike vehicle, riding high on four huge tires, five feet in diameter.

It rolled directly past Bolan's position in the brush. The man jouncing in the saddle and holding the wheel was big, bearded and had a strip of bandage wound around his head. He was the gatekeeper from the Bottoms Up Club. He wore a Double D security guard's uniform, and captain's bars gleamed from his shirt collar.

Lying hidden beneath the drooping leaves of a jacaranda, Bolan watched as the buggy rolled on. It swerved slightly and a beam of light from a handheld flashlight stabbed out into the darkness beyond the fence. The man was shining the light on narrow wedges of shadow where the spread of the floodlamps didn't meet.

The light vanished and the vehicle rumbled on, following the straight stretch of the building's outside wall. Bolan arose in a crouch and duckwalked along the fence until he reached the streak of darkness where the position of the floodlamps left an opening.

He crept to the bottom of the fence, examining it. It was twenty feet high, the top frame adorned with curls of razor wire. Scaling it was out of the question. He also saw a gossamer line running along the cross bars. It was obviously a trigger wire connected to an alarm.

Unzipping his war bag, Bolan removed a pair of short-handled wire-cutters. Lying flat, he began snipping metal strands. He had done this so often in so many places, the triangular pattern he cut could have been performed in his sleep.

When he was done, he had cut a two-and-a-half-foot-high pyramid shape in the fence, three feet wide at its base. He kept a couple of strands intact, one at the apex and one at the bottom, so the snipped area would remain vertical and pass a cursory inspection.

Returning to the tangle of foliage, Bolan moved fast despite bending in a crouch. With no guards patrolling outside the compound perimeter, it seemed as if Deveroux was either riding a high wave of overconfidence or he didn't intend to launch a rocket that night. The wind picked up as he crept along, the welcome hint of a chill within it.

Stepping out of the shadows, he startled Kirchov so much she jumped, but she didn't make an outcry. Neither did Nimchov.

"I found a point of entry," he whispered. "Doesn't appear to be any patrols outside the compound, so I think it's safe to move in."

"Lead the way," Nimchov said, drawing the big Colt pistol.

Bolan turned, parting bushes. There was a sudden rustle of leaves behind him and Kirchov blurted something. As he began to whirl, a loud crack and crunch filled his ears. At the same time, a hard, heavy weight descended upon his skull, slamming him headfirst into a deep, black pit.

DEVEROUX TAPPED a sequence of buttons on the keyboard and ran the simulation program for the third time that hour.

On the monitor screen, an animated Remora Three rocket approached an animated suborbital nuclear platform in a computer-generated simulacrum of outer space.

Pinpoints of flame lanced from the Remora's maneuvering thrusters. The nose of the rocket shifted, pointing directly at the flat, dark underbelly of the platform. A ring of nozzles encircling the body of the Remora danced with jets of fire. The retrothrusters engaged in a five-second burn, and the rocket's velocity slowed.

Like a log floating on the surface of a sluggishly moving river, the Remora drifted forward. A final one-second burn of the low-key maneuvering thrusters propelled the nose of the rocket into a metal-ringed port on the bottom of the platform.

The perspective on the screen changed. An enlarged, cutaway diagram appeared. The nose of the Remora raised open, and a metal probe extended from the tip. It pushed up, sliding into the access port. The probe turned and locked.

The onboard computer systems of the Hellfire Trigger were activated, penetrated, compromised and integrated within a nanosecond. Responding to a binary code transmitted from the Cheops Alpha, the targeting program booted up. A stream of telemetric signals and commands flooded the platform's simple binary cybernetic brain. It uplinked with the Cheops Alpha through a ground-based radio antenna.

The Hellfire Trigger responded to the commands, arming its warhead, executing a course-corrective program, recalibrating its systems and establishing a solid target lock.

The entire process, occurring completely in cyberspace, took 10.6 seconds.

Though he very much wanted to, Deveroux didn't laugh as the Remora's retrojets flamed again. Slowly, majestically even, the reverse thrust pulled the platform out of the invisible clutches of the Lagrangian point.

He kept his face impassive as he watched the simulation continue. The Remora's maneuvering thrusters fired, and the platform and rocket tilted together, spinning around with the midpoint of the Remora acting as an axis.

Following the blue, white and green curvature of Earth,

the Remora, seemingly pushing the Hellfire Trigger ahead of it, thundered across suborbital space.

Corrective signals continued to be transmitted into the Remora's guidance system. When the rocket reached the programmed angle of trajectory, the retrojets flamed once more, slowing the velocity, and the altitude control subsystem kicked in. The maneuvering thrusters brought the platform horizontal to the force of gravity, the nuclear warhead pointing downward. The retros fired for the final time, pushing the platform down until it entered Earth's gravity well at an altitude of one hundred miles.

The Hellfire Trigger, linked in physical and cybernetic symbiosis, began a free fall. On the screen, a bright yellow *X* was superimposed over the ragged, roughly foot-shaped outline of the Arabian Peninsula.

The blanket of atmosphere retarded the long tumble. Scraps of clouds whipped over the friction-red edges of the platform. Under the aerodynamic drag, the Remora and the Hellfire Trigger slowed to Mach 1 at 30,000 feet. A readout in the corner of the screen kept count of the altitude and rate of descent.

Three gigantic parachutes deployed from sealed boxes around the outer rim of the platform, opening fully at 10,000 feet. The free fall became a twenty-two mile per hour float.

At 3,000 feet above a section of Saudi Arabia, the simulations of the Remora and the Hellfire Trigger vanished in a brilliant fireball.

The legend Simulation Complete, Accuracy 93 Percent appeared on the screen. Deveroux leaned back in his chair. The chronometer at the upper right corner of the monitor read 20.09.

From the moment the Remora had made its rendezvous with the platform, the entire sequence leading to warhead detonation had comprised a little over twenty minutes. Though there were still variables to contend with, Deveroux was positive the process wouldn't take over twenty-five minutes.

"Why Saudi Arabia?"

Deveroux swiveled in his chair. Eberhardt stood over the accelerometer, precision tools in hand. "Pardon?"

"I asked why you chose Saudi Arabia as ground zero," Eberhardt asked, trying to smile. "A whim?"

Deveroux snorted. "Hardly a whim, though I am entitled to indulge them. No, there's a sound psychological reasoning behind my choice. Firstly there is the irony factor."

"The *what* factor?"

"The irony is that Saudi Arabia, so fiercely independent of Russia and America for so many years, is rendered uninhabitable by one of the cold war's forgotten toys."

"Then why not one of the Eastern Bloc nations?" Eberhardt asked. "Or even Cuba?"

"The Eastern Bloc is too remote," Deveroux answered, pushing his chair back from the keyboard. "And Cuba lies only ninety miles from the U.S. mainland, therefore, it's too close. Besides, neither Eastern Europe nor the Caribbean possess competitive natural resources. Saudi Arabia does."

"Oil?" Eberhardt asked. The smile was frozen on his face. He scratched nervously at a red rash on his wrist.

"Oil. Saudi Arabia is the richest nation in oil on Earth. Fortunes in the world economy are made and lost on the ebb and flow of Arabian oil. They have, for all intents and purposes, a monopoly on the energy resources of the entire planet. Half of Saudi Arabia's oil reserves, approximately seventy-five *billion* barrels, is located at the Ghawar fields of the eastern province. The defenses of that field are popularly believed to be impenetrable."

"Except," Eberhardt said slowly, "by a hydrogen bomb exploding above it."

"Now you're getting it," Deveroux replied. "Imagine the shock value of such a catastrophe, its unthinkable magnitude, its horrific long-term implications and consequences. No fuel, no gasoline, no heat, no electricity.''

Eberhardt cleared his throat. ''There will be worldwide panic, Dexter. Complete tumult.''

''Well, that's rather the point, isn't it? The destruction of the oil fields will terrify and arouse the population. They will seek, even howl for, an alternative to imported and expensive oil. And one will be offered.''

''How many people live around the Ghawar fields?''

Deveroux shrugged. ''No complete census of individuals has ever been conducted by the Saudis, and I can't see that it really matters at this point.''

Even through the thick, reinforced concrete walls, the thunderclap was very loud. Deveroux finally smiled. He stood and stretched. ''Button up the Remora and prep the tube. We're at T-minus zero and counting.''

Nelson Demille   135

clutter; he tortured to begin finkskwog: wit' ander
dhotius. Ms bill may it'd yrar rhia litet me bit row
Forward should dry mosrow raike; will toweg sayin'
pails; Larter Ceosijuem' hhi.
    Wirli; was a conx; wic'b hkraud' ar? The decodtion
a hignit; fall-will hereog nelly eyes the popation. Tsa
will snak; even is.jet hau thmalthre to expoded the
exponen'n off. And ouc will be cricked.
    "How many people.ly surond the Chway; dela?"

13

The crashing seemed to come from inside his skull, a ladder
of sound Bolan had to climb to reach consciousness. His
eyes opened and took in his reality.

He was lying on his back, looking up at a patch of dark
sky between swaying treetops. The night-vision headset
was gone, and he immediately sensed the absence of his
Desert Eagle and the Remington shotgun. The crashing
came again, this time punctuated by a flash of lightning.

Bolan's thoughts cleared, despite the pain in the back of
his head. He got his arms under him and pushed himself
to a sitting position.

"Easy, Belasko," Nimchov warned. "I'd prefer not to
shoot you. Killing you wouldn't bother me, but shooting
you would make noise and perhaps draw attention."

Nimchov kneeled about six feet away from him, the Colt
automatic in his right hand, the Desert Eagle in his left.
Beside him was the shotgun and the war bag. Kirchov sat
to one side, huddled between the two men, hugging her
knees. Though it was hard to tell in the murk, she appeared
frightened and angry.

"I had no knowledge of this," she stammered. "I did
not betray you, Belasko."

"No, I can attest to that," Nimchov spit. "She preferred
to betray her country."

"What do you mean?" Bolan asked. The night-vision
headset lay near him, the plastic helmet cracked, the infra-

red projectors broken. It had probably saved him from a fractured skull when Nimchov had rapped the gun across his skull.

"Not everyone serving in the Russian military or in government feared the Hellfire Trigger, or even considered it a bad thing." Nimchov grinned, his teeth showing whitely against the black combat cosmetics smeared across his face. "In fact, when some of us learned that Deveroux had the entire telemetry in his possession, we figured it might turn out to our advantage."

"Who are 'some of us'?" Bolan asked.

"Hard-liners," Kirchov replied, contempt dripping from every syllable. "Holdover Stalinists and supporters of Vladimir Zhirinosky who want a return to the old ways, who want the iron curtain dropped again."

Without looking at her, Nimchov casually reached over and swiped the barrel of the gun across her left kneecap. Though she tried to stifle it, a cry of pain was forced past her lips. Bolan didn't move.

"Assuming what she said has some truth to it," Bolan said, "how would allowing Dexter Deveroux to control the Hellfire Trigger be an advantage to your loyalist faction? At the very least, Russia's public relations with other countries would take a definite downslide. Worst-case scenario, if the bomb *is* dropped, your country will be universally censured, trade embargoes put in place and any number of economic sanctions could be imposed. The UN would probably demand you pay reparation to whatever nation is unfortunate enough to receive the platform's little thermonuclear love offering."

Nimchov shrugged. "That is what we hope will happen."

"You don't make any sense."

"I make perfect sense, American. You simply don't have the brains to comprehend."

"Then take pity on the brain-damaged American and explain," Bolan bit back.

"If any of the situations you outlined do occur," Nimchov responded smoothly, "the Russian people, their backs to the wall, will naturally remember the days when their motherland stepped aside for no other nation on Earth. They will beg the 'hard-liners,' as we are called, to return to power, to face down the self-righteous United Nations, to meet intimidation with intimidation. The Soviet Union will be reborn."

"So you actually want Deveroux to launch his pocket-rocket?"

"Yes."

"Are you doing this on the orders of your superiors?"

"Irrelevant," Nimchov replied diffidently.

Bolan's lips compressed, then quirked in a cold, half smile. "Not really a bad plan, Nimchov. You're assigned to partner up with Professor Kirchov and act in cooperation with American intelligence services. I smooth your path with the authorities, and take you with me in a probe of Deveroux's stronghold. The professor and I end up dead, the rocket is or is not launched, and you say, 'The security was very tight, I tried to save them, I was lucky to get out alive, and hey, casualties are part of the game.' Then you go back to Mother Russia, slug down a few vodkas with your ex-commissar pals and hope the boom will be lowered."

Nimchov chuckled. "I miscalculated. You *do* have some brains. At least until I blow them out. Now, on your feet."

Bolan arose stiffly, wincing at the pain in his head. All things considered, the injury could have been much more severe. Nimchov gestured with the Desert Eagle to Kirchov, who slowly climbed to her feet, favoring her left knee.

"We will go back to the beach," Nimchov announced, "where gunshots are less likely to be overheard."

He shifted position, getting behind him, and Bolan felt the tip of the .44 touch his spine. He'd hoped Nimchov would make that choice. In one swift motion, the Executioner stepped backward, stamping down hard with his heavy-heeled boot on the Russian's instep, pivoting on it with all his weight, his hand chopping at the gun. The Desert Eagle spun end over end into the brush.

Nimchov didn't scream, but he half roared, struggling to pull his foot free and bringing the Colt Government model to bear with his right hand. He squeezed the trigger. The firing pin clicked.

Bolan hooked his left fist into Nimchov's body. Starting from his hip, it smashed directly into the Russian's diaphragm. The punch bent the man in the middle, and his mouth and eyes flew wide. He slowly fell to his hands and knees, making a great effort to breathe, to blink, to even think.

The Executioner snatched the automatic from his nerveless fingers, hefted it and sidestepped over to the brush where his Desert Eagle had fallen. He squatted, pointing the Colt at Nimchov, and after a few moments of groping, retrieved the big .44 from the ground.

Kirchov gaped at him in astonishment, then by degrees, a hesitant, jittery smile played over her face. She picked up the Remington and the war bag. Nimchov forced himself to his knees, gasping with exertion and pain. His glassy eyes were questioning.

Jacking a round out of the Colt's slide, Bolan said, "I've crossed trails with too many Russian agents to have much trust in your fraternity, glasnost or not. Earlier today I took a round out of your gun, emptied the primer and replaced it in the clip."

Nimchov took a great shuddery breath, but said nothing.

"I took into account the possibility that you were legitimate, and that I might be putting you at risk if we walked into a fire-zone. That's why I insisted on taking the point.

I figured one misfire wouldn't necessarily jeopardize you, if I provided adequate cover. The rest of the ammo is live."

Bolan handed the gun to Kirchov and waggled the barrel of the Desert Eagle at Nimchov. "Get up, hard-liner. We're still going to the beach."

Grunting, the Russian pushed himself erect. Hands clasped over his middle, he walked in front of Bolan through the jungle. A stiff wind rattled the leaves and branches of trees. The sky rolled with thunderclaps and became illuminated by bolts of lightning. Before they had traveled more than halfway to the beach, the full fury of the storm front hit the island broadside.

Wind-driven sheets of cold rain blasted them, mixed with tiny fragments of hail. In a handful of seconds, the three were soaked to the skin. Bolan kept pushing Nimchov onward. The Russian fell once, but he pushed himself upright and went on.

As they approached the beach, using one hand to shield his eyes from the downpour, Bolan heard the murmur of voices. He forced Nimchov to a halt and strained his ears to hear over the constant pounding of the rain and the thrash of wind-whipped foliage. He picked up snatches of conversation from the shoreline.

They were male voices, more than two, he guessed. Prodding Nimchov with the Desert Eagle, they continued warily. When they reached the fringes of the undergrowth, they sank beneath a palmetto scrub and peered out at the beach beyond.

When lightning lit up the sky again, Bolan saw four men wearing hooded rain capes trudging along the sand, their faces hidden by the shadows of the cowls. They were heading in the direction of the compound. Two of the men cradled pump-action shotguns in their arms.

Nimchov suddenly exploded into motion, lunging toward the beach in a shambling dive. He shouted in a raspy voice, trying to catch the patrol's attention. Bolan aimed the Desert Eagle at the back of the Russian's head.

He didn't squeeze the trigger; there was no need. One of the shotgun-toting men whirled, weapon held at waist level. There were no "who goes there?" or "halt and be recognized" challenges. The man simply fired. The explosive report was drowned out by a crash of thunder.

Nimchov's chest broke open like a watermelon under a sledgehammer. Ribbons of blood gouted into the air and he fell backward, his face a ruined, wet mask.

Bolan turned, grabbed Kirchov by the elbow and rushed back into the jungle. They didn't bother with stealth; the storm was making so much noise, no one could have heard their blundering. A voice, as sharp as a whip-crack, shouted something behind them.

There was an explosion, and the bole of a tree on Bolan's right was transformed into flinders as a load of buckshot pounded into it. Flying splinters stung the side of his face, the back of Kirchov's head. She grimaced, but said nothing.

Not really aiming, still running, Bolan swung the big .44 over his shoulder and fired five times. He caught a brief glimpse of four hooded figures scattering in all directions.

Bolan changed course; struggling through thorns and vines, he dragged Kirchov into a bush. There was a depression beneath it, and they rolled into it. They lay side by side, bodies pressing together. He didn't believe the patrol had seen them alter their course, but the men fired blindly into the jungle anyway, pistols and shotguns both.

Bullets thudded through the air, knocking bark off trees, and buckshot slashed through shrubs and branches. Bushes bent and leaves fluttered to the ground. Bolan realized that his earlier sensation of being expected was correct; the security guards had been ordered to subscribe to the shoot-first-answer-questions-later school. He doubted it was Deveroux's standard policy.

More men were certainly on their way, alerted by walkie-talkies, and he had no idea how many might arrive. It would take them some time to rendezvous with this quartet. In the thick bush, they would have to proceed slowly, or risk shooting one another.

The firing ceased and a man shouted something in Spanish, then in English. He said they had to spread out and advance carefully. One guard, by the name of Carlos, was ordered to return to the beach and stake it out.

Kirchov huddled next to Bolan, trying to soften the frightened harshness of her breathing. The gun in her hand trembled. The sounds of men moving swiftly, if not noiselessly, through the foliage reached them. The rain abated for a moment, then poured down hard again. The storm's intensity showed no indication of slackening. Water dripped from the leaves of the bush and down the backs of their necks.

Bolan drew the Sykes-Fairbairn combat stiletto, holding it in his left fist. He tried to penetrate the dark, overgrown tangle with his eyes, searching for any movement.

Leaves crunched somewhere on the other side of the bush. Holding his breath, he waited for another sound. It came in the next few seconds. A man wearing a moisture-slick rain cape passed by, walking slowly, holding his shotgun in both hands. It was a pump-action Savage Combat Model 77E, a 12-gauge like his Remington.

The guard was within five feet of them, turning his head to and fro like a foxhound casting for a scent. He moved forward another few feet. Bolan wormed toward him on his belly, silently cursing the slight rustle the motion caused.

As the man passed his position, Bolan slipped to his feet and fell into step behind him. The cape's hood effectively cut off the guard's peripheral vision, so he was completely unaware of the big man's presence until a hand clamped tightly over his mouth.

The Executioner slid the blade between the man's third and fourth ribs, puncturing the heart. The guard's lips writhed against Bolan's palm, but he perished without making a sound.

Catching the sagging body, Bolan dragged it into concealment in the overgrowth. He removed the knife and wiped the blade against the grass to clean it. He considered giving the Savage to Kirchov, but he doubted she could withstand its recoil for more than one shot. He left it with the guard's body and gestured for the astrophysicist to join him.

Hair plastered to her head and face, clothing adhering to her body, Anastasia Kirchov looked extremely bedraggled and unhappy. Not frightened, exactly, but judging by the expression on her face, she fervently wished she could be someplace else. Bolan had no time or inclination to comfort her. She was the one who had insisted on joining the probe, after all.

Kirchov leaned into him, her left breast against his arm. He could feel her heart pumping hard and fast. Whispering into her ear, he said, "Our best bet is to get inside the compound. Stay close, keep your eyes and ears open."

He heard the voices of men muttering behind them. Reinforcements were arriving, so there were probably a few guards spread out ahead. Bolan and Kirchov crept carefully through the jungle, and though he was grateful for the steady patter of rain and the thunderclaps that masked the sound of their progress, he cursed the lightning lashing across the sky. It lit up the island as though it were high noon.

Immediately following one flash, a man appeared in their path. He had his back to them, but he was in the process of turning, scoping out the zone. He stepped to one side, and his upper body was concealed by the broad leaves of an elephant ear plant. Only his hips, legs and feet were visible.

Bolan immediately drove the butt of his Remington through the leaves into the man's throat. He fell backward, making a gagging, gargling noise. Before he could bring up his shotgun, Bolan butt-stroked his head several times. The guard made no movement afterward.

After pulling the man into a tangle of shrubbery, Bolan and Kirchov continued toward the fence. They moved slowly, carefully, skirting treacherous bog holes. To their left, a few hundred feet behind a wall of overgrowth, two almost solid-looking pencils of white light scanned the sky, intersecting and causing the falling rain to sparkle like diamonds. The security guards, a pair of them, were outfitted with Maxabeam xenon flashlights, which could project a beam of between three and six million candlepower.

Kirchov stumbled and fell, grabbing at dangling vines to catch herself. She had stepped on a fallen log that seemed solid, but it was rotted and hollow and broke beneath her weight. She didn't cry out, but from a point twenty feet to their left, a man called out, "Hey!" A white spike of blinding light splashed directly on Kirchov's face.

Bolan spun, saw the guard with the flashlight and lunged for him. The guard shouted wordlessly, voice full of alarm, and dropped the flashlight, swinging the shotgun in the soldier's direction. He pulled the trigger.

The Executioner swerved, and buckshot-shredded leaves showered on his head. He kept running, the treaded soles of his boots keeping him from losing traction on the wet ground.

The guard fumbled with his weapon, working the pump action and ejecting bright brass. As the barrel swung toward him, Bolan left the ground in a long dive. The man tried to dodge, but he moved right into Bolan's line of fire.

The guard went over on his back, blood pouring from a gash at his hairline. His head struck an exposed tree root with a sharp crack. Carried by his momentum, Bolan fell into a tangle of drooping liana. He fought back to his feet and lurched over to the motionless man. The flashlight shot a rod of incandescence into the sky like a signal, and Bolan turned it off. He flipped back the cowl shadowing the man's face. He was young, his forehead lacerated by the big automatic, his face slack-jawed and senseless.

There was a crashing in the brush behind them. Kirchov, back on her feet, joined him and they ran into the darkness, in the direction of the fence. They heard angry shouts, and the sporadic crackle of gunfire. The commotion wasn't near them, but they went to ground anyway, lying beside the deeply rutted trunk of an ancient post oak.

The wind was dying down to no more than a stiff, intermittent breeze. The rain was a hard drizzle, not a driving downpour. Lightning still arced across the sky, but it had moved away from the island, pushing farther into the Gulf. The humidity, rising in the wake of the storm, was oppressive.

They waited for two minutes, then rose to their feet and crept on. The glow of the compound's security floodlamps was much closer. There was a little *whup* of suddenly displaced air close to Bolan's right ear. Grabbing Kirchov, he hurled her into a clump of bushes. The report of the pistol shot reached him a fraction of a second later.

On all fours, they scrambled into a narrow V made by two Spanish bayonet plants. There was another shot. The small muzzle-flash briefly limned a hooded shape standing about a hundred feet away. Bolan didn't fire. He granted the gunman the next move.

14

Dexter Deveroux looked forward to a busy, tension-drenched night. In his private quarters, he sat in a swirling, steaming whirlpool, proofreading the mechanicals of the brochures and advertisements scheduled to go to the printer the following week.

He was happy with the way the new Ra Soltech logo had turned out, but he was a bit dissatisfied with the type-face chosen for the trifold, color brochure. Since he was devoting more than one million dollars, nearly every penny of his liquid assets, to the first phase of his promotional campaign, he demanded perfection.

The actual copy was fine; he had written it himself. The prose was persuasive without being treacly, forceful without hinting at menace. The graphics were solid attention-grabbers as well. He particularly liked the picture of the Three Mile Island nuclear complex stamped with a cross-barred circle.

With a blue pencil, he indicated a change here, circled a typo there. Because of his exceptional speed-reading skills, Deveroux proofed all the material in less than twenty minutes. Setting it aside on a table, he rose from the Jacuzzi. His nude white body was very nearly hairless, and thin to the point of emaciation. Picking up a towel, he dried himself, humming quietly. It was a song he had written years before, "Puke and Explode." Meriem, his second wife, had made it the sole hit of the Microcephalics, less than a year before he had arranged for her to fall victim to a fatal drug overdose. He still collected several thousand dollars a year in royalties from it.

Pulling on a terry-cloth robe colored in a lurid, psychedelic pattern, Deveroux padded to his bedroom closet and selected a spotless white linen suit and white silk shirt. He dressed carefully, noting that the muffled thunderclaps were decreasing in frequency. After knotting a silk vermilion tie around his neck, he left his quarters and went to the primary control room, just down the hall.

It wasn't very large, but it was packed with monitor screens and a nightmare collection of electronics. The monitors displayed different views of the exterior and interior of the vast building. The exterior views showed very little but rainy murk. Activating the camera on the far end of the roof, he gauged the wind speed by the fullness of the bright orange wind sock attached to a pole.

He depressed two tabs on the console before him. The roof split into a pair of very long, vertical panels, opening up, then sliding aside. The solar cell array didn't rise. Inside, an intricate steel-and-wire framework slid upward, topped by the circular grid of a huge directional antenna. It was pointed almost directly overhead, but at the touch of a button, it swiveled and tilted, first to the north, then to the south. He plucked a cellular phone from the console, pressed a button and waited for it to be answered.

"What's the word?" Jest said into his ear.

"I'm preparing a test for the command guidance systems," Deveroux replied. "Get to the Cheops Alpha and ready it to uplink with the Remora's homing equipment."

"Will do."

Deveroux cut the connection. Before he could put down the phone, it buzzed. Since he was busy, he didn't want to answer it, but his staff knew not to call his private cellular phone number except under emergency or crisis conditions.

He put the phone to his ear and opened the connection. "What?"

The voice was agitated, but trying to maintain a facade of crisp professionalism. "This is Croy, sir. We have a situation on the island."

"What kind of situation?"

"Intruders. Three of them, two men and a woman, we think. The shore patrol neutralized one of the men, but the other two are in the jungle."

"Isn't it within your job description to find the other two?" Deveroux snapped.

"Yes, sir, but I wanted to apprise you before I pulled more men to join the search detail. Do I have your permission?"

"Yes, of course you do. Take care of it." Deveroux started to disconnect, then he said, "Croy, wait a minute."

"Sir?"

"Take them alive if you can."

"Sir?" Croy's voice was puzzled. "The standing orders you gave us yesterday are to terminate with extreme prejudice all trespassers."

"Since *I* gave you the fucking standing orders," Deveroux snarled, "I can fucking well amend or rescind them as I see fit, is that clear?"

"Yes, sir. Clear."

"Alive, Croy. And if they're not apprehended in that condition, you'd better have some pretty snappy and believable reasons why not."

"Yes, sir." Croy hung up.

Deveroux would have far rather preferred that Phildercost's hit team had been successful than having to deal with Belasko and Anastasia Kirchov in his own backyard. However, since they were intruding on his home turf, he made the snap decision to keep them awhile. Both people's connections could prove useful, even after they were dead.

THE NEXT MOVE wasn't long in coming. A rain-caped man eased into view, moving in a crouch, but moving quickly. A Delta Elite pistol was held in a two-handed grip.

Not lifting his head, Bolan tossed a stick into the brush on his left. Three bullets beat the air, coming so close together the shots sounded like a single long *bam*. Then there was dead silence for the better part of a minute. Finally he heard a faint rattle of leaves, a crunch of wood. Bolan gripped the Desert Eagle tightly, finger caressing the trigger.

A voice wafted through the dark shadows. "Games are all over, folks. Time to come in."

Kirchov flattened her body against the ground, pressing her face into the wet soil. Suddenly the fine hairs on Bolan's nape tingled and lifted. He turned his head, first to the left, then to the right.

A figure charged through the brush, his rain cape spread like the wings of some bird of prey. The stock of a shotgun was jammed against his hip in a firing position. In a shaved sliver of an instant, Bolan realized the first man had tried to distract him with blind shooting and brittle conversation, while his partner skulked up from behind.

The guard armed with the pistol rushed forward at the same moment. Kirchov fired the Colt pistol at his legs, three squeezes of the trigger. The man's trousers burst into dark splashes, his kneecaps splitting under the .45-caliber blockbusters. He screamed, a ghastly gurgling wail, as his legs buckled.

Simultaneously the second man let loose with his shotgun, triggering a 12-gauge burst that swept the top of the Spanish bayonet plants clean of its needle tips. Pulped vegetable matter splattered Bolan's face. He squeezed the trigger of the Desert Eagle when the shotgunner was less than ten feet away. Caught directly in the chest by the round, the guard left his feet, back-somersaulting into the foliage.

He landed in a facedown, spread-eagled position over a bush.

Springing to his feet, Bolan searched the zone and then sprinted in a westerly direction, roughly parallel to the line of the fence. Kirchov easily kept pace with him.

"I thought you hated guns," he said.

"I do," she panted in response. "But that doesn't mean I don't know how to use them."

The sudden light was as bright and as unexpected as full dawn, and they skidded to a clumsy halt. Two searchlight beams burst from between the trees, catching them in near-blinding glares. A low droning rumble echoed in the darkness. Kirchov made a motion to bound into the nearest clump of brush, when a swamp buggy emerged from the jungle, headlights blazing.

The pair turned in the opposite direction, but the mechanical sounds of groaning gears came to them as a second swamp buggy rolled into view, the huge wheels smashing foliage. There was no escape on either side.

Bolan fired the Desert Eagle once at the vehicle bouncing toward him from the left. He heard a clashing of glass and one of the headlights spit sparks and went out. At his back, Kirchov fired two shots at the second swamp buggy. The bullets ricocheted off the front grille, whining into the night.

"Move!" Bolan snarled, and began to sprint back in the direction of the beach.

What looked like a solid wall of hooded, cloaked men materialized in his path. They whooped triumphantly, like Confederate soldiers charging the enemy at Bull Run.

The Remington sprang into his hand and the shotgun jerked and roared, unleashing round after round of 12-gauge, solid-steel pellets.

The security guards wilted, fell, stumbling, their war whoops turning into a garbled babble of screams and profanity. Return fire ripped into the foliage around him, whipping it in a frenzy like a ground-level gale. A bullet snapped past his ear, sounding like the crack of a bullwhip. Bolan continued working the trigger of the autoloader, swinging the flame-belching barrel from left to right. Hot brass spewed from the ejector. He glimpsed Kirchov on her knees beside and a little to the rear of him, blasting away at the swamp buggies.

Dimly Bolan saw a two-foot metal cylinder arcing down over his head from behind. It went off in the air between his position and his targets. The noise of gunfire and men's screams was overlaid by a painfully loud, sharp *bang!*

Synchronized with the bone-knocking concussion was a white light of such hurtful, blinding intensity that the shadows were washed out of the jungle. The white became gray and the gray became black.

Bolan didn't lose consciousness, but he hovered at its brink for what felt like a very long time. His stunned brain identified the cylinder as a flash-bomb, probably a French Alsatex model. Fired from an antiriot weapon, the combination of concussion and magnesium flare dazed and disoriented crowds. As it was, the flash-bomb had detonated less than five feet from him, almost at head level.

The Executioner realized he was lying on his side on the soggy ground. His ears kept replaying echoes of the detonation, and his head felt as if it were swelling to pumpkin size. He tasted blood running from a superficial, fragment-inflicted cut on his cheek. Though his eyes were open, all he could see were swirling, multicolored spheres of light.

Then, as if a great invisible boot had delivered a kick to his behind, he was in the real world again. He tried to get up, but a muddy boot sole slammed against the side of his head, mashing his face into the ground. Fortunately the wet soil gave a bit, acting as a cushion. Hands groped all over him, snatching away his knife and his war bag.

The heavy foot was removed and Bolan slowly sat up, spitting out bits of dirt and sludge. His vision slowly cleared. Though the noise level around him had to be high, he heard only distant echoes of voices. Men were scream- ing, groaning and cursing, buckshot-blasted bodies lay nearby, the rain washing the blood away from their shred- ded rain capes.

Other guards, expressions savage, stood over him. He saw one had appropriated his Remington and Desert Eagle. His mouth moved, and though Bolan couldn't hear more than a dim murmur, he understood him. Carefully he climbed to his feet, blinking away the last of the magne- sium flare-induced spots. Hands patted him down, fingers probed, and his watch was wrenched from his wrist.

Bolan realized he had been stunned for only a handful of seconds, since men were still rushing in from the jungle. Kirchov was hauled to her feet and roughly searched. Though she squinted and shook her head frequently, she had avoided the brunt of the flash-bomb's explosion.

A man swung down from the saddle of the nearest swamp buggy and swaggered toward them. He was the head-bandaged gatekeeper, shouldering a light-weight, big- bore Arven Ace 37 riot gun. The stun bomb had been fired from that. He wasn't wearing a rain cape, and his Sam Browne belt was discolored from the moisture. When he came closer, Bolan read the brass-finished name tag pinned over his left breast pocket. It read CAPT. CROY.

Looking him up and down with contemptuous eyes, Croy smirked and started to turn away. Then, he whirled, swing- ing the barrel of the Arven directly at Bolan's face.

The half-turn was a dead giveaway. Bolan had expected a payback strike and ducked beneath the barrel. Lunging forward, he planted his head squarely in Croy's midriff, hooking his fingers in his belt. With a flailing of arms and a roar Bolan could barely hear, Croy toppled backward into a clump of scrub brush, the Executioner atop him.

Gun barrels and fists hammered at him. A guard darted in, drew back his foot and booted Bolan in the side of the head. He was roughly dragged from Croy, punched and kicked and pistol-whipped. Kirchov stopped the beating by flinging herself over his body. Though she received a few kicks, the violence ceased.

Face and body bruised, Bolan allowed himself to be prodded to his feet and his hands bound behind him by nylon cuffs. Croy got to his feet, glaring venomously. Then he spun and gestured. Bolan and Kirchov were pushed ahead into the jungle.

Slowly Bolan's hearing returned. As he and Kirchov marched shoulder-to-shoulder through the drizzle, he mouthed to her, "Thanks."

"What were you trying to accomplish?" she whispered back angrily.

"I wasn't just 'trying,'" he replied. "I accomplished it."

A gun barrel poked her in the spine and she fell silent. They were directed onto a footpath cutting through the vegetation and ground cover, and they followed it in a wide, sweeping curve until they were stopped by a gate in the fence.

The gate didn't have a conventional lock, only a square of metal. Croy groped at his belt and cursed. "I lost my goddamn key in that shit back there."

A guard stepped forward, unhooking a small, black plastic device from his belt. He pointed it at the square of metal. A series of clicks sounded, and the gate swung open. Bolan and Kirchov were pushed through. After the guards entered the compound, the gate swung shut.

They marched around the corner of the long, low building. Bolan saw a streamlined, two-seater jet helicopter tied down to eyebolts on a concrete landing pad. Stopping at a recessed steel door, a guard poked one of the small sonic keys into it. When it swung open, Kirchov and Bolan, escorted by Croy and two security guards, entered a reception room that was so normal in appearance and furnishings, it appeared weirdly out of place.

The guard sitting at a desk squinted at them and said, "The boss wants to talk to our guests."

A man standing behind Bolan and Kirchov snorted. "Guests, my ass."

The guard at the desk said sternly, "That's what the boss called them. I suggest you call them that, too."

Braced by the guards, Bolan and Kirchov went through a door and along a high-ceilinged, well-lit corridor, past doors marked with many different labels. The air was cool, and it made Bolan's skin beneath his wet clothing feel clammy. They turned right under an arched doorway and into a giant room humming with activity.

Bolan's eyes were immediately drawn to a tall man wearing white, standing near a long, horizontal black cylinder. There wasn't a speck of color about him except for his bright red tie. The man smiled at them and lifted a slim, pale hand in greeting.

15

As Bolan and Kirchov were marched through the vast room, Bolan saw a lot of equipment he recognized and a lot that he didn't. Though there was the hum of sensor units and the steady click of rheostats, there were only three people in the entire huge room. One was a young Chinese woman working at a drafting table who regarded them curiously as they approached. The other was a middle-aged man in a white lab coat who looked at them in fear. He started scratching the back of his neck as soon as he saw them. Bolan figured it was a nervous habit. The guards dropped his weapons onto a tabletop and prodded him toward the man in white.

Dexter Deveroux didn't look much different than the twenty-year-old picture Bolan had seen on Kurtzman's computer screen. His green eyes conveyed a self-confidence that was rarely shaken, but they also contained the look of the wolf and the hawk. He was a few inches taller than Bolan, but the erect poise of his lean body made him seem still taller.

"Professor Kirchov. I'm so glad I finally have the opportunity to make your acquaintance." Deveroux's voice was quiet, modulated. "It's been a few years since you rejected my proposal to your government."

"That was a committee decision," Kirchov said levelly.

"And I assume it was the committee's decision to hijack my work, without proper compensation or recognition. I can't tell you how much I enjoyed reading the classified and confidential reports your Plesetsk installation has been making on the efficacy of my launch system.''

The emerald eyes swung to Bolan, direct and unblinking. ''Mr. Belasko, the mysterious 'Hardman.' I had hoped we would never meet. Our mutual acquaintance in Algiers caused our fates to intertwine, albeit only briefly. You are, I think, a clever man. You are also very ruthless and have incredible luck.''

Bolan didn't respond.

''However, you didn't stumble onto my island tonight of all nights by sheer luck. How much do you know, or rather, how much do your people know about me?''

''I think I'll let you worry about that,'' Bolan said wryly.

Deveroux sighed. ''That attitude is shortsighted, sir. You and the professor came here to learn what I am doing, and after that, you'd make a report to your people. If the authorities truly knew my plan, they wouldn't have sent you and an academic. They would have sent troops.''

''That could still happen,'' Bolan said, keeping his face impassive. ''You've made some mistakes, like using Phildercost as your assassination broker.''

Deveroux waved a hand impatiently. ''Using anybody is a risk. You must use people, and people are prone to mistakes and misjudgments. But none of this comes to the vital point—how much, or how little, your organization knows.''

''I suppose you'll tell me it's a matter of life or death.''

''Hardly. You must die and you will die. You know far too much, no matter how little. It's only a question of how and when you die. I doubt you will tell me anything, even if I choose to drug, hypnotize, dismember and disembowel you. Such things revolt me, although I will admit to a secret fascination with them.''

Deveroux turned his gaze on Kirchov, who met it unblinkingly. ''Besides, you're a professional and deserve professional courtesy. On the other hand, the professor is a common thief and though she has some technical expertise that might serve me, there is the penalty for stealing to be meted out.''

"Don't you intend to steal the Hellfire Trigger's payload?'' Bolan demanded. "What's the penalty for that?''

Deveroux returned his attention to him. "The Russians put the platform up there. I took advantage of it. Opportunity combined with profit. As a result, I'll be the most influential man on the planet. That scarcely fits the definition of a 'penalty.' On the contrary, it's my long-delayed destiny.''

"We know what you're planning to do, Deveroux. But we don't know the target.''

"Oh. Well...'' Deveroux smiled. "I intend to detonate the warhead over the Ghawar oilfields in Saudi Arabia.''

Bolan stared at him silently for a moment. "Do you realize how many people live there, work there? How many people you'll kill?''

"I'm not interested. Do you know how many of my employees you've killed tonight? No? I didn't think so. To compile a body count is flabby sentimentality and is not germane to my long-term plan.''

"Which is?''

Angling an eyebrow at him, Deveroux replied ruefully, "I've always hated contrived stories where the villain reveals all the information the hero needs to thwart his plan. In this scenario, there are no heroes, no villains. Only a world that needs saving.''

"With you cast as the savior?''

"Who better? I have devoted my life to free enterprise, to being a part of the corporation, the conglomerate that is America. But corporations and countries can only thrive, can only survive, with fresh ideas and concepts. At this point in history, free enterprise has been murdered by endless legislation and corrosive complacency.''

"Get to the point, Deveroux,'' Bolan said impatiently.

A sudden rage swirling in his eyes, Deveroux back-handed Bolan across the face. It wasn't an admonishing tap; the sound of flesh smacking against flesh echoed in the vast room. Bolan was rocked back on his heels. He stumbled and fell against a drafting table, jarring it on its stand. He fell to a sitting position beneath it, cheek stinging. Objects on the table clattered and tinkled to the floor around him.

Deveroux moved toward him. Bolan saw the great self-control the man exercised to keep from kicking him in the face. His foot lifted, quivered, then he took a deep breath and heeled away.

Trying to push himself up with his bound hands, he felt something small, metallic and very sharp. The point of it pricked the tip of his thumb. By feel, he identified it as a small, razor-keen cutting instrument used by graphic artists. When the guards helped him to his feet, he had the half-inch-long, flat splinter of steel concealed in the palm of his right hand.

He glanced over at the Chinese woman sitting at the adjacent table. She stared at him so intently, Bolan was sure she'd seen him pick up the blade and palm it. However, she said nothing and his worry ebbed a bit.

"I will not tolerate disrespect, Mr. Belasko," Deveroux said. "I said I will extend you professional courtesy, and I expect the same in return."

Bolan only nodded.

"The world suffers epidemics and plagues," Deveroux went on, "it stews and percolates in pollution, it bulges at the seams with people. Corporations and industries could end these fundamental evils, but they see no immediate profit in doing so. Make a profit in the present and discard the future, that is their credo. The sad fact is that civilization, on a global scale, is likely to fall apart in the near future without enormous changes and sacrifices."

"I can't argue with that," Bolan said.

"No one can. But to make these changes, cooperation is

essential. Even if that cooperation is coerced. I know, that seems like a redundancy. However, it will work if no one realizes they're being coerced.''

Deveroux waved to the long black cylinder. Getting a closer look at it, Bolan wasn't surprised to see it was a rocket resting in wheeled metal mounts.

"The first phase of the new spirit of cooperation," Deveroux said, "is represented by the Remora."

"Which will link with the suborbital nuclear platform." Kirchov's voice was flat, unemotional.

"Exactly. The second phase will occur when the supply of oil from Saudi Arabia is abruptly and shockingly cut off. Permanently.''

"There's a third phase, I suppose?" Bolan inquired.

"Actually there are four. The third phase is the period in which the people of the world, and primarily of this country, are faced with an energy crisis that makes the oil embargo of '74 look like a Barbie doll shortage. Can you imagine the terror, the outrage, the panic, the screaming demands for an energy alternative? That's where I and phase four come in.''

"Your solar energy technology patents and inventions," Bolan interjected.

Deveroux lifted a forefinger and tapped empty air with it. "On the money. Which is what I will make. A whole lot of it. I own the exclusive patents, rights, licensing and trademarks on an entire slew of Soltech devices. After my marketing campaign, I'll have international contracts to provide solar power to almost every industry, every nation on earth. I estimate that by the one-year anniversary of the destruction of Ghawar, Ra Soltech will be the primary power utility to half the world.''

"There's got to be another part to phase four."

Deveroux spread his arms. "The best part. I'll be one of the wealthiest, most influential men alive. All the super-powers will elbow each other aside for the chance to kiss my ass. I will direct the course of world events, establish new geopolitical and economic standards and dictate all the terms. I'll be the savior who rescued civilization from the second coming of the Dark Age.''

"Presupposing," Bolan said, "nobody reveals you're the same savior who brought the world to the brink of the Dark Age. My people are already aware of you, of the platform and your launching system. No matter what happens, you'll be the first suspect and they'll hunt you down.''

"As will my government," Kirchov snapped.

Deveroux shook his head. "You don't understand. Too many powerful people in the military-industrial complex will benefit enormously from the new situation. Think of all the government contractors who'll go back to full-time production. Only they'll be building solar energy convertors, not submarine plumbing systems.''

Bolan stared at the pale man in white, wondering if he was so completely delusional that he was unable to conceive of the horrific aftermath of a thermonuclear explosion in a population center. Or, more than likely he wasn't self-deluded, he simply didn't give a damn.

Deveroux's face creased in a cold smile. "Stop looking at me with such revulsion, Mr. Belasko. I've thought every angle through. In the long-term, humanity will benefit. That's worth a few lives consumed by atomic fire, isn't it?''

"So you can become a god?" Bolan's question was posed in a mild, almost disinterested tone.

Deveroux's eyes widened, then narrowed. He clenched his fists until his knuckles whitened. "Who is better qualified to be anointed with such a status? Less than a thousand years ago, the world was ruled by god-kings, monarchs who traced their ancestry back through the aeons to the deities of old. And though I can't do that, I can bring the glory of Ra, of Apollo, of Phaethon back to shine over the earth.''

Striding over to the Remora rocket, Deveroux rubbed his

hands over it lovingly, then walked back restlessly to face Bolan. "To qualify as a god, all one must do is exercise the power to nurture and destroy. I have that power. I will return the hand of Ra, the Egyptian sun god, to earth."

Bolan smiled grimly. "You don't have the power to foresee the immense catastrophe you'll trigger. You can destroy, but I doubt there'll be much left for you to nurture. You're a diseased, tricky weasel, Deveroux. Not a candidate for godhood."

Deveroux sprang forward, hands reaching in clawlike curves for Bolan's throat. His green eyes were wide and wild. "How dare you judge my vision, you cheap thug?"

Bolan didn't flinch. He kept his eyes fixed on Deveroux's face. Before Deveroux fitted his hands around Bolan's throat, he suddenly relaxed, dropping his arms to his sides. He smiled a faint, superior smile. "Violence. It's a kind of compulsion, an illness, isn't it?"

He stepped away. "I cannot express in words how I feel at this moment. I have waited and planned such an undertaking for many years, my entire life. I'll let my actions speak for my emotions."

He gestured to the observation level. "Put our guests in there, Croy."

Croy caught Bolan by the back of the neck and shoved him forward, while two guards braced him between them.

"Don't fight it so," Deveroux told him as he passed. "Although you're slated for oblivion in the very near future, I'm permitting you to witness the most pivotal moment in this—and the next—century."

The guards marched Bolan to a door opening up to the elevated observation deck. Docilely Kirchov followed them. They went up a short flight of stairs into a long, bare-walled room. At the far end of it, a large window was set in the wall. There was nothing to see out of it, only a drizzly murk.

Bolan and Kirchov moved to the transparent panel overlooking the work area. The guards took up a watchful position at the door. Beyond the window, Deveroux and the balding man exchanged a few words, and Bolan followed Deveroux's pointing finger to a perfectly round, metal-rimmed portal punched in the wall.

"The launch tube?" Bolan inquired quietly.

Kirchov nodded. She looked ill, her eyes darting wildly, like some frantic animal's.

"Don't go simple on me, Professor." He pitched his voice at a calm, unemotional level. "I'm not able to slap you."

Kirchov's eyes flicked toward him and she forced a chuckle. "That is a good thing. For you."

The white-coated man walked to a control box hanging by a thick cable from an overhead circuit junction. It was studded with two buttons, one red, one yellow. His thumb depressed the red button.

The wheeled mounts supporting the Remora rocket began to turn, slowly rolling toward the open hatchway. A squeaking creak reached them through the glass.

"I cannot believe this is happening," Kirchov said, her voice quavering. "If he is successful, the Saudis will blame Russia, and Russia will blame America."

Bolan didn't respond, but her words echoed his own thoughts. No matter if Dexter Deveroux was exposed as the real culprit behind the crime, America's enemies in the Mideast would undoubtedly label him a tool of big business. The situation would be terribly dangerous, leading to a very real threat of World War III and chaos across the planet at the same time. And if the aftermath of the destruction of the oil fields didn't lead to world war, it would probably leave Deveroux sitting exactly where he wanted—in the fabled god seat, at least for a time.

The nose of the Remora slid smoothly into the hatchway, small rollers on the mount propelling it forward. The diameter of the rocket was almost exactly the same as the tube. Deveroux stood beside the heavy metal cover, watching every centimeter of the rocket enter the portal.

"What kind of time frame are we dealing with?" Bolan asked softly. "How long after the launch will the Remora dock with the platform?"

Kirchov frowned, performing rapid mental calculations. "Hard to say. Since the platform is stationary, at zero velocity, matching the orbital trajectories will be difficult, very tricky. To achieve the rendezvous, the launch of the rocket needs to be timed precisely to reach a coplanar orbit."

Bolan listened as the scientist talked. Though she was taking the long way around the barn to answer his question, her voice was strengthening, her self-confidence returning. "When slightly below the platform, application of the rocket's braking thrusters will cause it to slow to near zero velocity. Then—"

She broke off and smiled. "That really doesn't tell you what you need to know, does it?"

"Not exactly."

Briskly Kirchov said, "I calculated that it will require approximately two and a half hours' flight time for the Remora to reach the platform's position. Without knowing all the variables, I estimate another ten minutes for the docking maneuver to be completed."

"And after that, how much time will we have before the platform is in position over ground zero?"

"Perhaps ten minutes. Perhaps less."

"Three hours," Bolan said.

"Approximately. A little less, a little more."

Below in the work area, the portal had swallowed up the last few feet of the Remora rocket. All that could be seen of it were its pair of conical thrust chambers.

The white-coated man pushed the yellow button on the control box and the hatch cover swung silently over the portal. It sealed with a muffled thud and a hiss.

"The next step is to pressurize the launch tube," Kirchov observed.

Fingering the blade he'd purloined, Bolan cast a wary glance at the guards. Though Croy was looking down into the vast work area, the other guards were staring at him. Out of the corner of his eye, he caught bright lights blazing into life. Glancing toward the far wall of the observation deck, lights shone brightly on the other side of the window. Beads of rainwater gleamed.

Deveroux waved, caught their attention and pointed toward the window, mouthing, "Go and watch." Then he turned and walked rapidly out of the huge room.

"Where's he going?" Bolan asked, staring after the receding figure.

"To control the launch sequence, I imagine," Kirchov answered. "His egomania won't allow him to trust anyone else with the task, no matter how qualified."

They walked together to the far window while the guards remained standing at the opposite end. Peering through the rain-speckled glass, at first Bolan saw nothing but a row of floodlamps glowing in a symmetrical curve, spaced at hundred-yard intervals. Then a motion from below the nearest light assembly commanded his attention.

What he first thought to be foliage was camouflage netting. It was being pulled from underneath, sliding and dropping into the shadows. Beneath the netting was a dully gleaming half curve of translucent pipe, made of some kind of opaque PVC material. The diameter was about five feet—the same as the interior portal. It looked molded from one piece. He couldn't see joints or couplings anywhere.

From his position, the other half of the great ring was blocked from view, but by squinting and looking toward the farthermost floodlamp he discerned a hollow cylinder extending up and out on an angle. It looked like a missile silo, and was at least one-eighth of a mile away.

Deveroux's voice suddenly vibrated through the observation deck, speaking over a public address system. "Countdown continuing. T-minus five minutes. Mark."

16

The floor trembled beneath their feet, a steady rising rhythm. The raindrops beaded on the outside of the window jiggled and vibrated in cadence with the continuous tremor.

"He's powered up the turbines," Kirchov said sharply. "Pumping the seawater into the vacuum tube."

There was a faint gurgling, bubbling noise, then a surging roar. Bolan saw that from a floodlamp-illuminated section of the half loop of the pipeline there suddenly erupted a geyser of water. For a hopeful second, he wondered if the tube had sprung a leak, then he realized that a pressure-equalization valve had been opened. The fountain of water quickly subsided.

Over the public address system, Deveroux spoke in a calm monotone, almost a parody of the men at Houston's Mission Control. "Generators at full output. Bleed-off valves one and two opened. Valves two and one closed. Pressure equalized. Liquid propellant at max capacity. Launch signal given."

There was a squeaking and hissing of hydraulics, then a new sound reached them—the continuous roar of a heavy body rushing past in a circular pattern, picking up speed with every revolution. The pipeline within Bolan's field of vision shook slightly every time the projectile zoomed around it.

"Buildup of thrust at one hundred thousand pounds,"

Deveroux's voice intoned. "One hundred and twenty...one hundred and thirty-five...one hundred and fifty."

As the rocket's centrifugal force increased, the roaring of its passage climbed in volume. Each time it whirled past the observation window, Bolan felt the floor vibrate.

"One hundred and seventy thousand pounds..."

A spotlight stabbed a shaft of yellow light into the darkness, fixing on a point just above the hollow mouth of the launch silo.

"One hundred and eighty...one hundred and eighty-five...one hundred and eighty-eight thousand pounds. Ejection jets activated. We have liftoff."

An explosive torrent of water, like an upside-down Niagara Falls, burst from the distant silo. Riding atop the foaming column of liquid, passing through the spotlight beam, was a black cylinder. The light centered on it for a moment, trying to follow its driving, upward course. The Remora rocket lifted into the sky like a needle drawn by a celestial thread. Its velocity was astonishing. Within a few seconds, the needle was but a speck and well beyond the spotlight's range.

Deveroux spoke again, a deep-voiced, reverential declamation. *"I am Ra!"* he thundered. *"And I carriest them all away captive. I am Ra, and though I am far away, my rays are upon the earth. Though I am far away, my footprints are the day."*

There was a long, meaningful pause. When Deveroux spoke again, it was in his crisp monotone. "Ceiling reached. Hot booster ignited. Solid fuel thrusters burning."

In the deep blue-blackness of the starless sky, Bolan glimpsed an almost imperceptible pinpoint flare of light. Then it was lost in the darkness and distance. "Three hours?" he asked.

"A little more, a little less," Kirchov whispered.

"Croy?" Deveroux's questioning tones came over the speaker. "Escort our guests to the control room."

The guards herded them from the observation deck at gunpoint. As they passed through the work area, the balding man studiously avoided looking in their direction, but the Chinese woman regarded Bolan solemnly as he walked by.

Back out in the corridor, which evidently ran the entire length of the building, they were directed down a side artery and into a small, well-lit room full of electronic tracking equipment and several video monitor screens. Deveroux sat before a console, like a master musician who had just performed to wild ovations.

"What do you think of my little place here?" he asked. Not waiting for a response, he added, "I built it to be the prototypical solar-powered manufacturing plant of the future. Presidents of corporations, sheiks, mercantile kings all toured it. None of them were impressed, so I refurbished it to serve another purpose."

Deveroux swiveled his chair around, facing them. "The Remora is on its preprogrammed flight path. The guidance system has built-in fail-safes, a triple redundancy. I can control it from here, or from my office. From this point forward, nothing can prevent the Remora from mating with the Hellfire Trigger. So, Mr. Belasko, I ask you again—who else knows about me and my project?"

Bolan stood silent. Deveroux sat placidly. No one moved. After thirty seconds, Deveroux snorted a laugh. "I'll keep you a little while, Mr. Belasko. Only until dawn. Then I'll have you strapped to one of this facility's solar cells and when the rising sun strikes it, I can guarantee there won't be so much as a handful of charred bone to commemorate your visit here."

"And if I answer your questions before sunrise?"

Deveroux shrugged. "Then I'll have Croy or someone else shoot you through the head and sink your body in the Gulf. It's a quicker, less painful death than experiencing your flesh scorch and peel, your bodily fluids boil and your internal organs explode. Think about it."

"I will," Bolan said.

Turning to Kirchov, Deveroux said, "As for you, Professor, I think I can find a place for you in my company. You're a brilliant astrophysicist and you're not hard to look at. I think, with a little pain, a little fear, you'll make an excellent addition to knob row."

"Knob what?" Kirchov's voice was faint.

Deveroux chuckled and pushed himself out of the chair. "A little inside humor. You'll understand in time."

Deveroux shook his right sleeve, as though he were shooting his shirt cuff. A small loaded hypodermic appeared in his right hand. In the same smooth movement, he injected its contents into Kirchov's upper left arm and jerked the needle free.

Crying out in pain and fear, she stumbled back toward the door. She struck out at Deveroux. Croy grabbed her, pulling her right arm behind her back in a painful hammerlock.

Bolan shifted position, but stopped moving when Deveroux cast a quick, ironic glance in his direction. He looked critically at Kirchov and the guns and decided it wasn't worth the risk. If he started something now, both he and Anastasia Kirchov would die.

"Just a sedative to make you a bit more tractable during our trip," Deveroux said. "You'll sleep for an hour or so. When you awaken, all the rules will be my rules."

Deveroux stared at Bolan and smiled. He waved one hand in an abrupt motion. "Take him."

Bolan allowed himself to be manhandled out of the room into the long corridor. They passed through a series of long rooms that smelled of chemical fuels and were crammed with pressure sumps and pumps. He saw many packing crates stenciled with the name of Ra Soltech.

He was yanked to a stop before an open metal door. Like all the others he had seen, it had no handle or lock. One of the guards planted a hand between his shoulder blades and shoved him into a dark, windowless room.

"See you in the morning," one of the guards said with a smirk. "When you're sunny-side up."

The door clanged shut, and the room was totally black. Bolan paced it off. It was surprisingly spacious for a cell, but then again, it probably was built to be a storeroom, not a holding tank for interlopers. Slowly his vision adjusted to the dark, but there was nothing to see but bare concrete walls and floors. Only a thin, hairline crack of light shining at its base showed the door's location.

Bolan's questing fingers closed on the blade he had held concealed in his hand for the past twenty minutes. It was sticky with sweat, but he managed to place the edge of the blade against the nylon binder encircling his wrists. He began working the blade in a back-and-forth sawing motion, as fast and as hard as his nearly numb hands could manage. The polymer strip was of a heavy gauge, but the razor-sharp edge of the blade scored it.

He concentrated on working the blade faster. He could feel the friction-induced heat on the sliver of metal between his fingertips. Pain inched along his wrists, slipped up his forearms and settled in his shoulder blades. In a very few seconds, the muscles were howling in protest, threatening to cramp.

Sweat trickled into his eyes and his breath was a harsh, rattling rasp in his throat. His tendons and muscles were shrieking at the strain placed upon them. Finally the strand parted, and he immediately dropped the blade on the floor and let his arms dangle, like lead weights.

After taking a few deep breaths, he massaged his arms and worked the stiffness out of his fingers. Then he reached down into the top of his boot, felt around and pulled out the small remote-control device he had torn from Croy's belt. Bolan had recognized it as a simple sonic lock switch that activated electronic doors. The Farm used something similar under emergency conditions.

Pressing his ear to the door, Bolan listened for sounds on the other side. He heard nothing, not even a man breathing. Dropping flat, he peered through the thread-thin crack at the base of the door, searching for shapes or shadows. He saw none.

Standing, he took a position against the wall beside the door, aimed the lock switch at it and pressed the stud. With a clicking of solenoids, the door opened outward. Bolan stayed where he was for the count of thirty, then he sidled around the door and looked both ways down the corridor. He saw no one, heard no sound of movement.

He left the cell in a low crouch, moving fast and soundlessly, taking advantage of every corner, every crate he came across to hide and check the zone. No one came down the corridor or through any of the rooms he had been marched through.

Bolan reached the control room, but it was empty. The monitor screens showed only exterior views of the compound. Seeing a shortwave transceiver in a corner, he examined it quickly. The sending and receiving frequencies were locked, so he was unable to make a distress call. He gave it a quick, hard kick. Glass dials shattered and the plastic housing split. No messages would be sent from here, or received, at least for a little while.

He moved out again along the corridor, a little mystified by the absence of activity. His sense of time was acute, and he reckoned he had been in the makeshift cell for only ten minutes, if that. The most likely explanation was that Deveroux had departed for the mainland by air, taking the sedated Kirchov with him. What was left of the security force had returned to patrolling the compound perimeter. The guards were probably under orders not to check on him until dawn, when it was time to talk or fry, or talk and die.

Bolan turned the corner to the cross hall leading to the work area and nearly trod on the toes of Croy.

The tattooed man stared, eyes wide and disbelieving. His hand made a reflexive move for the Delta Elite pistol holstered at his hip, but he had stared too long. The edge of Bolan's hand lashed out, catching him full across the neck. There was a mushy snap, as of a stick of wet wood being broken, and Croy dropped dead to the floor of the corridor. He uttered only one choked cry.

Gathering a fistful of uniform shirt, Bolan dragged the corpse around the corner, left him propped in a sitting position against the wall and relieved him of his gun.

Reaching the open archway of the giant workroom, Bolan peered around the frame. Only the balding, scratching man and the Oriental woman were there. They were talking, arguing, and though he couldn't hear what the man was saying, he picked up snatches of the woman's words. Her voice was high and shrill with passion.

"He's sick, Eberhardt! Insane! We can't let him do this. We've got to warn somebody."

The man addressed as Eberhardt replied in a nondistinct mumble. He waved his hands in a dismissive, helpless gesture. Neither of them saw Bolan's black figure glide into the room. He moved in a swift crouch between work tables and stands of equipment. His gaze was fixed on the table where his ordnance lay. Engrossed in their argument, Eberhardt and the woman paid no attention to what was happening behind them. As he drew closer, the man's words were more distinguishable.

"I swear I thought he was bluffing, Liu Weng. Indulging one of his egocentric whims, role-playing. Besides, we're just employees, we never participated in the actual planning—"

The woman, Liu Weng, broke in with a contemptuous laugh. "Plausible deniability? He'll throw us to the wolves, blame it all on us. Maybe nobody will believe him, but it'll buy the sick bastard some time to disappear.''

Bolan reached the table, squatting behind it. He put his hand on the stock of the Remington shotgun. At that instant, Eberhardt turned. His eyes widened, his mouth hung open. Liu Weng saw the change in his expression and spun. Bolan stood, the Delta Elite pistol held at arm's length. ''Keep calm.''

The Chinese woman's reaction wasn't what he expected. Relief flooded her dark eyes. ''Thank God. I was hoping you'd escape. When I saw you filch the blade—''

''I thought you did,'' Bolan interrupted. ''Why didn't you report it?''

She hooked a contemptuous thumb toward Eberhardt. ''My conditioning wasn't as deep as his. I upchucked the crap Deveroux crammed down my throat. Eberhardt and everybody else gobbles it down and asks for seconds.''

Drawing himself up in a posture of wounded dignity, Eberhardt squared his sloping shoulders. ''That's not true. I tried to talk Dexter out of this, but he kept the salient facts from me.''

''Bullshit!'' Liu Weng snapped.

''Enough,'' Bolan said sharply. He buckled on his belt and looped the Remington over his shoulder. ''Where is he now?''

''On his way back to the Double D,'' Liu Weng answered. ''His office building on Harbour Island.''

Bolan slid the Sykes-Fairbairn stiletto back into its sheath. ''Can the rocket be diverted from here?''

''No,'' Eberhardt said. ''He's transferred control to the Cheops Alpha.''

''The what Alpha?''

''A superfast, state-of-the-art computer,'' Liu Weng replied. ''A machine designed by that wacko who calls himself Dr. Jest.''

''The Cheops Alpha operates on algorithmic and stochastic mathematical processes, utilizing teraflop technology," Eberhardt put in. An accusatory note entered his voice. "She wrote some of the programs."

Liu Weng turned toward Eberhardt, looking like she was going to spit on him.

To ward off a continuation of the verbal buck-passing, Bolan asked, "Can the flight path of the rocket be aborted via the computer?"

"Yes," Liu Weng said. "But we don't have the telemetric self-destruct code. Only Deveroux does."

"What's the least-conspicuous way out of this place?"

Eberhardt shook his head dolefully. "Only one way in and one way out of the building. You'll have to pass a security checkpoint in the reception room."

"Besides," Liu Weng interposed, "you'll just find your way out into the compound. There's only way out of there, too. The gate is guarded."

"If I can get out of the building, I can escape the compound."

"What good would it do you?" Eberhardt asked sadly. "Deveroux's holed up in his building, and it's a fortress. Jest installed all sorts of crazy defense mechanisms."

"Like what?"

"No one knows for sure. Electrical traps and childish things like flame-throwers in the elevator shafts."

For once, Liu Weng was in agreement with Eberhardt. "To get to Deveroux," she said, "you'll have to get inside his penthouse, and you probably wouldn't survive entering the lobby."

Bolan barely heard her. His thoughts were leaping ahead, his tactician's mind considering and discarding a dozen options in the time between heartbeats. With the barrel of the shotgun, he gestured toward the metal hatch covering the launch bay. "Is there any way out of the pipeline other than the ejection silo?"

Both Eberhardt's and Liu Weng's faces brightened. They

began talking at once and Bolan was forced to shush them. He pointed at the man.

"There's a pressure-equalization maintenance valve a hundred yards or so from here." Eberhardt's words tumbled over one another in their haste to leave his mouth. "You'll find a wheel at the top of the tube. It'll pop the valve open and out."

Scrutinizing the breadth of Bolan's shoulders, he added, "It'll be a damn tight squeeze."

"I'm used to it. Let's go."

Eberhardt stalked quickly across the room to the control box dangling overhead. His steps were firm, full of resolve. Watching him, Liu Weng's lips trembled. "I'm throwing it all away, aren't I, by betraying him?"

Shouldering his war bag, Bolan said quietly, "It's no sin to betray a betrayer. Deveroux's not a god, and his delusions aren't a religion, no matter what he tried to force you to believe."

Eberhardt pressed the yellow button on the box. An electrical hum floated from the hatch covering. There was a prolonged hiss, like steam escaping from a ruptured boiler, as the interior of the tube depressurized. Air rushed from around the rubber seals on the inside of the hatch.

"I always wanted to get away from him." The woman's voice was thin and small. "I was studying for my Ph.D. before Deveroux hired me. He made me what I'm not, and he kept me from finding out who I really am."

She looked up at Bolan, tears of shame glimmering in her eyes. "Do you understand?" Her question was a fierce whisper.

"I do. But you've found yourself. You reached the crossroads and chose the right road."

The aspirated rush of air ceased. The heavy cover slowly creaked open. Bolan started toward it when loud frantic voices shouted from the arch behind him. Three armed guards raced into the work area. They were yelling, their expressions a mixture of anger, surprise and fright.

17

Before the first gun blazed, Bolan opened fire with the Remington. The cluster of buckshot caught the center man in the upper chest, slapping him off his feet amid a flying arc of blood.

His comrades returned the fire, and in an instant, the work area was a battlefield. The sound of gunfire echoed through the vast room. Liu Weng screamed. Bullets smashed into equipment, bouncing off with high-pitched screeches, or shattering the more delicate devices.

Bolan pushed the woman to the floor and bounded between benches and tables, a series of 9 mm slugs tearing long gouges from their corners. The hatch cover was open just enough to allow him to squirm past it into the vacuum tube. Bullets struck sparks from the steel door.

Eberhardt still stood with the control box in his hand. Bolan tossed him the Delta Elite pistol he had taken from Croy, but he didn't waste time watching to find out if the scientist caught it. Bolan pointed the shotgun at the guards, keeping up a continuous pattern of hammering fire. He heard the sharper crack of an automatic from his right.

As he squeezed between the hatch cover and the mouth of the tube, he hazarded a quick glance toward Eberhardt. The man had indeed caught the Delta Elite and was squeezing off a surprisingly steady series of shots. With his free hand he pushed the red button on the control box, and the heavy portal began to swing shut.

Then Eberhardt was hit in the chest, the bullet striking a blossom of bright crimson against the white coat. He jerked sidewise, but he kept his grip on the box. He tried to raise his pistol, but it fell from his fingers. Still hanging on to the control box, his head drooped and blood spilled from his lips. Then the hatch cover closed and sealed with a muffled boom.

All sound from the outside ceased, as if a volume knob had been turned all the way down. The pipeline stretched away into darkness. Bolan took his flashlight from the war bag to light his way.

He had no choice but to walk in a stooped posture, and the bruises from the beating he had sustained pained him. The tube curved ahead, featureless except for water dripping from its circular walls. The smell of brine was very strong.

Bolan didn't allow his thoughts to dwell on Eberhardt or Liu Weng. He expected the hatch cover to open at any moment, admitting the gun-toting guards. However, nothing of the sort occurred, and he wondered if Eberhardt had done something to jam or disable the controls.

Playing the beam of the flashlight ahead, he searched the roof of the tube for the valve wheel Eberhardt had mentioned. From far away, from the darkness before him, he heard a whine. Before it became a rumble, he recognized the sounds of the turbines warming up. The guards intended to flood the tube, planning to eject his drowned corpse from the launching silo.

He felt a tremor run the length of the pipeline and he increased his speed, splashing through puddles of standing water, feet sliding on the curved surface. He shone the light ahead and saw a deluge of water pouring through the tube. At the same moment, he glimpsed a white-painted wheel recessed in the roof of the pipeline a hundred feet or so ahead. He ran forward, grimly determined to either beat the flood, or at the very least, meet it halfway.

Since his eardrums didn't register a change in the atmosphere, the guards hadn't bothered depressurizing the tube. Bolan reached the valve release just as water rushed over his feet. It rose quickly and steadily, lapping at his knees, then his thighs.

Grasping the wheel with both hands, he gave it a counterclockwise twist. It didn't move. Roaring water continued to flood the pipe, the current dragging at his legs. He wrenched savagely at the wheel with all his strength, with no results. The water licked at his waist.

Water spumed and splashed around him. Since he was standing in a stooping posture, the water level swiftly rose above his chest. He took several deep breaths, hoping to saturate his lungs with oxygen. The floodtide drove against his mouth and nose.

Acting on a sudden impulse, Bolan turned the wheel clockwise and it moved. He should have expected Deveroux to take perverse pleasure in designing even the smallest items backward.

The water rose against him, trying to force him up to the ceiling of the pipe. Due to the weight of the autoloader, the ammo drum in the war bag and his Desert Eagle, he was able to maintain his footing, bracing his legs firmly against the upcurving walls of the tube.

Hand-over-hand, Bolan spun the wheel, shutting his eyes against the stinging brine of the seawater. His lungs began to ache with the effort of turning the wheel while holding his breath.

The current suddenly doubled in speed and force, sweeping his feet out from under him. He managed to retain his grip on the wheel, but the current caught him, pulling him into a horizontal position, his back bumping the top of the tube, the shotgun banging against his thighs.

He fought the rush of water with flailing legs, turning the wheel slowly, fearing that he would lose his grip and be smashed against the hatch portal a hundred yards to his rear. Suddenly there was a shrill screeching of metal breaking loose from metal.

His lungs felt as though they were on the verge of collapsing when another current, this one eddying up from below, slammed him upward. The valve cover sprang open from the water pressure and the sudden water displacement was like a punch in the stomach. He was swept up, and he burst out onto the rounded surface of the tube, his shoulders scraping against the edge of the opening.

The lip of the release-valve cover fetched him a painful crack across the crown of his head as he was forced up and out. Water gurgled, sprayed and foamed all around him, his lower body buffeted by the surging, upward current.

Bolan managed to keep one hand on the wheel as he was pushed out, half drowned and coughing. The pipeline was elevated, and he had no desire in finding out if a fall from it was survivable or merely bone-breaking.

Scrabbling along the surface of the tube, Bolan drank in great lungfuls of air and fingered salt water from his stinging eyes. Surveying the zone, he saw he was still inside the compound's fence, sitting about twenty feet above the ground. He was also sitting inside the funnel of light cast by the high-intensity floodlamp.

Looking to his right, toward the building, he saw a dim man-shape behind the window of the observation window. Even as his gaze settled on the figure, it bolted away in a frantic run.

Climbing to his hands and knees, Bolan saw a support pylon directly beneath him. Steadying himself with the lamppost, he swung his legs over and down, putting his weight on the steel cross-braces. He quickly clambered down the pylon, dropping from strut to brace, sacrificing safety for speed. He jumped the last ten feet and hit the ground running.

The section of snipped-out fence was less than fifty yards away, but it faced the entrance of the building, where he was sure he would encounter the remnants of the security force. He had fixed the position of the fence section in his mind, and he doubted anyone else had noticed it. He tried to coax more speed out of his pumping legs, but the night's exertions had taken their toll. His legs ached, his chest was tight and little fireballs of pain bespoke of strained or torn ligaments in his shoulders and upper back.

As he rounded the corner of the building, racing for a flat stretch of shadow, a muzzle-flash mushroomed from his right and a little behind him. Bolan dived to the ground, taking the impact on his shoulder, sliding across the wet ground. As he slid, he triggered the Remington.

The last two rounds of the buckshot in the autoloader caught the guard in the groin and belly. He fell back into the shadows he had used as cover.

Bolan ejected the spent drum, but didn't expend the time to take the spare from his war bag. Letting the shotgun hang from its strap, he unleathered the Desert Eagle and plunged on toward the fence. Behind him he heard shouts, but the words were unintelligible.

Reaching the fence, he ran along the side of it until he hit the wedge of darkness between the mounted pair of security lights. Dropping to his belly, he hooked the fingers of his left hand through the interlocking links of wire and pushed. A triangle opened at the base of the fence, and he squeezed his body through it. The shoulder strap of his war bag was snared by a jagged point of wire, but he jerked it free without slowing.

Then he was outside the compound and in the jungle again. Immediately he felt better, despite the sound of bullets splintering against the fence. For a split second, he considered hunkering down in the shadows and picking off the gunners while they carelessly exposed themselves in the light. He chose, instead, to melt into the wet, dripping darkness.

Eyeing the sky, he was relieved there was no sign of

dawn. If the raft had been discovered, or the *E.G. Robinson* disabled, then thousands would die shortly before sunrise.

Bolan refused to dwell on the possibility. He began to run, his booted feet churning up leaves and breaking twigs. He knew he was making enough noise to enable a blind person to track him, but it couldn't be helped. He vaulted over fallen logs and jumped muddy patches. Leaves batted at his face, vines tried to tangle and trip him up, but he kept running, the Desert Eagle tight in his fist. He realized that he should slow down; a sprained ankle would mean death, but he kept running.

Then, he burst out of the undergrowth onto the sandy sweep of the beach. He sprinted toward where the raft lay buried. A blocky figure in a rain cape stepped out of the brush, and Bolan remembered a man named Carlos had been ordered to patrol the shoreline. He aimed a Delta Elite pistol and yelled something.

If Carlos expected Bolan to either come to a halt, or veer away from him in a panic, he had seriously misjudged the strength of the shadowy man's resolve. Bolan increased his speed, heading directly for him.

Carlos squeezed the trigger of his weapon just as the Executioner fired the Desert Eagle. He heard a bullet thumping the air, missing his head by a fractional margin. The Desert Eagle's single round struck home, directly between the man's eyes, the impact hammering him off his feet, dropping him dead at the shoreline. A wave broke over his broken face.

Bolan rushed toward a clump of brush and kicked at the sand, uncovering the rubber raft. He dragged it loose and pulled it across the beach to the water. He waded into the sea, breasting the waves. When he was free of the breakers, he rolled into it and began to paddle. He could just make out the anchored *E.G. Robinson,* bobbing on the waves.

Over the crash of the surf, he heard an engine throb into life behind him. The white explosion of a searchlight turned the rippling surface of the Gulf into a shimmering silver. The patrol boat was heaving away from the pier, fanning the light in the direction of the beach.

Bolan sucked in gulps of air as he slid the paddle into the water and pulled, then repeated the motion in a fast, almost frantic rhythm. His brow beaded with sweat, which dripped into his eyes, making it difficult to focus on the distant outline of the runabout. He hazarded a quick glance over his shoulder.

The patrol boat was cutting through the breakers, sidling as close to the shoreline as possible without running aground. The cone of light played over the corpse of Carlos lying on his back in the surf, and Bolan thought he heard a yell of outrage.

When the light swept across the beach toward the foliage, Bolan knew his tracks leading to the sea would be noticed. He couldn't tell how many men were aboard the craft; he hoped it was one, to make the task of steering and firing the U.S. M-60 machine gun mounted amidships an impossible one.

Bolan kept up the paddling, but his arm muscles and shoulder blades ached with a burning pain that got worse with every stroke. Sweat rivered down his chest beneath his shirt.

The blaze of white lighting up his way and the sharp climb in the sound of the diesel engines were simultaneous. Bolan instinctively flattened in the flexible bottom of the raft, looking behind him. Blinding light shone full in his face. The patrol cruiser planed across the surface of the Gulf, the prow splitting it into two great sheets of flying foam. There was no gunfire, but Bolan rapidly calculated the speed of the boat to his relatively motionless position.

When the searchlight was a dazzling orb filling the night, and the engine roar nearly deafening, he took several deep breaths and rolled his body over the side of the raft.

He swam down as far as he could, clawing water aside.

The weight of his weapons helped to keep him submerged as the boat roared over him, the propellers tearing the raft to scraps. The backwash tumbled him about like a piece of driftwood.

He came up in the churning wake. The boat made a wide, roaring curve for a return run. As it turned, Bolan saw that there was only one man aboard. He was forced to cut the rpm of the engines so he could swivel the searchlight. As the blade of white light cut toward him again, Bolan dived.

The cruiser shot overhead, within arm's reach. Measuring the distance, Bolan kicked himself toward it. One flailing hand managed to secure a grip on a length of nylon rope trailing from the stern.

The craft surged forward, dragging Bolan in the wash, his face only inches away from a whirling propeller. Water forced itself into his nostrils, and he had to keep snorting it out as he hung on. He was slapped and buffeted by the turbulence, but he dragged himself forward and up. His arms strained in their sockets.

Hauling himself hand-over-hand, he got a firm grip on a cleat at the side of the boat and wrenched himself up and over and onto the deck. The pilot of the craft was the heavyset, goateed man Bolan had seen the morning before. One hand was at the wheel while the other aligned the searchlight to shine out over the sea.

The pilot hadn't seen or heard Bolan's arrival, which was just as well. His clothes were heavy and sodden, his arm muscles dead. It was all he could do to keep from gasping as he dragged himself to his feet, swaying a little on unsteady legs.

Bracing himself in a corner, he unholstered the Desert Eagle, drew a bead midpoint on the man's broad back and said loudly, "Looking for me?"

The guard's head snapped around so violently and quickly, it was a wonder he didn't dislodge a few neck vertebrae. The expression on his face was of such baffled horror that Bolan almost felt sorry for him. His finger tensed on the trigger. He expected the guard to react in one of two ways: to either twist the wheel to throw Bolan off-balance, or to engage in a macho quick-draw contest, snatching futilely for the Delta Elite pistol at his right hip.

The guard didn't try either option. He crashed to the deck on his knees, covering his face with meaty, shaking hands. Bolan stared at him for a second, then cautiously crossed the deck.

The man made retching sounds beneath his hands. At first, Bolan thought he had timed the announcement of his arrival with an onslaught of seasickness, then he realized the man was trying to ask him something.

"No," Bolan said. "I won't kill you. That is, if you agree to a midnight swim."

The guard lowered his hands. "Huh?" The word bubbled from between his chattering teeth.

"You heard me. Up and over. Now, stand up."

"Y-yes, sir."

The guard lumbered to his feet, hands above his head. His eyes shone with terror of the man in black.

"With your left hand," Bolan said, "thumb and forefinger only, take out your side arm and chuck it over the side."

Slowly, and with exaggerated care, the guard obeyed the command. As the Delta Elite plunged into the water and sank toward the bottom of the Gulf of Mexico, Bolan made a motion with the barrel of the Desert Eagle.

"You next. I hope you can swim."

"Yes, sir," the man said huskily. "I used to be a lifeguard."

"Then you shouldn't have any trouble making it to the island. Watch out for barracuda, though. They hunt at night."

The guard swallowed hard, poised himself on the side,

eyed the water below him and jumped overboard. For such a large man, he didn't make much of a splash.

Bolan watched him until he was stroking steadily back toward the island. Then, leathering the Desert Eagle, he took the wheel and steered the patrol boat to where the *E.G. Robinson* lay at anchor. He bumped the side of the cruiser harder into the runabout than he intended, but it was the least of the damage he planned to inflict to government property over the next couple of hours.

He weighed anchor, started the runabout and had it roaring at twenty knots back to the mainland inside of five minutes. Powering up the transmitter, he made sure the channel was on the proper frequency, and he spoke into the microphone. "Sonny, this is Bubba Boy. Come in, Sonny. Do you copy?"

He had to repeat the hail several times before a voice Bolan didn't recognize responded sleepily, "This is Sonny, receiving you."

"Alert Falcon Station to prep for a flight. Stat. Do you copy?"

The voice was puzzled. "A flight? Who is this?"

"Belasko. Where are Heath and Akins?"

"Home in bed."

"Wake them up. Tell them and George Tam to meet me at the airfield."

"Meet you when?"

Bolan's voice was like the crack of a whip. *"Now."*

The flight to the Osiris Tower was short in duration but
long on discomfort. Deveroux held the limp, sedated form
of Anastasia Kirchov on his lap, and though she wasn't a
particularly large woman, she was solid. Both of his legs
had gone to sleep somewhere over the bay.

Kindzierski, the pilot, didn't voice an objection about the
extra weight in such a small aircraft, but he did comment
sourly on how sluggishly the helicopter seemed to
maneuver.

When the chopper alighted on the landing pad atop the
building, Jest was there to meet it. Deveroux handed out
the sleeping woman, and Jest threw her over his shoulder
in a fireman's carry. Kindzierski climbed from the helicopter, and Deveroux started to dismiss him for the rest of the
day. He thought better of it and said, "Stay close until
further notice."

As they walked toward the entrance cupola, Jest said
worriedly, "I can't raise the island."

Palming open the door, Deveroux demanded, "What do
you mean?"

"I mean their receiver is dead, and they haven't called
in, either. They're about twenty minutes overdue with a
security-status update. I called them, and no one answered,
not Croy, not Burtis."

Crowding into the stairwell, Deveroux took the lead.
"The storm must have damaged the receiver."

Jest shifted the woman's weight across his shoulder. "It worked fine through the worst of it, Dex. Our tight-beam frequency barely had a speck of static in it."

Deveroux turned to look sharply at Jest. He knew the tall, bony man was thinking the same thing he was, but he refused to put his suspicion into words. Words carried power, and Jest smelled of sweat and tension as it was. "Calm yourself, Doctor," he said. "We're in control."

They entered the operations center. Kindzierski took a seat at one of the empty desks, stretching his legs and looking as if he intended to take a nap. Deveroux's fingertips unlocked the door to the King's Chamber, and Jest moved past him to drop Kirchov into the single chair with a sigh of relief.

Deveroux pressed the cartouche at the base of the statue of Ramses, and as it slid aside, he said, "Fetch one of the sterilized coveralls and put the professor in it."

Jest's eyebrows rose. "Why?"

Pushing a strand of loose hair from her eyes, Deveroux answered softly, "I don't want her out of my sight until this is over. She'll go into the strong room with us."

As Jest entered the narrow passageway behind the granite sculpture, Deveroux sat at his desk and touched the inlaid intercom key. "Security station."

"Security," came the immediate response. "Ramirez here."

"This is Mr. Deveroux." His voice was smooth, unhurried. In the tension of any operation, Deveroux always strove to exude a calm self-confidence. It came from long years of studying yoga and practicing meditation. No matter his inner turmoil or excitement, he made a fetish of appearing unconcerned and completely in control to his subordinates.

"Anything unusual this evening, Ramirez?"

"No, sir."

"No low-flying aircraft buzzing the building, or strangers driving by the lobby?"

"No, sir. Everything checks out normal."

"Good. But just the same, double the frequency of the foot patrols in the parking garage. How many men on duty tonight?"

"Ten, sir," Ramirez replied. "The usual complement."

"I wonder if you could send one of them up to the penthouse in a few minutes. Have him bring a nylon wrist binder."

"Will do, Mr. Deveroux."

Jest returned with a coverall and crossed the room to the sleeping Kirchov. Kneeling in front of her, he asked with a grin, "Want me to undress her first?"

Deveroux considered it for a moment, then shook his head. "I think not. The humiliation of awakening helpless, a prisoner, and being forced to watch my plan come to fruition will suffice for an initial lesson. For the time being, anyway."

Jest stuffed her feet into the leggings of the coverall, then dragged the garment up over her hips. As he slipped the thin fabric up and over her arms and shoulders, he commented, "Kind of a tight fit."

A guard rapped on the open office door and came in when Deveroux beckoned to him. He placed the nylon binder on the desk, then quickly left, studiously avoiding looking at Jest as he dressed the unconscious woman.

Deveroux stood from his desk, pointing to the white strip of nylon. "When you're done, tie her wrists with that, suit up yourself and bring her into the strong room."

Deveroux entered the passage behind Ramses, tugged on the coverall, adjusted the surgical mask over his nose and mouth and walked into the domain of the Cheops Alpha. The machine made a faint hum of purpose.

Sitting in front of the master keyboard, he gazed at the bead of green light inching along the grid pattern glowing

on the big monitor screen. In less than a half hour, the
Remora would dock with the platform.

All the accumulated tensions of the past six months of
planning were swept away by a surge of triumph and ful-
fillment. There were no longer any problems to solve, only
a routine to complete.

HEATH AND AKINS came out of the little office when they
spotted the headlights of the Sable. They eyed the car warily, hands on pistols holstered at the small of their backs,
until Bolan parked and got out.

He entered the shack, and when Heath got a look at his
battered face, he winced and said, "Jesus, Belasko. If that's
what you look like after a soft probe, you must look like
hell after a hard contact."

"The soft got unexpectedly hard," Bolan replied tersely.
"Is George prepping the SWIFT?"

"Yeah," Akins said. "He's complaining like hell. Says
it's too dangerous to take her up when it's dark. It's not
outfitted with running lights."

Bolan nodded impatiently. "That's one of its advantages,
and the fact it's silent."

Akins stared at him curiously. "George wants to wait
until daybreak."

"That'll be too late. I've got to take her up now."

"Why? What's so damn urgent?"

In simple, unadorned language, Bolan told the pair of
FBI men everything that had transpired on the island. Their
expressions were stunned, incredulous, but not disbelieving.

"Shit," Heath said. "We'll call in for a warrant, get a
strike team together—"

Bolan cut him off with a quick gesture. "You're talking
a minimum of three hours to put all that together. If we're
lucky, we've got maybe an hour and a half. If we're
lucky."

He turned and left the office, stalking across the dark

airfield toward the hangar. Lights shone within. Heath and Akins dogged his heels, peppering him with questions and demands.

"Why don't we alert NORAD or the Saudi embassy—"

"How well defended is the bastard's penthouse—"

"You need to brief us on the layout of the island—"

George Tam was adjusting the left-hand winglet when Bolan walked into the hangar. Though he made no comment, Tam obviously found the differences between the casually dressed, soft-spoken man he had met the day before and the grim, heavily armed warrior in black very disconcerting.

"George, I need the SWIFT. Can you pilot the tow plane?"

Irritation displaced the fear in Tam's eyes. "The SWIFT is private property. I'm the only one qualified to fly it."

"I don't have the time to argue with you," Bolan stated in a low, icy voice. "You'll have to accept it as an article of faith that I wouldn't ask this of you unless hundreds of thousands of lives weren't at stake."

Tam hesitated before inquiring, "I'll do what I can, but I'll have to be the one to do the flying."

"No." Bolan's tone brooked no debate. "You're not a field man, not a soldier. What I have in mind is more than a recon flight. I can't even promise I'll return the SWIFT intact, but I can promise you'll be compensated for its loss."

"You're not authorized to promise anything of the sort," Akins protested. "Hell, George has more than a million bucks invested in the SWIFT!"

"Call Brognola in Washington," Bolan snapped, fixing him with a cold stare. "He'll tell you what I am and am not authorized to do."

Facing George Tam again, he asked, "What's your answer?"

Tam met his gaze unblinkingly. "I have a feeling that if I refuse you'll just 'requisition' the thing anyway."

"That's probably true."

"In that case—" Tam smiled wryly "—if there's any chance at all of you bringing her back to me in one piece, I'd better give you a crash course in its operation. I hope you're a quick study."

"At this point," Bolan said, "the world better hope the same thing."

ANASTASIA KIRCHOV came out of a forced sleep to find herself in new surroundings. It was a small, low-ceilinged room, coldly lit by overhead fluorescent tubes. The room was dominated by a computer with a huge, four-foot-wide monitor screen. Its support systems spread out from the master keyboard. Though computers and cybernetic hardware wasn't her field of expertise, she saw at a glance that the machine filling the room was enormously advanced.

There were two people in the room, their attention focused on the computer console. One was sitting, the other standing, and the murmur of their voices were male. Both men wore hooded coverall garments, like those worn in operating theaters. The standing man was exceptionally tall and thin.

Kirchov shifted position on the high-backed chair in which she was seated and looked carefully around. She wore a duplicate of the men's coveralls, but her white-clad wrists were entrapped by a nylon binder. A surgical mask covered her nose and mouth. The only exit was behind her, a narrow doorway blocked by hanging static-guard strips.

Her garment rustled as she moved and both men turned toward her. "Ah, so you've awakened," the seated man said. "Excellent. I wanted you to be fully cogent for this, Professor Kirchov. I can't help but enjoy a touch of irony to start the day."

Indicating the other man, he said, "This is Dr. Jest, my biographer and lieutenant, you might say."

The man pulled down his surgical mask as he gave her a courtly bow and a macabre grin. "Enchanted."

Kirchov started to say something, but Deveroux raised an imperious hand. "Before you rattle off a stream of wearisome questions, allow me to explain a few wheres and whats. You are in a strong room in my penthouse atop the Osiris Tower. And the Ghawar oil fields have perhaps forty minutes of life remaining." Smiling, he added, "I trust that satisfies you?"

"Not quite," bit back Kirchov. "Belasko."

"Oh, yes. I almost forgot about him. It would be best if you did so as well."

"Why?" Kirchov silently cursed the shrill note in her voice.

"He'll be fried or head shot in a few minutes. Or both."

Kirchov didn't respond. A chime from the computer console commanded Deveroux's attention. "Marvelous. The Remora has uplinked with the suborbital platform."

A series of digits flashed rapidly across an amber screen. The numbers vanished, and the chime sounded again.

"The platform's reprogramming is complete," Deveroux announced. "Come here, Professor. You might find this interesting."

Kirchov uneasily stood over Deveroux's shoulder. On the monitor was a shimmer of white light. Superimposed over that was a number: 865.

Deveroux tapped the number with a white-gloved forefinger. "That is the present height of the platform in miles."

Even as he spoke, the number changed to 863, and the light shimmer acquired a faint blue tinge. "The light indicates the position of the platform. As it changes its orbital trajectory and descends, the color of the light will change accordingly."

Deveroux smiled up at her. "OPEC has nothing to worry about until the light becomes red. Rather appropriate, I think."

Kirchov stared at the screen, the image burning into her eyes. Thousands of people were about to be wiped out by a flicker of light and a number.

"Doctor," Deveroux said, "to be on the safe side, why don't you run a security scan?"

"Will do, Dex." Jest strode over to a bank of monitor screens and turned them on, one by one. Images flickered across them.

"Street-level parking garage secure," he intoned. "Building lobby secure. Private lifts secure."

Dexter Deveroux wasn't even bothering to look at the monitor screens. He was totally engrossed with the computer displays.

"Long-range scan," Jest continued. "Jet liner on approach run to Tampa International…man, looks like the smog will be bad today…*hold it!*"

Not turning his head, Deveroux murmured, "What?"

Jest peered at the screen intently, adjusting the focus. As far as Kirchov could see the monitor held only the images of buildings and a sky turning a faint orange from the rising sun.

"I'm not sure," Jest muttered. "Something's just coming into camera range from the northeast. Coming low and coming fast."

"A plane, probably," Deveroux offered.

"No, it's too low for a plane."

"Then it's a bird," Kirchov ventured.

Jest spared her a single, contemptuous glance and said, "It's way too big for a bird."

He fastened his eyes on the screen again. "Coming in closer now." He stiffened and bleated, "Kee-*rist!*"

Deveroux lunged from the computer console as if the keyboard had suddenly become scalding hot. He wheeled his chair to the monitor screen. Kirchov stared over his shoulder at the distant, but still recognizable winged figure on the screen.

Deveroux's eyes above the surgical mask blazed with emerald anger, but his voice was unhurried. "Alert security, inform them to prepare for an assault. Tell Kindzierski to get to the roof and wait for word. Have him seal the exit door. Standby to activate defense mechanisms."

He glared furiously at the image of the winged shape barreling across the sky, skimming the skyline, soaring out of the predawn darkness. "Not this time," he breathed. *"Not this time."*

19

The SWIFT handled far easier than Bolan had expected. The controls were simple, consisting primarily of handles and cables to lift and drop the flaps and a foot pedal for the rudder. Though the spread of the cantilevered composite wing was nineteen feet, the air drag was negligible. The only sound was the faint hiss of wind sliding over the streamlined fuselage. Peering through the plastic bubble covering the cockpit, Bolan reflected that the SWIFT provided the next best thing to free, unaided flight. It was no surprise why George Tam was so devoted to it.

Following Tam's instructions, Bolan kept the speed at fifty miles per hour and the altitude at a thousand feet. Though the SWIFT was capable of attaining an 8,500-foot flight ceiling and a redline speed of eighty miles per hour, he hadn't pushed the craft's capabilities during its ten-mile flight from the airfield. Though he hadn't slept at all in nearly forty-eight hours, a few cups of coffee while Tam had briefed him on the flight operations had allowed him to catch his third wind.

The Double D building looked normal enough from above. It looked like any other fairly modern, midsize office building, but he wasn't comforted. Eberhardt's words echoed in his mind, "It's a fortress."

Arrayed on the roof at forty-five-degree angles were a dozen solar energy panel cells. A small, gleaming jet helicopter rested peacefully on a concrete slab at the array's outer perimeter.

As the aircraft circled one hundred feet above the penthouse, Bolan saw an entrance cupola and a skylight. The door to the cupola slid aside, disgorging a quartet of uniformed security guards. They spread out across the roof in a well-ordered drill. They were armed with Heckler & Koch 94 autocarbines, and the SWIFT was well within range.

Bolan pulled a handle, engaging the pair of upward-pointing winglet flaps into flying station. As soon as he felt the lift of the winglets, he curved the SWIFT away from Deveroux's eyrie—just as the guns were triggered. The weapons were silenced, the muzzles equipped with flash-hiders so Bolan heard and saw nothing beyond wisps of smoke and the glinting rain of ejected cartridges.

However, he felt the SWIFT shudder beneath multiple impacts before he was able to whisk the craft up and away. A stitching of bullet holes had appeared in the port wing. He twisted the aerolons, kicked the rudder and the SWIFT gained speed, soaring over rooftops, then the black surface of the bay. As he forced more altitude, air whistled through the bullet holes and the wings shook with the strain. He notched down the speed controls to thirty miles per hour, only ten above stall speed. The altimeter read two hundred feet.

He made the SWIFT skim the roiling waters of Tampa Bay for a few miles before he dared let it surge upward toward the skies again.

Since the SWIFT had no means of offense or defense, landing atop the penthouse would be futile, as well as lethal. Staging a frontal assault from the lobby would fail as well.

Bolan reviewed his inventory of ordnance. Because of the exceptionally light weight of the SWIFT, he was carrying only his Desert Eagle and the Remington shotgun, both strapped to his body. His pilot's harness doubled as a sail parachute. At the touch of a lever, the plastic cockpit bubble would be ejected and a rocket would deploy the parachute, dragging him up and out of the craft.

Grimly Bolan recognized that the SWIFT had to be sacrificed. He felt a stab of sympathy for George Tam, but the alternative would be far, far worse. Pulling the handles of the control cables, he put the craft's nose up, swinging it in great circles as it gained speed and altitude. The air made a keen hissing through the bullet holes in the wing.

When the gauges read six hundred feet and sixty miles per hour, Bolan glided back toward Harbour Island. Twice he circled the Double D building, watching the men on the roof. He kept well out of weapons range. If he took too many hits too early, the SWIFT would be ruined, the wings flying apart, and the craft would crash far short of its target.

He made the ship descend and as it completed one final circle, he kicked the speed to maximum. He made an almost vertical bank and the SWIFT plunged directly toward the Double D. He was careful not to whip stall the ship, or its backswept wings would be torn off.

The craft vibrated dangerously as he continued to push it at peak speed. He saw the members of the security force racing to the edge of the roof, putting the H&K-94s to their shoulders. Lead cracked into the fuselage. Bolan kicked the rudder and waggled the wings, tilting the craft from side to side. He steepened the angle of the dive to gather momentum.

When the SWIFT was only two hundred feet from the top of the tower, Bolan wrenched at the lever beneath the seal of the canopy. At the same moment, he yanked the cord attached to the pilot's harness.

The explosive pop of the rocket deploying the parachute was almost swallowed by the scream of the wind. The glider chute opened with a loud whip-crack as it caught the air. Bolan didn't have to kick himself free of the cockpit. A pair of giant hands seemed to close over his shoulders and catapult him out and upward. He had performed dozens of parachute jumps, so he was prepared for the stress and strain against his upper body. His long experience enabled him to grasp the guide cords and gain a stable altitude, despite the eighty mile per hour wind slapping against his unprotected face.

The SWIFT continued on its downward course, on a direct heading with the pair of huge, overlapping *D*s. It plummeted into the letters fronting the penthouse with a screeching, grinding crash. Red-tinted plastic, steel and glass spun in all directions, cascading into the street five hundred feet below.

Bolan heard the shouts of the security guards as the craft skated into them on its belly. Grisly jangling and crunching noises told him that the solar energy panels were being crushed and uprooted from their moorings. Though the SWIFT was light, its momentum had turned it into a scythe, its wingspread sweeping the roof clear.

Even as the air still shivered with the echoes of the impact, Bolan slipped the glider-chute sideways toward the windows of the floor beneath the penthouse. With his right hand he unlimbered the Remington and began pumping the trigger, sending round after round of the 12-gauge buckshot against the tinted window. The glass quivered, shivered, shuddered, cracked and sparked.

Though Eberhardt had told him that the Double D had electrified defense systems, it hadn't occurred to Bolan that the windows were protected by some type of an electric field. As he glided closer, sailing along at close to thirty miles per hour, he saw tiny blue flashes arcing in a dancing pattern around and even through the window. In a fraction of a second, he realized Deveroux had sandwiched a metallic mesh or screen voltage carrier between the double-glazed panes of glass.

Lifting and spreading his legs, he held his rubber-treaded combat boots out before him like a pair of battering rams.

He continued to blast with the Remington, aiming between his feet.

The window shivered, then collapsed with a hiss of electric current just as Bolan hit it feetfirst. A fractional spillover of the voltage caught him as he crashed through the ragged remains of the mesh. It wasn't powerful enough to harm him severely, but he still burst through the window in a shower of splintered glass, convulsed in pain.

Bolan's breath was driven from his lungs as he fell to a thickly carpeted floor. He fought off the blackness trying to claim him and forced his legs and arms to push him erect. With numb fingers, he unlatched the chute harness and struggled out of it. The silk chute canopy, tangled in the jagged edges of the window, flapped uselessly in the breeze.

Perspiration filmed Bolan's face with the effort of climbing to his feet. By degrees, his nerves recovered from the terrible stunning shock and he surveyed the zone.

It was an empty office, containing only a desk, a few chairs, a computer terminal and a potted plant with drooping, brown leaves. He knew he was on the floor just below the penthouse, so he had to find either an elevator or a stairwell.

The door was unlocked, and he moved out into a wide, wood-paneled corridor that stretched to his left and his right. It was shadowy and dim, with only a straight thin line of neon light running down the center of the ceiling. He turned right, moving rapidly, his feet silent on the nap of the carpet.

Bolan passed two doors, which were locked. He came to an intersecting corridor and peered around the edge. To the left, a few hundred feet away, an Exit sign glowed red from the ceiling, right above a varnished wooden door.

He paused beneath the square ceiling grille of the ventilation system and considered using the ductwork to make his way unhindered and unseen into the penthouse suite.

He considered the option for only a second before discarding it.

No matter what was shown in the movies, most air-conditioning ductwork in modern buildings was very narrow, barely wide enough to admit a child, and designed with long vertical drops, internal grille baffles and circulating fans. Besides, it was more than a little likely that intruder defense mechanisms were rigged inside the ducts, maybe even lethal devices like the cyanide cartridge he had encountered in Algiers.

Gripping the Remington tightly, Bolan eased down the hallway, careful to keep his body to one side. He had crept half the distance when the door swung open violently and three uniformed security guards stampeded into the hall. Bolan glimpsed stairs leading upward behind them. Though the men weren't carrying the submachine guns, they fisted Delta Elite pistols.

The guards rocked to a surprised halt when they saw Bolan. One of the men barked, "Cut the son of a bitch to shreds!"

As one, three gun barrels were lifted and trained on him.

20

Bolan dropped to his stomach, catching himself on his elbows, steadying the Remington in a double-handed grip. His first target was the man who had barked the order.

He worked the trigger, and the uniformed man catapulted backward, his torso squirting blood like a squeezed sponge. The man beside him yelped in terror and reacted by firing his automatic blindly, without even attempting to aim it. Bolan fired again, the shotgun's roar painfully loud in the corridor.

The buckshot took the guard in the chest and spun him in a grotesque pirouette. Blood streamed from the wound, draping his companions and the walls with red, liquid ribbons.

The remaining Delta Elite cracked and spit flame. Bolan felt two bullets tug at the padded right shoulder of his blacksuit. Wood chips tore loose from the wall paneling above his head, and scraps of carpet jumped up from the floor.

Bolan continued to pump the Remington's trigger. The man received the shot in the head and careened backward with a red smear where his face had been. He slid to the floor and sat heavily.

The Executioner reached for the handle of the door, turned it and gingerly pulled it open. It led onto an empty, bare-walled landing. Carefully he crept up the wide concrete steps, careful not to touch the metal banister. His nervous system still retained vivid memories of the electric shock it had received.

He reached another landing and a voice, so finely amplified that it might have come from beside his ear, asked, "'Hey, Joe—where you goin' with that gun in your hand?'"

Bolan skipped around, eyes and shotgun questing for a target. He saw nothing but a video camera bracketed to the wall high in the corner. A small speaker grid was connected to it. The voice spoke again, and he recognized the lilting tones of the man calling himself Dr. Jest, "Sorry, Hardman. You've entered a Firearm Free Zone. No armament allowed. Company policy."

"Are you prepared to enforce that policy?" Bolan asked.

"Are you prepared to die?" came the laughing reply.

Bolan assumed the question was strictly rhetorical. "Where's Deveroux?" he demanded.

A new voice blasted from the speaker, thundering and menacing. "Right here."

"What have you done with Professor Kirchov?"

"She's here with us. Unharmed. For the moment."

Bolan eyed the stairway stretching up before him, just in case guards lurked there to shoot him down. "I suppose you'll promise me you'll release her if I surrender."

"Do you think this is some stupid movie?" Deveroux's suddenly maddened voice roared. He sounded insulted. "I don't give a damn if you surrender or not! I'll still have you killed. The Hellfire Trigger is under my control and there's not a thing you can do about it."

"A little premature, aren't you?"

"I am one of the most intelligent men on this planet. You're a thug, a sanctimonious killer-for-hire. You have no right to meddle in my affairs, affairs concerning the future welfare of the world."

"You're the most intelligent mad dog on this planet,

Deveroux. But you're still a mad dog. You claim you're concerned about the future?''

"I do," Deveroux responded vehemently. "Solar power must supersede fossil and nuclear fuels as a worldwide energy source. Or else we will have a return to feudalism and barbarism.''

Bolan affected a sneering laugh. "And you think by the murder of innocent millions you'll gain your objective? The nations of the world won't turn to your solar energy patents for salvation. They'll blame each other for the energy shortage, struggle with each other, war with each other for possession of coal and oil, even food.''

"You're ranting," Deveroux snapped. "You waste my time. I will not be diverted from my path.''

"Good," Bolan replied flatly. "We know where we stand.''

Lifting the Remington to his shoulder, he squeezed off a round that blew the video camera and the speaker grid into fragments and scraps of metal.

Bolan went up the flight of stairs, taking two at a time. The stairs terminated at a door. Testing the handle, he found it was unlocked. Slowly he shouldered it open.

There was no warning at all, but suddenly the door was wrenched wide and something cracked across his right arm. His hand went numb. He was bowled over by a rush of bodies, shoved sideways into a large room. An out-thrust foot tripped him, and he went down heavily on the floor, unable to catch himself with his right arm. The Remington swung from its strap at his shoulder, banging his knees and shins.

Snarling and swearing, three security guards hurled themselves atop him, clubbing down at him with long batons. Bolan tried to bring the shotgun to bear with his left hand, but the end of a baton hit his biceps. The stick hummed and popped as it touched Bolan's arm. The muscles convulsed and spasmed, and a numbing pain raced from fingertips to shoulder socket.

The guards were armed with SAS 121 Shocksticks. Designed for crowd control, the batons delivered a 6,000-volt localized shock. The batons were a little under two feet in length and powered by batteries inside the molded plastic grips. They bore no other weapons.

A guard seized Bolan by the hair and attempted to twist his head back, leaving his throat exposed to a baton. The man was very strong, and his grip was painful. Bolan kicked at his leg, and the subsequent cracking of bone and shriek of pain was loud and ugly. The guard collapsed to one knee, half-falling across Bolan and taking a shock meant for him.

He managed to throw the man's body aside just as a boot rebounded from his chin and a baton stroked across his rib cage. Streaks of fire lanced up and down his side, and it took all his focused willpower and survival instinct to keep from curling in a fetal position.

Sensation was returning to his right hand and, with fingers that felt like sausages, he clawed at the butt of the Desert Eagle at his hip. He unleathered it, forcing his finger through the trigger guard, striking sideways with the long barrel. It splintered one of the batons with a flare and flash of sparks. A guard snarled and his baton slashed down, humming like a wasp. The big pistol seemed to vibrate, stung Bolan's fingers and flew from his hand. He heard it thud against the carpet.

Using his elbows as levers, and swiveling his hips, Bolan flung out one leg in a roundhouse kick. His boot found a target in a soft gut. As the guard choked out a curse and bent forward at the waist, Bolan hurled himself to the right in a frantic roll, as if his clothes were on fire and he was trying to smother the flames.

As he rolled, he received a whirling, dizzy impression of the large room. He caught fragmented glimpses of desks, computer terminals and a huge Mercator projection of the world spread across one wall. He managed to wrench himself to his feet with a corkscrew motion of his hips and legs. An instant later the three guards slammed into him.

Gripped by the guards, Bolan staggered from one side of the room to the other, trapped inside the thrashing, cursing mass. They sought to swamp him by sheer numbers. All three crashed against the map with a snap of fragile metal and a tinkling of glass. The network of lit lines shorted out, the tiny bulbs exploding.

Using the map as a brace, Bolan grabbed the man with the injured leg in a headlock, keeping his body between him and the other two guards. Though he was outnumbered, he was in perfect condition, and the three guards had gotten soft in the time they had done nothing more strenuous than watch security monitors. Their faces were red, their breath came harshly, and sweat stains were forming under their arms.

Crouching slightly, bending his knees, Bolan gathered his legs under him and surged forward, carrying the injured guard with him in the rush. A Shockstick baton touched his lower back, but the touch was too light, and he barely felt the streak of voltage.

Bolan flung the man ahead of him, and he tumbled head over heels across the top of a desk, taking the computer terminal with him. The other two men jumped him, one clutching his right wrist and attempting to twist his arm behind him. Bolan kicked himself backward off the floor, slamming the man against his comrade. All three went down, with the Executioner on top. A baton slid along his neck and pain rippled through him.

Bolan wrenched himself to one side and threw his body into a shoulder roll. Feeling had returned to his left hand, and he managed to drag the shotgun up from where it dangled by the strap against his right thigh. When he came up on one knee, his finger pressed the trigger.

Deveroux's voice, high and wild, shrilled from somewhere above. "No, not in there, you bastard!"

The remainder of his scream was drowned out by loud, hammering blasts from the Remington. The power of the shotgun hit the guards like sledgehammers, shredding organs, hurling them off their feet and splashing the big room with blood and viscera. More than one computer terminal was damaged beyond all hope of repair by buckshot. Ragged, silver-dollar-size holes were punched through the huge wall map. The Western Hemisphere fell with a clang to the floor.

When the firing pin struck the empty chamber, only Bolan was moving. The smell of cordite hung in the air. The bodies of the guards lay like disjointed puppets, leaking fluids all over the carpet.

Standing, he retrieved the Desert Eagle and jacked a round into the chamber. Bolan surveyed the room. His eyes rested upon a door at the far end. It bore no knob or handle, but it did have a small, rectangular strip of black glass where one would be. He wondered how many rounds it would take to blast the door open.

DEVEROUX HAD HIS FACE buried in his hands, his shoulders shaking. "That bastard," he murmured.

Anastasia Kirchov smiled beneath her mask. Bolan was refusing to play Deveroux's god-king game—he wasn't lying down and dying by royal decree.

Deveroux raised his head, his green eyes blazing with a venomous fury. The expression of madness in those eyes caused Kirchov's smile to vanish. She glanced at the computer's monitor screen. The number read 385. The bead of light was a pinkish hue.

Turning from the video screen that held the image of Bolan in the buckshot shattered office, Deveroux grabbed Jest by one arm. "We've got to do something. We can't allow him to reach this room."

Jest laughed, a high-pitched titter that puffed out the mask over his nose and mouth. "I'm waiting for the word, Dex."

"Go out there," Deveroux commanded. "Stop that son of a bitch. Kill him. I don't care how you do it, but stop him!"

Jest moved toward the exit. He slipped off the mask and cast Kirchov a wide grin. The grin caused frigid fingers of terror to close over her heart. She averted her gaze.

Pushing aside the static guard strips, Jest pulled off the coverall and left it in a heap on the floor. He entered the King's Chamber, and his eyes searched the shelves holding the Egyptian objets d'art. He quickly found the two items he was looking for. His hand plucked the long-handled "Scorpion King" ax from the shelf. Of Coptic design, it bore a crescent-shaped copper blade and dated from 3200 B.C. According to Deveroux, it had once been the favorite weapon of King Nar-Mer of the upper Nile regions. Obviously the wooden handle was of much more recent vintage.

From the shelf beneath, he took a leather cord sling and an oval lead pellet, inscribed with an anchor. The pellet was heavy, about the size of a robin's egg. The ancient Egyptians were believed not to have used slings, but Deveroux insisted otherwise. He claimed he had purchased both at great price from a merchant in Memphis, one of Egypt's largest seaports, hence the anchor on the pellet.

Looping one end of the sling over his right index finger and hooking the other end over his thumb, Jest fitted the pellet into the pouch. He moved to the marble desk and touched one of the inlays. The skylight darkened, making the King's Chamber almost too dim to navigate. He pressed another hieroglyph, and the lock solenoids of the door clicked open. Jest began whirling the sling vigorously over his head.

He kept it spinning, humming through the air, eyes fastened on the door. Slowly it was pushed open, an inch at a time. Light spilled in from the room beyond, as well as the sharp stink of gunpowder. By degrees, the long barrel of a pistol appeared around the edge of the door. Jest grinned and waited until its full length was visible. Then he released the loose end of the sling, spewing out the lead bullet at sixty miles per hour. Centrifugal force had quadrupled its relative mass.

For one of the few times in his life, Bolan had no idea what hit him. An object cracked loudly against the barrel of the Desert Eagle with terrific force, and sent shivers of pain through his finger and wrist. The .44 was torn from his grip.

Bolan went to the floor, using the door as a shield. Jest laughed in genuine delight. Recognizing the laugh, Bolan asked, "You did that?"

"Me and my slingshot. David has nothing on me, Hardman."

The soldier got to his feet. His eyes caught the tall, narrow outline of Jest standing behind a desk and he raced toward him. His move wasn't as impulsive or as reckless as it might seem. He remembered Jest's spoken antipathy to firearms, so whatever the man had chosen as a weapon, it wouldn't be a gun. However, Bolan didn't intend to grapple with the man. Their brief struggle in Algiers had demonstrated that Jest was deceptively strong and agile. With his knowledge of the nervous system, he could incapacitate or cripple Bolan with his bony fingers.

Jest bounded over the desk eagerly, as though rushing to meet a long-lost loved one. Both men came together in the center of the room. Jest kicked upward with his right leg in a long arc. His foot slammed into Bolan's chest and flipped him onto his back. He rolled with the blow and wasn't injured by it.

Bolan bounced to his feet as Jest lashed out with another kick. His foot glanced off Bolan's forearm, and in a blur of motion he hooked the thin man's heel and gave it an upward push.

Jest started to fall, but in a lightning-like explosion of reflex and sinews, he turned the fall into an gymnastic back-flip. He landed gracefully in a crouch. At the same time, he launched a blow with the fighting ax toward Bolan's unguarded midriff.

With animal quickness, the Executioner sprang away from the notched head of the weapon, but he wasn't quite quick enough. The dull blade scraped his belly. It was only a graze and didn't cut the fabric of his blacksuit, but the force was sufficient to make him swallow a grunt of pain.

Jest rose to his full height and spun the ax by the handle in his right hand. Both men circled each other.

Jest swept the ax at him, and Bolan ducked the first swipe and stepped inside the backswing. He put his right fist into Jest's belly and pounded his left in an uppercut that rocked his adversary on his heels. Blood sprang from his nostrils.

Snorting crimson droplets, Jest came boring down, swinging wildly. Bolan weaved, spun and backstepped, letting the ax go over his head or past his belly. Balancing on the ball of his left foot, Bolan spun his right leg up and around in a crescent kick. The sole of his boot caught Jest solidly on the point of his jutting jaw.

The skinny man staggered the length of the King's Chamber, arms windmilling. He came to a bone-jarring halt against a six-foot-tall, free-standing étagère that had shelves holding clay jars and pots. The entire display case teetered and fell. Glass jangled, and thousand-year-old jars and pots shattered. Though off-balance, Jest managed to keep his footing.

The two men circled each other again. Jest made a number of feints, lunges and thrusts with the ax, but Bolan avoided them all. They danced and counterdanced around the King's Chamber, and Bolan watched as Jest called upon all his reserves of strength. He left no killer's tricks untried, but the copper ax sank lower and lower, threatening Bolan's thighs and knees instead of his head and body. Breathing in whispering gasps, Jest lumbered around Bolan. His knees wobbled. The man was an excellent hit-and-runner, his reflexes and speed were little short of inhuman, but he didn't possess the stamina to participate in a prolonged conflict.

"Give it up," Bolan said. "This isn't your field."

Jest gasped out a laugh and lunged forward, swinging the ax in a deadly half circle. Stepping back, Bolan's heel caught on broken glass and shards of pottery. He half stumbled. The notched edge of the copper blade and the wooden haft smashed into Bolan's right side, grating on bone. As he staggered backward, he felt blood flowing warmly down his ribs. He would have fallen if not for catching himself on the marble desk.

Gasping for air, Bolan pushed himself erect, probing his rib cage for fractures. Jest bounded to him before he could recover his wind. Holding the handle with both hands, he brought the ax down on his head. Bolan shifted to one side and the blade crashed into the desktop, biting out a chip. At the same instant, Jest snapped a kick into a clump of ganglia behind Bolan's left knee. He knew exactly where to strike.

His leg went momentarily weak beneath him, and Bolan didn't try to stay standing. He went to the floor and rolled away. He got to his feet, dragging his left leg like a sack of birdshot, wondering where his Desert Eagle might be.

Jest, tittering breathlessly, came at him again. Bolan sidestepped a vicious roundhouse with the ax. The force of his unconnected blow turned Jest around completely, and Bolan swept the man's feet from under him with his right leg. Moving in, favoring his left leg, he booted Jest beneath his prominent jaw with his right foot. The back of the man's head struck the floor with a solid thud. His long, lanky body went slack, and Bolan was sure Jest was unconscious. He lay prone on the floor, unmoving, and as far as Bolan could see, unbreathing. Rubbing the back of his left knee, he limped toward the door, looking for the Desert Eagle. At the sound of a low groan, he turned.

Jest stirred, feebly pushing himself up with his elbows, grunting with the exertion and the pain. Looking at Bolan, he croaked out, "Hardman, indeed."

With sweat pouring into his eyes and pain flaring all over his body, Bolan waited until Jest climbed to his full, formidable height, measured him off and drove his right fist fully into the man's mouth.

With a liquid, gurgling squeal, Jest lurched backward, stopping short against a granite statue Bolan recognized as a replica of one in the Abu Simbel valley. Jest slid down it a few feet, but he didn't fall. He pushed himself erect again, his back pressing against the statue for support. The ax dropped from slack fingers, the copper head clanging loudly on the floor.

"T'ain't over, Hardman," he mumbled.

"The hell it isn't," Bolan said quietly.

He dived at Jest in a plunging rush. Tucking his chin against his chest, he left the floor in a long dive, cannonballing his entire weight into Jest's upper torso and head, smashing them against the head and upper torso of Ramses. The snapping and splintering of bones were heard plainly. Not a sound came from the bloody lips that flew wide in agony.

The impact very nearly stunned Bolan, and he stumbled to one side, across the King's Chamber. Jest slowly and grandly bent at the middle, as if bowing gallantly to Bolan, then he crumpled to the floor, like a tallow sculpture suddenly exposed to a great heat.

As he fell, his fingers scrabbled briefly at the base of the statue. Silently it slid to the left on well-oiled pivots, revealing a narrow doorway in the wall behind it. Bolan searched the room quickly and found his Desert Eagle. He inspected it briefly, making sure it was undamaged, then stepped through the doorway and into a cramped stretch of corridor. It was so narrow he had to walk along it sideways, shuffling like a crab.

21

Bolan stepped over a white coverall wadded on the floor and pushed aside the hanging static guards. He sacrificed stealth for the chance of having a head-on, face-to-face confrontation.

He stepped into a room dominated by a computer system. Deveroux and Kirchov were there, wearing the sterile white coveralls and surgical masks. He was able to differentiate the two people by the way the Russian astrophysicist filled out her garment.

"Get out of here!" Deveroux squawked. "You'll contaminate the Alpha's subprocessors!"

Bolan stared at the man for a moment, then strode toward him. Deveroux backpedalled until he was pressing against a hard drive. Fixing a hand in the front of the coverall, Bolan jerked him around and pushed him into a chair before a large keyboard. "I'll have the detonation code for the warhead."

"Not a chance."

Bolan snatched away the surgical mask and pressed the bore of the Desert Eagle against the pale man's thin lips. "Then I'll have the most intelligent brain on the planet splattered all over your precious Cheops Alpha."

"Belasko," Kirchov said. For the first time he noticed her wrists were bound. "There are only a few minutes until the platform reaches its detonation point."

Bolan thumbed back the hammer of the pistol. "The code."

Deveroux cast a glance at the long, heavy barrel of the Desert Eagle. He started to speak and Bolan pulled the muzzle away from his lips. "You don't dare kill me."

"I dare. Trust me on this, god-king. At the very moment that warhead detonates, I'll empty this clip into your head. So much for guiding the destiny of humanity. I suggest you think about it."

Deveroux thought about it, for approximately fifteen seconds. In the final analysis, he was a pragmatic man, despite his dreams of attaining godhood. He had lost battles before, but not one—as he argued with himself—of this magnitude. However, the loss of his life would be an irreversible setback.

With the gun still trained on his mouth, Deveroux spit out a series of numbers. Bolan ordered him to repeat them. Deveroux did so, but added, "It may be too late."

Bolan glanced toward the computer's monitor screen. A blob of reddish light glowed upon the grid pattern, as well as a number: 115. "Why too late?" he asked.

Kirchov answered for him. "The warhead has to be detonated at least ninety miles above Earth or the fallout will contaminate the atmosphere. And it'll require a few minutes for the telemetric signal to reach the platform's onboard computer and respond to the programming change."

With a contemptuous hand-shove to his face, Bolan pushed Deveroux out of the chair and onto the floor. Turning to Kirchov, he asked, "Do you know how to work this thing?"

Kirchov seated herself before the console, studying the keys and buttons. "I know a little about computers, but this one is so unusual in design—"

Picking himself up, Deveroux snorted diffidently.

Bolan took his Fairbairn-Sykes combat knife from its

sheath and slashed the nylon binder around Kirchov's wrists. "Do what you can."

The woman began to tap out the telemetric detonation code sequence. Even as she began, the number on the screen changed to 110 and the red hue of the light grew deeper.

After a moment, Kirchov pushed back her chair. "That's it. All we can do now is wait."

"My long-range scanner might pick up a trace of the explosion," Deveroux suggested contritely. "I'm bouncing the signal off a communication satellite."

Bolan glanced at him with slitted eyes, then nodded. With the Executioner watching his every move, Deveroux walked over to the monitor bank and flipped a few switches and adjusted a knob. The image of a dark sky appeared on the screen. The scene shifted to a high, aerial view of streamers of white clouds above a blue ocean.

"It's focused on the general vicinity of the Arabian Peninsula, set on maximum magnification," Deveroux said. He stepped back so Bolan and Kirchov could have an unobstructed view.

On the computer monitor, the number changed to 105. Bolan tensed, not moving, keeping Deveroux covered with the pistol. Every nerve was wire-taut. All the scanner screen revealed was a panorama of blue sea and wispy clouds.

A tiny red spark suddenly gleamed against the clouds. Bolan squinted, hoping his eyes weren't deceiving him. The light was so small, it could have been a star. Then, the spark slowly expanded to a flare, like a matchhead flaming up. Slowly the light faded from sight.

Bolan hazarded a look at the computer display. The red dot was stationary. The digits remained frozen at 105.

"That had better be it," Bolan said. Tension drained out of him, leaving him weary in every limb. To his surprise, Kirchov turned and caught him in a crushing embrace, murmuring something in Russian.

Bolan started to disengage himself when there was a quick scutter of feet and a flashing movement of white. Deveroux plunged through the static guards and into the narrow corridor.

Pushing Kirchov aside, Bolan rushed after him, though his progress through the corridor was considerably slower than Deveroux's. Kirchov was right behind him. He raced into the King's Chamber just in time to see a wall panel sliding shut behind Deveroux.

Snatching the ax dropped by Jest, he forced the blade into the almost invisible crack between the door panel and the wall and heaved back on it. The muscles of his arms bulged. There was a grating sound as the panel was pushed open a bit.

"Belasko!" Kirchov's scream was sudden, galvanizing.

Bolan snapped his head around, still maintaining pressure on his makeshift pry bar. Jest was on his feet and reaching for Bolan's throat with his talon-like fingers. He was a nightmarish figure. One eye was but a slit in his face, his lips oozing bloody pulp. His nose was completely flat. He was grinning with broken, red-stained teeth.

A muted crack sounded, and the door panel rolled open without resistance, rocking Bolan on his heels. Instantly his ears were deafened by a crackling roar and his eyes dazzled by a sudden flash. A torrent of orange fire spurted from the open door and engulfed Jest. Jesse El-Hamid perished without so much as a cry of surprise or indignation.

Coughing through the stink of roasted human flesh and hair, Bolan looked at the blackened, smoldering figure on the floor. Kirchov averted her eyes, making strangling noises deep in her throat. At least she was wearing a mask over her nose and mouth.

Very cautiously, Bolan examined the portal. It was an elevator shaft, very economical in size. The lift was probably designed to hold a single person. Attached to the wall of the shaft was a network of copper tubing, shiny canisters and a dozen nozzles. The sharp, metallic odor of propane gas cut into Bolan's nostrils.

It was one of Jest's over-the-top defense mechanisms, triggered in the lift to discourage pursuit. Pressurized jets of gas were pumped through the nozzles and when ignited made a very functional, one-shot flamethrower.

Glancing down, Bolan saw the shaft stretching away into deep darkness. Tilting his head back, he saw the bottom of the elevator car barely twenty feet above him. Faintly he heard the whine, cough and sudden droning roar of a powerful engine. It was a familiar sound, and he guessed the jet helicopter on the roof had survived the SWIFT's scythe-like landing.

Whipping back into the King's Chamber, Bolan grabbed the étagère lying lengthways on the floor, upended it and wrestled it to the desk.

"What are you doing?" Kirchov asked.

Bolan didn't reply. He dragged the display case atop the desk, making sure it was secure on the smooth surface. He heard the chopping whir of helicopter vanes.

"Come here," he ordered Kirchov. "Anchor this thing."

The woman gripped the bottom of the case as Bolan climbed the shelving like a stepladder. It swayed and creaked beneath his weight, but he didn't hesitate. Raising the Desert Eagle over his head, he squeezed the trigger. The room filled with thunder as he blazed away at the sky-light canopy.

The plastic half dome shuddered under the withering .44-caliber impacts. It didn't so much shatter as explode. Tinted shards rained down, clattering against the marble desktop. Bolan fired off the entire clip.

Grasping the rim of the skylight frame, Bolan heaved himself upward, kicking off from the top shelf. Kirchov moved aside as the case toppled over, crashing to the floor.

Pulling himself through the bullet-blasted opening, Bolan took in the scene with one quick, piercing glance. The wreckage of the SWIFT lay across the roof, crumpled wings butting up against the smashed solar energy panels. Uniformed bodies were mixed in with the debris. In the distance, down below, he heard the wail of approaching sirens.

The air was filled with a chopping drone. The helicopter rose from its landing pad, pushing up into the sky. Deveroux, seated next to a man at the controls, acknowledged Bolan's arrival with a silent snarl.

Holstering the emptied Desert Eagle, Bolan sprinted across the roof, pistoning feet grinding against glass. Several of the solar energy panels still stood intact. He bounded toward one, leaped, his feet gaining uncertain purchase on the up-tilting, slick surface. He ran up it as if it were a ramp, and, using the topmost edge as a springboard, he launched himself off the roof, arms extended.

His hands closed around the helicopter's port-side landing gear. With a whiplash motion of his body, he swung up onto the metal rail, right arm and leg hooking the struts.

Deveroux turned in his seat. The pilot uttered a cry of fright, fighting the controls. The aircraft lurched, then righted itself. Deveroux drove a foot in a straight-leg kick at Bolan. His heel rebounded off the crown of the Executioner's head.

Grunting in exertion and fury, Deveroux unlatched his safety belt and half slid out of his seat, delivering a flurry of stomps and kicks. Deveroux's eyes were wild with terror and panic. Bolan had seen men react like this before—the arrogant death-merchants who loved their power over others, who, when faced at last with the possibility of their own deaths, turned into mindless, gibbering animals.

Hugging the rail, Bolan defended himself instinctively, and Deveroux's feet hit only his arms, elbows and shoulders. One penetrated his guard, a sideways kick that split the corner of his lower lip. At the sudden blaze of pain, the taste of blood, Bolan grabbed Deveroux's right ankle in a death grip. With every iota of his strength, he slammed it against the landing rail. Even over the rush of wind and the chopping beat of the blades, Bolan heard bones crunch and the mushy popping of tendons.

Deveroux threw back his head and screamed in agony, throwing himself backward. The back of his head struck the control stick, knocking it from the pilot's hand.

The helicopter yawed and went into a prolonged, stomach-turning spin. Bolan very nearly lost his grip. Beneath him he glimpsed a stretch of black water, wharves and warehouses, all wheeling crazily.

The aircraft's spiraling descent slowed and finally ceased, a bare twenty feet above the roof of a waterfront warehouse. The pilot had regained control. Bolan clawed atop the landing gear, hands gripping the edge of the open hatch, bracing his feet against the struts.

Deveroux lay sprawled across his seat, his head very nearly in the pilot's lap. His face was ashen, his eyes were closed. Bolan opened his mouth to voice an order to the frightened pilot, and Deveroux erupted into furious life. His left foot came up, slamming hard into Bolan's sternum. The soldier lost his balance, his feet slipping from the landing rail. He teetered on it, trying to tip himself forward, toward the hatch.

Deveroux lunged from the seat, using a shoulder as a wedge, ramming into his adversary and knocking him out into empty air. As Bolan fell, he slapped one hand around the coverall Deveroux still wore. The flimsy material ripped beneath his fingers, and Bolan plummeted toward the black water below.

The dark surface of Tampa Bay sped toward him. He didn't have time to slip into a vertical position, to enter the water in a dive, so he curled himself into a tight ball.

The brackish water smashed at him, and, at the same time, he was aware of a white shape splashing into the bay near him. The fall had been less than fifty feet, so the impact didn't daze him. He stroked to the surface, spitting the salty, oil-seasoned water from his mouth. The brine stung his cut lip like acid.

The jet thrust of the helicopter engaged, and it shot across the dark sky. A few yards away, ripples were moving in the water in ever-widening concentric rings. At the center of the ripples, a few small bubbles roiled, then vanished. Deveroux had been so close to the hatch that Bolan's sudden yank had dumped him out.

Looking toward Harbour Island, Bolan saw scores of flashing blue-and-red lights. Emergency vehicles were converging at the base of the Osiris Tower. Even now, the cops would be storming up into the penthouse, demanding to know what was going on. He hoped Kirchov invoked her diplomatic immunity.

Overhead he heard the sound of search and rescue helicopters, their colored running lights dancing against the darkness of the sky.

By swimming steadily for ten minutes, Bolan reached the barnacle-studded pilings of an ancient wharf. Despite the drag of his wet clothes, the weight of his pistol and his water-filled boots, he managed to climb one of the pilings. Heaving himself up on the splintery edge, he sat there, resting and panting. He was so exhausted, so completely wrung out by fatigue, all he could do was sit and stare.

Other craft were visible near where he and Deveroux had hit the bay. They shone searchlights over the surface, and helicopters buzzed the area. One chopper, equipped with pontoons, settled down very near shore. Bolan watched it. He saw no markings on the fuselage.

A few moments later, the helicopter rose from the bay, water streaming from its pontoons. It turned and beat the air over the Tampa skyline. As the drone of the blades faded, Bolan realized that the brief landing could have been more than a whim of the pilot.

It was possible that Dexter Deveroux had survived the

fall into the bay, contacted one of his many conduits and was even now being whisked to a safe haven. Bolan tried to dismiss the notion as melodramatic, but he found that he couldn't. If he were still alive, Dexter Deveroux would never forget how Bolan had snatched the crown of godhood from his brow.

Bolan stared at the dark surface of the bay, eyes narrowed, seeing nothing but an early-morning fog close in on him. If Deveroux had survived, he knew the man's delusions would demand vengeance. He supposed gods and kings, and people desperate to believe they were greater than both, had a sick need to see the world tremble in terror of their wrath.

The Executioner had visited some very human wrath on Deveroux's microcosmic Olympus, and if ever they met again, he would topple the entire mountain.

**A powerful cult leader triggers a
countdown to terror....**

STONY
MAN™ 36

STRANGLEHOLD

Trouble is brewing in the Land of the Rising Sun as a powerful
cult leader has assembled a fanatically dedicated following,
ready to do his bidding and deliver his gospel of death on the
rest of the world.

It's up to the counterterrorist commandos of Stony Man
Farm to act quickly to keep the world safe from this
displaced doctrine.

Available in September 1998 at your favorite retail outlet.

A preview from hell...

JAMES AXLER

DEATH LANDS®

Dark Emblem

After a relatively easy mat-trans jump, Ryan and his companions find themselves in the company of Dr. Silas Jamaisvous, a seemingly pleasant host who appears to understand the mat-trans systems extremely well.

Seeing signs that local inhabitants have been used as guinea pigs for the scientist's ruthless experiments, the group realizes that they have to stop this line of research before it goes too far....

James Axler

OUTLANDERS™

DOOMSTAR RELIC

Kane and his companions find themselves pitted
against an ambitious rebel named Barch, who finds a
way to activate a long-silent computer security
network and use it to assassinate the local baron.
Barch plans to use the security system to take over
the ville, but he doesn't realize he is starting a
Doomsday program that could destroy the world.

Kane and friends must stop Barch, the virtual assassin
and the Doomsday program to preserve the future....

One man's quest for power unleashes a cataclysm
in America's wastelands.